
★

THE TELEPHONE RANG
STRIDENTLY

When she lifted the receiver a chill, flat man's voice said, "I've been talking to your pretty little daughter, Rachel. Happy little child. Very fond of Smarties. Leave things alone, Mrs. Simms, while you still have two children."

Air rushed fast into her lungs, coming out in a gasp. The receiver clicked and hummed in her ear. She thought of ringing Morrissey, but instead dragged on her jacket and fled to the kindergarten, insisting on taking Rachel home. From there she went to her son's school. She took her children into a quiet café and let them eat chocolate biscuits and drink cola, until she stopped feeling sick.

When she put her key in the front door at four-thirty, she'd missed Morrissey's visit by ten minutes.

★

Kay Mitchell

ROOTS OF EVIL

W⊕RLDWIDE®

TORONTO • NEW YORK • LONDON
AMSTERDAM • PARIS • SYDNEY • HAMBURG
STOCKHOLM • ATHENS • TOKYO • MILAN
MADRID • WARSAW • BUDAPEST • AUCKLAND

ROOTS OF EVIL

A Worldwide Mystery/February 1995

First published by St. Martin's Press, Incorporated.

ISBN 0-373-26162-4

Printed in U.S.A.

ROOTS
OF
EVIL

ONE

MALMINSTER SLUMBERED and dreamed its dreams.

Under the amber lights the streets were bare and echoing, especially on the pedestrian precinct where a skittish breeze rattled an empty cola tin from shop-front to concrete-sided flowerbed and back again. Around the outskirts of town an occasional car moved along, its lights breaking up the darkness into shadows, and on the Industrial Estate off the Middlebrook Road the bakery night-shift were packaging bread for the next day's deliveries, the rich, yeasty smell of baking drifting as far as the motorway.

To the north of the Industrial Estate, well past the busy streets that led down to Queen's Road, a half-dozen rows of brooding terrace houses ran at right angles from the circular access road. The smell of warm bread embraced them too, and then filtered over a wildly overgrown parcel of derelict land, where squalid back-to-backs and a flop-house had stood until the Council sent in bulldozers.

The intention had been to replace them with slab-built maisonettes but then the Council got cold feet. Publicly, the failure had been blamed on the new government policies, but the truth was that a slippy rug had been pulled from under certain feet, and that, coupled with overspending in other areas, had made rebuilding impossible. Now the land lay barren. Here and there jagged mounds of rubble penetrated the invading overgrowth like stumps of decaying teeth, and at night a pack of feral cats hunted the jungle of weeds and debris, silent among tall willow-bay and couch grass until they found some small furry thing that screamed before dying.

The six rows of terraced houses wedged between the Industrial Estate and the waste land were occupied mainly by Asian immigrants. A week ago bricks had been thrown through three windows and a half-dozen doors had been daubed with crude swastikas while their occupants slept. Since then a police Panda had cruised the streets several times a night, and everything had been quiet.

The rich scent of warm bread filled the police car too, making PC Pearce hungry as he cruised quietly, bumping over cobbles and pot-holes, down one terraced street and up the next. When his stomach rumbled again he pulled into the kerb and dimmed his lights; he was reaching for the coffee flask under the front seat when breaking glass told him the brick-thrower was busy again, and he came upright in his seat, hand empty, in time to see the bright flash and glow of flame near the top of the street that said this time it had been no brick.

Swearing, he turned the lights to full-beam and picked out two running figures near the junction with the access road. Pearce accelerated after them, blue light flashing. When he swung out into the path of the articulated lorry he was talking urgently into his radio, telling Control that he needed a fire-tender and back-up, fast. The force of impact flung the Panda against a concrete lamp standard that sliced it in two, and the lorry jack-knifed, demolishing the end wall of the next terraced row as the two running figures reached the same spot.

INSPECTOR BECKETT seemed to have spent the night counting bodies, he was weary and also hollow-eyed and haggard, knowing that the night's images would stay in his mind when he slept. *If* he slept ...

The first fire-tender had taken only minutes to arrive, and when the crew saw the extent of the carnage, more fire units and a pale line of ambulances had come, trailed by Beckett and a team from the Accident Investigation Branch.

The house fire had been given first priority, but blazing polyurethane-filled furniture had already released enough cyanide gas to kill two children and their grandfather before they could be got out. Three older children and their mother had been rescued from an attic bedroom and were in hospital.

It had been Beckett who'd broken the news to the father working on the bakery night-shift, and it had been Beckett with a pale-faced WPC at his side who had woken Pearce's wife and taken her to the hospital to learn that she was a widow.

When it was all over he stood in Osgodby's office, and with as much profanity as he could muster wished out loud that he had never become a policeman.

The chief superintendent let him get it off his chest. When the flow of words ended he suggested Beckett take a few days' holiday. The inspector turned down the idea, from choice he wouldn't have gone home at all. Without Jean the house was noisily empty, every sound magnified by its surrounding silence. He ached for her to come back to him, and stubbornly refused to bend enough to tell her so.

Better by far to just get on with the job.

On his way to the canteen he tried to remember the statistics on broken police marriages.

THE KITCHEN RADIO was tuned in to the local news broadcast, and Morrissey saw the flare of anxiety in his wife's eyes when she heard the words 'a police driver died,' and saw too how she hid it from Katie and Mike by moving away from the table to open the window.

'There, that's better,' she said, coming back and taking her place again. 'I think we could be in for a hot day.'

'It must have been some accident,' Mike said unthinkingly. 'Getting wasted by an arctic. Wonder if he hit it side on or head on?'

Kate turned on him.

'Shut up, moron. All you're bothered about is how much blood there was. Ian's on nights too. Sometimes you're so stupid.'

Mike blinked. He said uncomfortably, 'Ian's all right. He wasn't there. I don't know why you're steaming.'

'Because you're thick!'

'That's enough,' Margaret said firmly. 'Katie, you aren't being fair.'

'But...'

'But me no buts.'

Katie shut up but the look she bestowed on Mike did nothing to mend things. After a couple of minutes she said grudgingly, 'All right, you're not thick, Mike. Sorry.'

'I know I'm not. So what's *your* problem?' He pushed his empty plate away and stood up, saying to his mother with unusual politeness, 'I need a few things from my room, excuse me please.' A few minutes later the sound of an old Prefab Sprout tape echoed down the stairs.

Katie, elbows on the table, fingers buried in the shock of hair, said: 'If this is what it's like to be adult I think I'd rather be a kid.' Then she pushed back from the table to follow Mike upstairs. When he heard her bedroom door slam Morrissey looked at his wife quizzically.

Margaret said, 'I think Katie could be getting serious about Ian Hicks. How would you feel about that?'

'Worried,' said Morrissey. 'She's too young.'

'Funny, I seem to remember my father once said exactly the same thing.' Their eyes met across the table and the chief inspector felt a belated sympathy for his father-in-law.

'It could be a passing fancy.' He spoke the words hopefully, and his wife smiled.

THE MORNING NEWS broadcast had been sketchy; only later did the media learn about the fire-bombing, and make the obvious link with racism. That they did so suited the man in the Council Committee Room very well. It had shocked him that things had gone so badly wrong the previous night, and it bothered him that with a policeman dead all the stops would be pulled out to find the fire-bomber. Then he learned that the two youths responsible were among the dead and his relief was tinged only slightly with remorse.

He hadn't actively suggested or agreed it should go so far. Harassment had been the name of the game. Broken windows, upturned dustbins, nasty things pushed through letter-boxes—not petrol bombs. *That* couldn't be laid at his door. But he had been given a fright and the liquid heat in his bowels was a consequence of it. He excused himself, moving from his position at the end of the heavy oak table with the haste of discomfort.

During his absence the Planning Committee continued to discuss whether a proposed local discothèque extension should be allowed, and when he came back it was put to the vote. He caught the chief planning officer's eye and his mouth twitched slightly as he added his own 'No' to make a majority veto.

No doubt in good time, plans for the extension would be passed. When the owners discovered which were the right wheels to oil.

TWO

MUSTAPH ALI had never before known such a depth of sorrow; neither had he known such wealth. A stringer on the local paper sent news of the multiple deaths round the tabloids, and because there was little else happening right then, and he'd provided some good pictures, it made front page on three nationals and got a mention in the rest. A fund was thoughtfully set up by one editor in search of better circulation figures, and given a kick-start with twenty thousand pounds from the newspaper. At the end of a month the fund had netted half a million pounds. Substantial interim payments were made to the survivors of the fire, and to the families of the dead policeman and the lorry driver.

Mustaph, not having learned the British art of cynicism, thanked Allah and planned a better life for his family, whom he moved to the more substantial terrace house kindly offered to him rent-free, for a year, by a property developer who insisted on having his generosity remain anonymous.

The inquests were held and bodies released for burial. Four deaths were found to be by misadventure, and the three others, those of the grandfather and two children, were declared to be by manslaughter. The dead youths had been in trouble before, for petty thefts and public affray after heavy Saturday nights in the town centre. The uniformed police knew them well, and knew all about the rest of the gang who went around wearing Union Jack emblems and calling themselves National Patriots. In sleeveless leather vests, metal-studded boots, and semi-shaved heads they were hard to miss. The warnings-off were not gentle.

In the first few weeks after the fire-bombing other tenants on the fringe of the derelict land took fright and moved away; the narrow streets began to take on a decayed look as windows were boarded up. It was rumoured that the local philanthropist who had helped the Ali family had also helped in rehousing the others. All these things were quietly noted at police headquarters, but no particular interest was paid, other than to make sure the regular police patrols continued.

When the inquests were over Inspector Beckett did as Osgodby had suggested and took some leave, locking up the house that was full of accusations and disappearing north with his fishing-tackle. Behind him the whole of CID heaved a collective sigh of relief. Maybe when he came back he'd be less touchy.

The day after Beckett left, Malminster's social elite attended a party. Not all were Labour supporters but that didn't prevent them celebrating the local MP's twenty-fifth year in office. Grey-haired and dapper, Gerald Mason wore a red rosette in the lapel of his dinner jacket and greeted everyone with the same quick handshake before steering them to where the drinks flowed freely, and melting away.

Jack Thewlis was one of the guests and he revelled in being there, knowing that nine-tenths of the milling people wouldn't have given him the time of day if he hadn't been chairman of the Planning Committee. Now they smiled at him nicely and chatted him up on the off-chance that one day he could do them a favour. Not long since, if they'd met him in the street in his pit muck, they'd have turned their noses up.

He gave his wife a sherry, pale and dry, knowing she disliked it and would rather have a port and lemon, but asserting his authority over her, as he'd asserted it over his daughter until she'd married. It pleased his ego that Ange-

line still did as she was told when he was around, married or
not. He had inherited a lot of character traits from his father and the liking for dominance was one of them. The
lesson had been learned when he was young that a big stick
was more effective than a carrot, but there was something
in his wife's eyes when her husband's back was turned that
made for discomfort. Mason noted that and wondered
about it, fingering his rosette. It was more than resentment. Hatred then? Thewlis hadn't even given her a name
when he introduced her. Instead he'd said, 'This is me lady
wife,' and left it at that, dismissing her as so much property.

Mason moved away, still thoughtful; grudges could
sometimes be dangerous. It entered his mind that if Thewlis were careless enough to take home papers connected with
certain things outside Council business, and if the plumply
corseted woman was able to understand them, a lot of people could find themselves hung out to dry.

He was talking quietly with Sam Richardson when he
learned they had a weak link.

WHEN THE CANAL was thriving the old warehouses had been
filled with grain and provisions, and wool for the mills, but
that had been a long time ago and for years they had stood
empty and neglected until, just recently, a property development company had taken several off the Council's hands.
Luckily, Malminster citizens weren't aware of how much the
buildings had been under-valued, and neither were many
members of the appropriate committees. By the time they
found out, it was too late, the deal had been struck.

Soon after the papers were signed, Thewlis enjoyed an all-
expenses-paid holiday in Marbella, and certain other people were enabled to increase their bank balances.

One of the buildings, the smallest, had already been converted into eight flats; the rest were earmarked for office development.

Detective Sergeant Barrett had moved into one of the new flats. It was smaller than the slightly shabby furnished rooms he had rented until two weeks ago, and cost him ten pounds a week more, but it carried a lease and he could furnish it as he pleased. When he thought about his near-empty bank account he had an occasional twinge of worry, but not enough to spoil his pleasure. The development had already become known as Malminster's mini-yuppyland and that suited him fine. Young, upwardly mobile, and successful were all things that Barrett desired to be.

Tucked away on the top floor he could see part of the town spread out like an animated map. To the left where the canal basin joined the river, a weir dropped in three steps of foaming water, and spanning both it and the canal a wide road bridge carried six lanes of traffic, three in each direction, north and south.

Barrett found the view especially good at night when the lights from street-lamps and passing traffic reflected in the water, and the pleasure of standing at his window looking out at it all hadn't yet dissipated. It was a little after Friday midnight when he saw the south-bound Sierra begin to weave erratically, its lights shifting wildly. There wasn't much in the way of traffic heading into Malminster, but when the car crossed over the central line it struck the back of an oncoming Cavalier and knocked it sideways into the ring road traffic. A pizza delivery van veered sharply left. The Sierra's speed didn't appear to slacken as it crossed the north-bound lanes and hit three ornamental stone pillars head on, before falling in a curving roll into the basin of water under the weir.

BARRETT'S DESK was in Morrissey's office, and he regarded it as his own property. He wasn't best pleased when he went into work next day to find the bulky Inspector Lister from Traffic Division teetering in his chair, feet up on a corner of the desk.

Morrissey greeted the detective sergeant with sour humour. 'I told you nothing good would come from moving house. Now you've been up half the night you'll know why.'

'Baptism of fire,' Lister said. 'Not likely to happen again.' He heaved out of Barrett's chair. 'I'd appreciate a report when you have a quiet five minutes. Pity it happened in just that spot; anywhere else and the unlucky sod might have stood a chance.'

'Drinking spree?' asked Morrissey.

'Don't think so. Working late and on his way home by all accounts. We'll have to wait for the post-mortem, but the label so far is a coronary. Not that old either, only thirty-eight.'

'Working where?' asked Barrett idly. 'One of the clubs, I suppose, not much else going on at that time.'

'You'd be surprised! No. He might have called in somewhere but he'd been in his office until after eleven, we know that. Name of Richard Simms, one of Malminster's town planners. Don't suppose you know him.'

Morrissey felt the chill nudge of mortality as his mind dredged up a mental image of the dead man's face. 'I've met him,' he said.

'Ah.' Lister waited, but the chief inspector didn't elucidate. His wife chaired the local Oxfam committee, and Claire Simms was one of its active members, but neither fact could have anything to do with Simms' death.

Barrett said, 'The whole sequence took less than a minute, so it'll be a short report.' He dusted off invisible scuff marks where the inspector's feet had rested.

Lister raised his eyebrows. 'I'll leave you to it then,' he said, and went out.

'Feeling touchy this morning, are we?' queried Morrissey.

Barrett got out a report sheet. 'Not especially.'

'Something I don't know about, then?'

The detective sergeant glanced at the door. 'Nothing important.' He began to write, hoping Morrissey would shut up. What lay between him and Lister had nothing to do with the chief inspector.

'It's too quiet,' Morrissey mused, half to himself, and recognised the illogicality of thinking it; having local crime drop to near zero would be a pleasure, not a burden. 'Either something clever's going on that we don't know about, or we're getting too efficient,' he worried, and scowled at Barrett's bent head. 'And it can't be that, can it?' Getting up restlessly, a tall and taciturn man whose face transformed itself when allowed to smile. 'Anybody wants me, I'll be in the canteen.'

'Yes, sir,' said Barrett, and didn't look up, which gave Morrissey more food for thought.

Mentioning the word canteen would ordinarily have turned the sergeant's thoughts to food. Remembering that Barrett had started his policing in Bradford, and Lister had just come from there.

An old score then?

If so, it was one that couldn't be allowed to get in the way of things here. With that thought at the front of his mind, Morrissey went to the basement canteen to soothe his acid stomach with junk food.

MONDAY MORNING Inspector Beckett woke to sunlight shining in through a gap in the curtains. The brightness threaded a path across the rose-patterned carpet to the untidy bed, and woke him with palely gilded fingers. Unthinking he reached out an arm and felt beside him, but all his hand found was an empty space. For a moment he lay quite still. He was alone, and had been for three months now. How long before he got used to it?

He drew back the hand and rolled onto his back. Outside on the street milk bottles clinked and an electric motor whined, high and grumbling. Grunting, he swung his feet out of bed and padded downstairs to the empty kitchen, to put the kettle on.

When he came out of the bathroom ten minutes later it was pumping steam out of its spout. He remembered the tea-caddy was as empty as his bed, and made strong coffee instead. It made the dull ache in his stomach worse.

Wherever he looked there was an air of neglect; if Jean came home now she'd look around and think she was in the wrong house. He could write his name in the dust. And the only real thought in his head was that he was alone there.

The cornflakes tasted stale after his ten-day absence, and soaked up long-life milk like blotting paper. He spooned more sugar on and ate doggedly and without pleasure. Then he bathed, shaved, and dressed and went out of the front door, leaving the used pots as they were, on the table.

There was a bottle-neck on the ring-road where red-and-white-striped cones forced two lanes of traffic into a single file. Anger and frustration fumed. When he got to the police building the dull stomach pain that had bothered him for two weeks had turned into sharp, burning nausea, so that instead of climbing the two flights of stairs to CID he went down to the basement canteen and tried to assauge it with milk. But this time it didn't work. Chief Inspector Morrissey, coming in through the swinging doors, saw Beckett's grey and perspiring face and got him upstairs to the surgeon's room.

A few minutes later Beckett began to vomit, and the morning food returned bathed in bright red. When an ambulance came and took him away, its siren blasting a path through the traffic, the normally pristine room looked like a charnel house.

Morrissey followed the speeding blue light in his own car, and hoped that Jean Beckett could be found quickly.

THREE

THE LAYOUT of the hospital was uncomfortably familiar to Morrissey, with its recent memories of Katie lying against white pillows, livid bruises on her neck painful evidence that his family was as vulnerable as the next.

In common with many general hospitals, emergency admissions went in via Casualty, but in Malminster that particular department had also to cope with a system of daily clinic appointments, and the seats were full to overflowing. Magically all the available staff bunched around Beckett's trolley, disappearing with it down a stump of corridor where flapping curtains screened off cubicles and all that lay within them.

The acidity in Morrissey's stomach rumbled and rose hotly behind his sternum, reminding him that he had gone to the police canteen with a purpose as yet unfulfilled. He eyed the drinks on offer from the automatic machine and fed it with coins. It was difficult to recognise the bland soup as anything but seasoned cornflour, but his stomach accepted it with gratitude and quieted.

There was a great to-ing and fro-ing of white coats and frilled caps into and around Beckett's cubicle. Half an hour went by. Another drip-stand was wheeled in. Eventually a doctor emerged, shedding his white coat. Morrissey noted the red patches. One had stained the man's blue shirt and he looked harassed, overworked, his thin olive face still showing stubble.

'No next of kin yet?'

'We're trying to find his wife.' Apologising. Only they didn't know where to look. Beckett hadn't been forthcoming about his marital troubles and, grizzly at the best of times, it had seemed politic not to press.

'No one else?'

'A daughter in Leicester. If it's that bad...' He let the words trail off, waiting to be told.

'What we're doing right now is stabilise him enough so we can get him into theatre. If you get his wife here in the next half hour you'd be doing him a favour.'

Morrissey looked at the dregs of soup. 'Ulcer?'

'Probably,' agreed the doctor, and went back to Beckett.

Ten minutes later Jean arrived, looking in her own way as harried as the doctor had been. Osgodby had come with her, gravely solicitous.

'John!' She came to Morrissey and laid a quick hand on his sleeve. 'Is it really that bad?' Her eyes said plainly that they didn't want it to be, and he guessed instinctively that part of the worry came from fear that in walking out on her marriage, some blame for Beckett's collapse lay with her. No one could tell her differently; but neither could anyone, knowing how bloody-minded Beckett could be, say she might not have had reason to leave.

And she was looking better and healthier than she had for months before the break-up, despite this new worry.

A nurse came through the cubicle curtains and Morrissey hailed her, saved from awkward questions.

'How bad is it?' asked Osgodby, when Beckett's wife was out of earshot, and when Morrissey told him the chief superintendent's glumness increased. 'You'd better get back and keep an eye on things,' he said in sour resignation. 'I'll need to hang on here.'

From the side of the hospital where Morrissey had hurriedly parked his car the single-storey mortuary building was visible, sticking out obliquely behind its screen of trees. Seeing lights gleaming behind the small, high, thickened glass windows of the post-mortem room, sent him inside to ask about Richard Simms' death. Unable to explain his interest even to himself, except by admitting a degree of morbid curiosity, he was glad not to be asked to explain it by Gibson.

The hospital pathologist was writing up reports, and looked surprised to see Morrissey. 'I've had one of your lot here already,' he grumbled mildly. 'Lister?'

'I'm unofficial,' the chief inspector said. 'Nothing sinister in mind unless you've turned up something.'

'Simple heart attack,' Gibson said with the casualness of everyday acquaintance with death. 'Dead before he hit the water, but if you'd thought it was any different you'd have had one of the Home Office lot down here to carve him up; not me.' He squinted at Morrissey obliquely. 'Or is it that you knew him personally, and old mortality's breathing down your neck?'

'Call it interested curiosity,' said Morrissey. 'I'm admitting to nothing else. Thanks for your time.'

As the chief inspector moved away, Gibson observed philosophically: 'It's a good way to go when you think about it, fast and furious and no regrets.'

And no time to say goodbye either, thought Morrissey, walking back to his car. Something to be said for keeping one's affairs in order.

BECKETT HAD BEEN in hospital three days, and the news was good, but that wasn't at the forefront of Morrissey's mind, instead it was occupied with Simms' inquest.

They'd been having a mild autumn, an Indian summer extending well into October, and because the winds had come with only brief skirmishes instead of the usual gales, the trees bore summer green leaves instead of brown and gold. It couldn't last of course and when the weather broke it would probably be with a vengeance, but for now the late October days were warm and sunny and Morrissey rose early to make the most of them.

The garden was his joy, and had been since they moved into the solid, 1930s' semi with its mullioned windows when Katie was born. Since then he'd watched the tangle of overgrowth give way to order, seen his spindly young fruit trees mature and give rich harvests, and it satisfied him. It was a large garden, and it kept both himself and Margaret busy. But the results were worth it.

That morning Morrissey had got up and shaved with a sense of unease. He didn't know why that should be, but the unease was tinged with premonition, and he tried to shake it off by doing some vigorous mulching. Morrissey's sixth sense bothered him rarely and he couldn't see a reason for it to be active now. Simms had died a natural death. Tragic maybe, unexpected, but not suspicious. He shovelled out a mix of compost and leaf mould, spread it, and shovelled some more.

A flight of birds in V-formation overflew the garden, heading south, and he leaned on the spade and watched them. There was a stillness to the new day, a breezeless waiting, and instinctively the chief inspector knew that the weather was changing; that the birds knew it too and that was why they were winging south. Another sensation rose and held him captive, a sharp, throat-catching nostalgia that came from knowing the late flowerings had to end. As he surveyed the bright greenness of lawn, and the multi-hued heads of hydrangeas, morbidly the thought came that it was like standing beside a death-bed. He pushed the idea away and lifted the last of the dahlias.

Barrett, having been called out to an early morning break-in at the Miller's Arms, was in the office when Morrissey got there, blearily writing out a report. The thieves, both canny and cheeky, had cleared out the stock of spirits in anticipation of a Christmas demand, and left enough money on the counter to pay for two pints of draft ale they'd drawn and drunk.

'You know what?' Barrett growled. 'They even washed the bloody glasses.'

'Can't be local then,' said Morrissey gravely. 'Not if they've got a sense of humour.' Barrett looked at him with suspicion and went back to writing.

Simms' inquest was scheduled for eleven in the Courts building. For three weeks now, Malminster's criminal sub-culture had taken a virtual holiday, and although he knew the state of affairs was simply a lull before the storm, it left Morrissey, like everyone else in CID, with time on his hands. Which was why at eleven o'clock he had time to sit quietly and unremarked, at the back of the long, narrow room, with its high arched windows that let in light but not sun because the building next to it was tall enough to block out the rays. Idly he stared at the yellow-cream walls and pine furniture and wondered if it had been deliberately chosen to compensate for the missing quality of light.

There were not many people in the room. Morrissey counted ten heads, one of them Claire Simms, sombrely dressed. He listened to Accident Investigation Team's assessment of road measurements and skid marks and the angle of impact, and heard the Cavalier's driver, whose car had been knocked sideways, and the swerving pizza-van driver, give their brief evidence. When Barrett's turn came, his was the more graphic account, viewed as it had been from his high window like the eye of God.

But when Gibson the pathologist, tubby in a grey striped suit, began to talk about the cause of Simms' death, Claire Simms' head shook from side to side in denial. When he had finished and was gathering his papers, she stood to say vehemently that her husband's cholesterol level had been checked a week before his death and it had been well within the recommended safety limit of 5.2mmol/1. Richard simply could not have had a heart attack.

The Coroner sympathised with her, but took pains to point out that he was adjourning the inquest only to allow time for the police to finalise their reports, and that he had no doubt the final verdict would be death by natural causes.

When it was over and Morrissey moved to leave, Claire turned and saw him, staring at him without acknowledging his brief nod, but watching until he was out of the room.

THEWLIS DIDN'T ATTEND the inquest. He'd thought about it, wondered whether in his role as Chairman of the Planning Committee he should be there to show proper concern for paid Council officials, from what was, when all was said and done, his sphere of influence. But then he'd had second thoughts about it. Best not to show too much interest perhaps; no sense giving nosy tongues more to talk about. But it might be as well to show some sympathy with the widow afterwards. Pity about Simms, but fortuitous too.

He told that to the mirror in the bathroom, saying the words out loud as he gave his chin a close and soapy shave.

It could be said that the little cartel he was in were lucky to have him aboard. He thought about that, his hand poised in mid-stroke; Thewlis didn't normally believe in abstracts—if you couldn't feel it, see it, hear it, or taste it it didn't exist. Something else then, not luck. Coincidence or circumstance. He liked the sound of that; it rolled off the tongue and sounded like educated comment. Not luck.

He had an ashtray he'd picked up at the seaside years back, when they'd put funny drawings on them like picture postcards. This one had a young boy cowering in a corner, covering up his privates, and an ugly-looking rabbi waving scissors. The legend on it said: *There is a destiny that shapes our ends.* Thewlis had liked that, bringing arty-farty notions down to their proper level.

Forget luck then, nothing to do with it.

He continued to shave, concentrating on the lather, his tongue curved gently out at the corner of his mouth. There'd have to be a new area officer of course, a replacement for Simms; but no rush about that, no sense in making mistakes. Skill and judgement, that's what mattered, leave education for office boys. He preened in the mirror, studying his profile, stretching his neck, pulling back the gut. Not bad for fifty-five, not bad at all. When he stepped into the shower the cascade of water over his still well-muscled, full thighs brought other things to mind, and he went back into the bedroom to wake his wife with perfunctory clumsiness and take his rights.

It didn't enter his head that her purpose in life was anything but to be used for his comfort.

FOUR

'You want me to disappear then?' Barrett asked as Morrissey put the receiver down.

'No, I do not!' The chief inspector said it with unusual vehemence. 'Make yourself look busy but stay put. I think Mrs. Simms has come to tell us the inquest got it wrong.'

'She was certainly uptight enough this morning,' Barrett acknowledged. 'But it seems to me her GP could help her more than us. Pills or something.'

Uptight, thought Morrissey. *Pills or something.* Out loud he said, 'Always supposing she doesn't know something we don't.'

'Like what? For my money, it's shock, and probably a bit of guilt thrown in.' Barrett got an A4 pad and laid it on his desk, then he set his pen on it carefully. 'Lister was investigating officer in Simms' death,' he said, looking at the pen. 'Be one in the eye for him if there was more to it.' He straightened the pen a fraction of an inch, lining it up with the edge of the pad.

Morrissey watched the small adjustment thoughtfully. It confirmed his earlier view that there was something between Barrett and Lister that shouldn't be there, but it wasn't for him to ask what. Not yet, not until it interfered with Barrett's work. Time enough then to dip an oar in. Pig-headed the detective sergeant might be, but resourcefulness and efficiency made up for that particular failing. Not that Morrissey would have admitted it within Barrett's hearing; no sense adding vanity to vanity.

He speculated on that until a WPC brought Claire Simms in and waited, eyebrows raised, for Morrissey's nod of dismissal before she went away. Against the silence in the office her feet made rhythmic sounds of descent on the rubber stair treads.

Morrissey said, 'Mrs Simms, I'm sorry about your husband. Come and sit down and tell me what we can do for you.'

She came without hurry to the chair he had set at the side of his desk, a woman in her mid-thirties, soberly dressed in the grey two-piece she had worn that morning, looking totally different to the person he had met socially, bright then in peacock colours, a-bubble with small-talk. Only the fashionably short cut of her light brown hair seemed unchanged. But then the chief inspector saw a difference there too; grey showing up in random strands. Had it been there a month ago, or was it the stress of her husband's death bringing it out. He'd seen that sort of thing happen before and marvelled at the way mind and body interacted. She let herself lean back in the chair, seeming more relaxed than he had expected, and he took that to be a good sign. 'Well, then,' he encouraged.

She said, 'I saw you at the inquest. I want to know why you were there.'

'It isn't an unusual event for me to attend an inquest,' he parried, and turned the question around. 'Is there any particular reason why I shouldn't have been there?'

Her smile shadowed itself slightly. 'None. I've been hoping there was a reason why you should,' saying that with a kind of eagerness evident in the way she tilted her body towards him, fingers curled round the arms of her chair. 'There must have been some sort of doubt in your mind about Richard's death; some shadow of an idea that it wasn't as simple as everyone says.'

Some sort of doubt.

Remembering how unease had plagued him that morning, Morrissey forced it to the back of his mind, and added his own voice to the rest. Gibson was a good pathologist. The police investigation had been thorough. Telling her that, reinforcing the official view, and when he'd done, trying to ignore the way her face flattened with disappointment.

Gruffly he advised, 'Give yourself a bit longer to come to terms with what's happened, a month say; then if you're still not satisfied come back.'

Her eyes showed bright points of anger. 'What for?' she flared. 'So I can be fobbed off again.'

'No,' he said. 'No, not that; that would be patronising, and I won't be that, I promise you. All I'm suggesting is you give yourself some thinking time.'

'The week before he died Richard doubled his insurance policy,' Claire stated with quiet emphasis. 'But of course that was just a coincidence. He was also more preoccupied than I've ever known him. Another coincidence.' She stood up and held out her hand. 'Thank you, Chief Inspector, I'm sorry if I've wasted your time.' Morrissey took the hand in his big clasp.

'I'm sorry, too,' he said with a bluntness he couldn't avoid. 'But there isn't anything from the accident scene, or the post-mortem, to suggest the preliminary verdict this morning might be wrong. I hope when shock and anger lessen a bit, you'll understand no one was to blame. Not Richard, and not anyone else.'

'And I'm sure you honestly mean that, even though I know you're wrong,' she said, and moved away.

'Funny about that insurance policy,' commented Barrett when she'd gone. 'What do you reckon? Premonition?'

Morrissey, wondering the same thing himself, said grumpily, 'Like Mrs Simms said, coincidence. So we forget it and get on with some work.'

'What work?' Barrett asked, laconically leaning back and pulling on the corners of his waistcoat. 'There is none, the villains are on holiday.'

That was something else that worried at the chief inspector. He liked the local crooks to stick to normal practice, to keep up with the usual breaking and entering, with petty fraud and thuggery, and all the other things their particular subculture got up to. For it to be as quiet as this was unnerving.

'Then you'd better go and fish some old files out, solve a few things that got by us before,' Morrissey snapped in sudden ill-sorts. His teeth bared in a mean grin. '"There is a purpose to all things and a time for everything under the heavens,"' he misquoted unkindly, 'and before you start solving, round up somebody to fetch tea.'

That, he thought with grim satisfaction, watching Barrett go stiffly out through the door, bristling with resentment, would bring home the error of smart comments about having no work.

FIVE

IF MORRISSEY thought he had persuaded Claire Simms to sit quietly at home and come to terms with her husband's death he was mistaken. Even without the presence of her two children for whom she had to put on a brave face, it would not have been her way to sit in reclusive silence. For her, to *do* had always been infinitely better than to wait. But hers was the problem of limitation rather than of will.

It wasn't that Richard had been a secretive man—there had always been an open forum of discussion between them—Claire couldn't have borne being married to someone less gregariously open than herself. But there were areas of his work that he couldn't talk about, even to her, because if he broke the silence of confidentiality with his wife, then the urgency of discretion with other people would also be lessened in some subtle way. Claire had understood and respected that.

She hadn't known about the insurance policy being jacked up, though, until after Richard's death, when the grey man with his briefcase had come from United Life and Equity and asked questions she couldn't answer. Things like—Did Richard have a medical check-up recently that might have worried him?

If he had he would have told her. That was the only answer she could give, but she hadn't given it with much certainty.

Had he then, said the grey man, incurred some heavy debt that needed repayment?

In the ten years of their marriage they'd never managed to save much, and sometimes they'd been short of cash for a few days before the monthly paycheck went into the joint account, but they had never been dramatically overdrawn. She had shown the grey man—what *was* his name?—their last three bank statements, indignantly angered by half-stated insinuations.

But she hadn't been able to sweep his visit from her mind; it rolled around in her thoughts like a thorn-ball, and as hurtfully.

There were only two ways by which Richard could have anticipated what might happen to him; either he really *had* learned his heart might fail any minute, or he had deliberately contrived his own death, and it was the first that caused Claire the most pain, because knowing her husband as well as she did the second was unthinkable. But for her to suppose Richard had known of something as terrible as his own imminent death, and kept it to himself, uncomforted by her, was more hurt than she felt she could bear. Searching for an alternative—because there always were alternatives if one searched hard enough—she had concluded that some other outside force must be to blame. And that was as far as her mind would take her, because to put a name or a reason to her belief had so far proved impossible.

Alone in the house until her children came home from school, she lay on the big double bed and hugged Richard's old woollen sweater, burying her face in its rough texture. Why else would he have increased his insurance cover, except to make certain she and the children had a breathing space when he was no longer there to look after them? Tears held back since morning soaked the soft wool and released a lingering scent of him.

It was all so stupid, so bloody, bloody stupid!

THEWLIS WENT to see Simms' widow the following day, three days before Halloween. He didn't stop to wonder if she would want to see him. Money made the world go around—offer her a little, do it with a show of good will, tell her how much her husband was thought of by those who knew him, and she'd be eating out of his hand.

Claire, ironing in the front room, saw his car stop at the bottom of the drive. The grey insurance man had come in a black Sierra too, and at first she thought it was him come back again. Then she saw Thewlis and recognised him without pleasure. She'd had to be civil to him three times at social functions and thought him an odious bully, sorry for his wife with her nineteen-fiftyish curls and sad eyes, and the bruise not quite covered up by concealer the last time they'd met.

With a muttered, 'Oh hell!' she turned off the iron and went to open the door, her face tightly unwelcoming. But Thewlis wore his sober face and spoke her husband's paean, and in the end she had no alternative but to ask him in and give him a cup of coffee.

He sat in the chair by the window looking out at the lawn that needed cutting, except that she hadn't been able to take the lawnmower from the shed since Richard died. Cutting the grass had been his Sunday ritual. To do the task herself seemed a near-Judas act. But she would have to do it, soon.

Forgive me, Richard, she thought bleakly, *I'm already putting patches over all the places you used to be; it's the only way we can survive.*

'...unofficially, of course,' Thewlis was saying when she dragged her mind back. 'But I know better than most how tight things can get financially, and Richard had some good friends who owe him favours. In fact,' he gestured magnanimously, 'I'm glad to say I can count myself one of them. So...' He put the cup and saucer on the carpet and felt in his inside pocket. 'I thought maybe a cheque to tide you over until things are sorted out...'

She asked sharply, 'What favours? What did Richard do that needs to be paid for?'

His ferret-sharp eyes, black as the coal he used to dig, closed down while he reviewed what he'd said. Nothing, he decided, nothing it hadn't been safe to say. He changed tack.

'Perhaps I used the wrong word; rightly I should have said kindnesses, not favours. You'll know how Richard would put himself out for people.'

Yes, I do, she thought, *but I can't believe he would do it for you.*

She said, 'Tell me about them, the kindnesses he's done, and then I'll decide if they're worth conscience money.'

'No conscience money about it; it'll go back in my pocket if that's what you think,' he said brusquely, with his own brand of truth. Only fools were troubled by a conscience, a strong man had no need of one.

Claire shrugged. 'I haven't been through Richard's papers yet. When I do, if there are any from the office, I'll pass them on to wherever I think they should go. That would be the best thing to do with them, wouldn't you think?' She watched him struggle and give in, and felt elated to read in his face the thought that there might be something she shouldn't see among them.

He had trouble trying to override annoyance with an insincerity of concern.

'I can save time and bother if you've got the things handy. Planning schedules and such have no place at a time of grief. Have you got them handy?'

'No,' she said, 'I haven't. I'll get around to them myself in a week or so.' His eyes speculated. He held out the slip of paper again.

'This cheque . . .' he tried.

'Don't you know there are things that can't be paid for, Mr Thewlis,' she said. 'Even though it's nice to know how much Richard will be missed. Perhaps his death will turn out to be a mistake after all.'

On his feet now, and ready to go, he was taken by surprise again, worried. 'Mistake? How so a mistake? It was his heart. You can't make mistakes out of heart attacks.'

Claire's smile was without either warmth or humour. 'Then call it a cock-up in heaven,' she invited, 'but don't offer me that bit of paper again, because money is the last thing I need.'

Of all she had said, that last comment shocked him most, told him better than anything else that she wasn't quite right in her head.

On tranquilisers maybe. He knew GPs doled them out like sweets; there'd been a long piece on it in the *News of the World,* a week or two back. No, Simms' wife wouldn't pose any problem. Making his exit, thinking as the door slammed shut behind him that they'd have to get a look at those bloody private papers all the same.

SIX

AT THE BEST of times there were things to be disliked about Guffey, but at the worst of times, when he was bored and short of cash, there were a lot more. And he was both those things now, a yob to be avoided, over-tall, loose-lipped, unco-ordinated after two pints, his pug-nose lost in the plains of his face. Only the sheer size of him stopped the urge to laugh. That and looking in the dead eyes that said Guffey didn't care much about anything, except Guffey.

Two nights ago he'd gone out with his leather-vested Patriots to cause a bit of wreckage, aiming to make it known they were still around, a force to steer clear of. But for once Guffey picked on the wrong pub, throwing his weight around The King Billy when it was full of miners with heads as hard as his own, and a lot more savvy. Sore in defeat, Guffey was out looking for an easier target.

He found it on North Street.

When Azar Khalid took his blond girl-friend to the cinema, he knew his father wouldn't approve, but that added to the delight. Azar had been born in England and behaved in the same way as every other A-level student at Fisher Comprehensive, speaking with the same flat-vowelled accent, his skin colour either ignored or unnoticed. In Malminster that wasn't an unusual thing to happen. Until Skeggy and Beano threw their fire-bomb, the town had considered itself free from prejudice. Now it was a subject talked about uneasily in pub bars and pulpits.

Guffey saw Azar come out of the Odeon with his arm round Karen Gosnay, and kiss her good-night at the bus-stop. When the Westmoor bus pulled away with her on it, Azar tucked his hands in the pockets of his jacket and headed home, turning right onto Queen Street, crossing at an angle to Carter Street and then along the ill-lit ginnel that led onto the Industrial Estate's circular access road. He was happy, his mind flitting from Karen to the school football team and back again, and relaxed as he was the footsteps behind him held no significance—there were always footsteps because there were always people.

Then Guffey loped past and turned to block Azar's path, setting up a chant of, 'Curry-head, curry-head, curry-head,' that was taken up behind Azar too.

Pleasure died, and Azar's mind emptied of everything except fear. Cornered, all he could do was brace himself against the high wall, and wait.

Insults came.

'Crap-head wog!'

'Shit-face!'

Spittle hit him on the cheek, and ran, warmly obscene. He wiped it with his sleeve. The heel of Guffey's hand slammed Azar's head hard against the brick wall. Azar struck back in reflex and a fist took him full in the mouth, knocking back his teeth, splitting his nose and lips, crashing his head into the wall again. A boot rose and he screamed out with the agony of it, falling awkwardly. Red pain rushing through his shoulder spread through his body with the crushing thud of boots. He was going to die, he had done nothing wrong, and he was going to die: hearing the dark wings of Azrael beat above his head.

AFTER THE FIRE DEATHS, Azar's father had thought long and earnestly about moving his family away from the terraced houses, but the shame of admitting he was afraid had outweighed the fear itself.

'The perpetrators are dead now,' he had told his neighbours, trying thereby to convince himself, 'and although I am very bloody worried, we must trust the police who say we shall be safe.' And Abdhul Khalid had done that, even when three families directly across the street moved away. Seeing the empty houses boarded up, he had raised his hands in something like despair. 'It is bad,' he told his wife, 'to be forced from a home by fear alone.'

Now, Abdhul Khalid was angry with his son. Azar had been told to be in the house by ten-thirty and it was midnight. Azar's mother Nazir was weeping in her chair. There was nothing to be done but for Abdhul to go and look for the boy, although where he should begin to look was a problem. Abdhul had tried to embrace Western ways, to give his son some freedom, but this was not a just repayment. Uneasily he watched the clock, and when ten more minutes had gone by he went to the houses of two close friends, and together they left the huddle of streets, discussing where Azar might be.

It had been a terrible mistake on Azar's part to use the short cut. Between night-shift workers coming on at ten, and day-shift workers at six the next morning, no one used the ginnel.

Azar's uncle Iqbal, who had a small taxi business off Queen Street, had said he would gladly drive his nephew home should the need arise. The offer had been made when Iqbal, having once lived for three depressing years in Solihull, remembered how paint-daubing and the emptying of dustbins often led to worse.

Abdhul had told his son he must either accept his uncle's kindness or walk home the long way. Knowing that had been his instruction, and having expected obedience, he looked everywhere before he was persuaded to enter the ginnel and look there. When he found his son, the only way he could recognise him was by his clothes.

WHEN THE 999 call was made just before one-thirty in the morning, it took the emergency operator awhile to understand what the man on the other end of the line was telling her, he spoke so rapidly and was in such obvious distress. Hicks took the call in his patrol car, putting his foot down and starting the siren. He entered the ginnel warily, because at that time in the morning, when clubs were closing their doors, hoaxes were not uncommon.

When his white torch beam picked out Azar cradled against his father, the boy looked already dead. Blood had spattered over the cracked and grimy paving stones, and in one place had pooled. Squatting, searching for a pulse under chilled and clammy skin, trying not to feel sick, Hicks almost missed the thready flutter. Not murder then, not yet, but it would be, he told himself, and maybe even before the ambulance got there. But Azar was still weakly clinging to life when he reached the hospital.

MORRISSEY REACHED his office at eight and found the two reports on his desk. One hand written, the other hacked out on the CID Remington, the misaligned 'e' evidence of its source. He knew what their content would be before he looked. *'Another racial attack at Malminster'* had been the news-reader's opening words on the breakfast bulletin. He lowered his buttocks into the ancient desk chair, comforted by its groan, and read the two reports grim-faced. Ian Hicks seemed to make a habit of being first on the scene.

Grudgingly, Morrissey admitted to himself that Katie's latest conquest had turned in another copy-book example of correct procedure; he should go far, not in Malminster, though, not while he went out with the chief inspector's daughter. Promotion, when he earned it, would have to come at some other division where favouritism couldn't be said to have a hand in it.

Barrett came up from the canteen and set a mugful of coffee in front of Morrissey that looked surprisingly unlethal.

'Made it with my own lily-white hands,' he said. 'Freddie was too busy to care.'

Morrissey took a wary swig and approved. He shoved the reports at Barrett.

'You'd better read them. It's one for you, something you should be able to handle on your own.'

Barrett looked gratified. 'I'll do my level best.'

'You might need to do better than that, Neil, and be careful where you put your big feet, they'll be treading in sensitive areas.'

Like Morrissey's did.

Barrett picked up the reports and retired to his desk, trying not to scowl. It was always the same, hand him half a compliment with one hand and squash it flat with the other. He read in silence then said stiffly, 'I'll take Copeland, unless you've other plans for him.'

'Take Woods as well. Teach him the way we like things done.'

Barrett perked up again. 'Glad to,' he said. 'I'll keep him with me. That way he can't pick up bad habits.'

Morrissey swallowed his grin, and hoped DC Woods appreciated the favour.

AT HIS HOME in Bradford, a man whose carefully channelled appetite for violence could make Guffey's outbursts seem like school-boy pranks had also been listening to the local radio, and he didn't like the way his mind made an immediate link between last night's violence and Guffey, because if his mind made the link, others would too. Vic Duttin had been paid to act as middle-man, and if anything went wrong, all the weight would fall on him.

He'd hired Guffey to have his scabby bunch of Nazi-loving farters burn a row of lock-up garages, not torch a bleeding house!

He was irked too, to think he'd had the wool pulled over his eyes. Guffey, sweating and swearing under near-neck-breaking pressure, had sold him a lie. 'I told 'em,' he'd squirmed, 'I told 'em garages. Honest, I never sent 'em out to do an 'ouse.' Oh yes! Only last night's little do said it hadn't been the flattened kids who'd got it wrong, the slobbering pug-face had given the wrong order. Vic had said to lay off now until it quietened down—given an extra little twist to reinforce he meant it.

Now this. One sodding mistake too many.

Goodbye, Guffey!

He swung his legs out of bed and sat naked on the edge, heavy-shouldered and thick-necked, the Torremolinos tan fading. The woman in the bed was naked too, glad to see him reaching for his underpants, but too much of a professional to let it show. Instead, she ran an exploratory hand along his spine, touching the three-inch scar that had healed white and pearly. If the knife had done better, Vic wouldn't have had many mourners.

'It's early, come back for a bit.' He shrugged away and she withdrew her hand. So what? She'd earned her money already, and then some. Maybe next time she'd let someone else have a turn. He took two tens from a thin wad and dropped them on the bed.

'Here,' she said. 'You said thirty for the night.'

'Piss off,' he said. 'You wasn't even worth that.'

BARRETT HAD been gone an hour and Osgodby expressed surprise that Morrissey wasn't out with him. Rocking a little on his heels, whistling air in through his teeth in a way the chief inspector particularly detested, he finally said bluntly that which he hadn't been able to find diplomatic words for.

'Not because the boy's a Pakistani, is it, John, that you've let Barrett have it on his own?' Back-tracking when Morrissey's eyes turned to slate, cold as the distaste on his face. Saying defensively, 'That wasn't meant the way it sounded.'

Morrissey barked back in brusque anger. 'If I didn't think Barrett could handle it, he wouldn't be out there. I'm surprised you had to ask. As far as I'm concerned he's acting up for Beckett; it isn't a murder inquiry, not yet.'

'From what I've heard . . .'

'Critical but stable, that's the latest,' cut in the chief inspector. 'If that changes it'll be time for a re-think—if Neil hasn't already got results by then.'

'Ah!' Osgodby made a second wrong connection, assuming Barrett had already had instructions from the chief inspector on where to look for a fast arrest. His thoughts ran on some. No harm then in going back upstairs and telling his visitor it was all in hand. Better still, he could let Morrissey do it. He suited thought to action. 'If you've got a minute to spare, John, I'd appreciate it,' he said. 'Up in my office.'

Having come in heavy-footed, the chief superintendent went out lightly. That was the only warning Morrissey had before he found himself facing Ishmal Habib, endeavouring to explain why a senior officer like himself wasn't out hunting Azar's attackers, instead of it being a detective sergeant.

Habib had been only recently chosen as spokesman for Malminster's small Asian community, and he felt honoured by such a mark of respect. A courteous man and well-fed, with sparse grey hair and round, rimless glasses, he wore his best charcoal suit and white shirt to show how serious was his worry. Habib owned a thriving Texaco garage near the roundabout on Middlebrook Road, and two out of his three sons worked there. The youngest son, like Azar, had stayed on at Fisher Comprehensive. This was the first time Mr Habib had needed to talk to the police on a matter of such profound importance, and he took his responsibilities seriously.

He shook Morrissey's hand briefly and said politely, 'You understand, it is not that I doubt the ability of a junior police officer, but it is very important for the reassurance of my community that these people are caught and punished.'

'Detective Sergeant Barrett is a very competent officer,' said Morrissey. 'I expect someone to be in custody before too long.'

'Then the chief superintendent is right and you already know the culprit?' Habib said eagerly. 'That is the best of all things. It will comfort Azar's father.'

Morrissey gave Osgodby a baleful look, and told Habib, 'I'd prefer that what I say to you stays in this room.'

'Then what shall I say to my friend Mr Khalid?'

'Tell him we're working hard and we expect good results. As soon as we have the right person in custody, Mr Khalid will be the first to know. That I promise you.'

'You were dancing backwards a bit there, John,' said Osgodby when Habib had gone. He steepled his fingers and brought out his harassed 'the buck stops here' look. 'I thought you said you knew who it was?'

'*You* said it, I didn't. I know where my first call would be, and I wouldn't expect to be making a second, but it's Neil's case, and unless I'm much mistaken he'll end up in the right place.'

'I don't think that's good enough.'

'Then you'll just have to override my judgement. You have the authority to do that,' said Morrissey shortly.

Osgodby glowered again at that. Morrissey wasn't often wrong, but at the same time, he couldn't always be right, and if this was one of those times, the whole bloody shooting match would land on his, Osgodby's, head. He stared at the chief inspector's stony face, and slammed the pencil he'd been turning end on end down, hard.

'I'll leave it as it is,' he said, and leaning over his desk towards the chief inspector lapsed into one of his rare displays of crudity. 'But I'll tell you this; if any shit hits my fan, there'll be a whole bloody sewage works fouling up yours.'

ABDHUL KHALID had told the police his son was a good boy, that Azar had spent the evening with his friends from school. But since Khalid's knowledge hadn't extended to which friends, Barrett had packed Copeland off to Fisher Comprehensive to find out. In control of things for once, Barrett started his investigation methodically, and with Wood in tow he went to see the ginnel; the SOCO team, called out in the middle of the night, had already done their work once under arc lights, but now they were going over the ground again by daylight, the ginnel sealed off behind yellow tape barriers.

The pattern and spread of stains on the paving coupled with clumped hair adhering to the brick wall, gave a grim picture of how it must have looked when Azar was found.

'Poor little sod,' said Woods. 'Got a right kicking by the look of it.' He squatted down, balancing on his toes. 'Segged boots. I suppose that's a help.'

'What?' Barrett squatted to see the imprint. So much for the lecture he'd been going to give on keeping your eyes open. He gave Woods a pep talk on not jumping to conclusions instead. The marks could, he pointed out, have been left innocently, other people wore segs in their boots—and shoes too, for that matter—besides yobs. The boy's father, or one of his friends; an ambulance man, even one of their own lot. Having impressed his superior knowledge he let his own mind leap from A to Z without worrying about any steps in between.

Painting swastikas, throwing fire-bombs, and beating up Asian school-boys all fitted into the same kind of warped pattern of mentality. It was a short step to take from there to Guffey and his mob. Barrett got to his feet and dusted himself down.

Walking back to the car he expanded on the difference between deduction and assumption. Woods, whose right knee, while still in uniform, had once connected with Guffey's boot, beat Barrett to the punch-line.

'Going to find Guffey, then, are we?' he said cheerfully, and started up the engine.

IN THE COLD light of a new day Guffey was beginning to reassess things. What had been a laugh with a six-pack circulating through his brain, looked a lot different now. He'd spent the night in Badger's bed-sit, and at about the same time as Vic Duttin caught the news bulletin in Bradford, Guffey was working on how to get out of sight. He had a favour owing in Barnsley, so he could doss there for a bit, and then move on down to Brum, get in with one of the outfits.

Yeah—that sounded good.

Down at the bottom of Canal Road where lorries parked overnight, there was a transport cafe. When Guffey got his head together he went there at a fast lope, thinking he might hitch a lift. It was a place he knew well, his office, where he conducted whatever little business deals came his way, like the bargain he'd struck with Vic Duttin for the harassment campaign.

Duttin himself, driving south from Bradford with an urgent need to rid himself of a problem, played a hunch in going straight to the cafe, guessing what might be in Guffey's head. Vic regretted the mistake he'd made in using local talent; he should have brought in from outside, kept away from amateurs. Now there was a mess to clean up before it spilled over onto him. He pulled onto the rough-surfaced car-park and waited.

A few minutes later a tipper truck drove in and parked. Its driver leaned out and saluted. Duttin left the car and went inside.

Guffey was wary when Vic hooked out a chair and sat down at the same table; he'd already had grief from that direction. But Duttin today was being helpful, making the same suggestion Guffey had already come up with himself.

Lie low for a bit.

'This'll help,' said Duttin generously, and saw the slack mouth grin.

With a fat wad of tenners filling his pocket, Guffey felt secure. 'Anything else you need doing,' he said, 'anytime. Don't matter what.'

The tipper truck driver had come in soon after Duttin. Now he brought his food over, dripping juices from a bacon butty.

'Sure,' Duttin was saying, still busy humouring Guffey. 'Soon as anything comes up I'll be in touch. Where you making for?'

No longer skint, Guffey scrapped thoughts of Barnsley. 'South.' He leaned sideways, nudging the truck driver. 'You heading south then?'

'Yeah. Why?'

'Give us a ride if you like.'

The driver eyed him without breaking the rhythm of his jaw. Duttin said, 'See you, then,' and left them to it.

IN A QUIET lay-by half-way to Doncaster, the trucker dropped Guffey off. It'd been one of Vic's rush jobs, on the phone one minute and expected to find the right wheels the next. When he'd asked about the money, Duttin had given that low, nasty laugh of his. 'He'll have it on him, won't he.'

Heading the tipper north now, up the A1, he patted the tenners he'd taken from Guffey. A couple of miles further and, still grinning, he ditched the stolen truck and caught a bus back to Leeds.

Like Vic said. Easy money.

EIGHT

No ONE had actively expected Claire Simms to go ahead with her coffee morning, but like a juggernaut with only one way to go, Claire had determined to keep to an organised path, only in that way could she hang on to any sense of purpose. And so, the notices had stayed where they were in the local shop windows, and the library foyer, and Claire herself had telephoned the rest of the Oxfam committee members, reminding them there were cakes to be baked and things to find for the bring-and-buy.

More people turned up than she expected, reflecting that oddity of human nature, a fascination with the surroundings of death. Her bright blue dress caused flurries of speculation over the coffee cups, her bright smile even more, except to those who knew her well enough to see past the disguise. To Margaret Morrissey, pouring coffee while Claire sliced cake and offered biscuits, the facade was fragile enough to break at any minute. She knew how Claire had reacted at the inquest, and understood—or so she believed—the mechanics behind it. She didn't know, until Claire told her, about the visit to Malminster police station, and Morrissey's gentle but firm refusal to dig more deeply into Simms' death.

'It isn't imagination,' Claire said as they cleared up the morning's debris. 'Richard stumbled onto something that worried him, and now it's all being covered up. You know who came to see me yesterday? Thewlis. Chairman of the Planning Committee, making sympathetic noises. Richard didn't like him, you know, but to hear Thewlis talk you'd have thought they were like that.' She wrapped her first and second fingers together. 'It wasn't even part of Richard's job to attend committed meetings—area officers aren't involved in that kind of thing, only the chief planner. What Thewlis really came for was to find out what kind of papers Richard kept at home.'

'What kind did he?'

Claire stopped what she was doing and stared.

'It's all right,' Margaret said. 'You don't have to tell me. I'm not a spy.'

Claire reddened and looked away. 'I'm becoming paranoid,' she admitted. 'But you know, no one's talked to Richard's GP; no one's asked about his medical history. Why is that, do you think? I told Thewlis I hadn't looked in Richard's papers.'

'But you had.'

'There's reams of stuff, some of it from way back, before we came to Malminster. I'll need to have a bonfire.' Margaret waited, but Claire had finished with the subject. Not until everything was done and Margaret was ready to leave did Claire say with quiet emphasis: 'Persuade John I'm not insane with grief. That would be the biggest act of friendship anyone could do me right now.'

FINDING GUFFEY turned out to be a lot harder than Barrett had anticipated. 'I bet he's half-way to London,' Woods offered. 'Hitchhiking, most like. What about trying transport caffs?'

Through the windscreen Barrett stared at the road, thoughts of being Woods' mentor vanishing fast. Teaching the new DC the ropes was turning into a salvage operation for Barrett's own dignity. 'I'd been hoping you might work that out for yourself,' he said, and borrowed a leaf out of

Morrissey's book. 'Good thinking. We'll make a policeman out of you yet.'

Woods dawdled at the T-junction. 'Which way then?'

'Back to the office, and when we get there you can put a
call out on Guffey.'

'What about the caffs then?'

'The Pandas can check them out.'

'Good idea,' said Woods encouragingly.

'All-night launderettes too.'

Woods turned his head. 'What?'

'Blood,' said Barrett, in tone superior. 'It'd be all over
their clothes, wouldn't it? That's the sort of thing it takes
experience to know about.' Confidence restored he relaxed
in contemplative silence until Woods swung into the police
yard. Copeland's car was back. If he'd been lucky at Fisher's, they could probably get the whole thing wrapped up in
one day. A fast result would look very good on Barrett's
record sheet.

Eagerly taking the stairs two at a time, pleased to find
himself barely out of breath when he reached the top, he
pulled on his waistcoat, lying flatter now since Michelle,
giggling, had patted his developing paunch and said he reminded her of a cuddly bear. Cuddly didn't fit with Barrett's view of himself in the lover league.

Copeland was at his desk, pecking at the Remington with
a look of concentrated effort. He detested the machine and
stopped all activity when he saw Barrett, thinking that
maybe, with a bit of luck, he'd be sent back out and not
need to look at the damn thing again until tomorrow.

'Well?' asked Barrett.

'Well,' answered Copeland. 'It took a bit of persuading,
because they didn't want to get him in trouble with his father, but Azar's been going out with a girl called Karen
Gosnay; used to go to Fisher's but left last year to work in

Woolworth's. I went and had a talk with her, and it seems she went to the pictures with him last night. Just before ten Azar put her on the Westmoor bus and started walking home. She was looking out through the window and saw three toe-rags following him out of the bus station. She said one looked like Frankenstein.'

'Guffey,' said Barrett with satisfaction.

'Want me to pick him up?'

'Uniform have it. What I want you to do is round up the rest of Guffey's lot. Organise a van and back-up, and take Woods.'

'A pleasure,' said Copeland, and meant it. Anything that kept him and the old finger-breaker apart had to be good.

INSPECTOR BECKETT was walking the corridors with a thin hollow tube taped to his cheek. The tube went up his nose and down through his naso-pharynx to his stomach. Every few hours someone came along with a giant syringe and sucked up his gastric juices. He longed for a plate of fish and chips.

The wound from his operation had reduced his normal buoyant stride to what seemed to him a near-shuffle, but was actually a careful walk. He had listened to seemingly endless lectures on lifestyle and diet, all of which had gone in one ear and out the other. But he was less depressed now, than when the ambulance had delivered him in through the Casualty doors. Jean was talking to him again.

Reconciliation hung in his mind like a tantalising prize, but he was stepping carefully, as unsure of himself now as he had been when they first met. He didn't know it but it was that air of uncertainty that made Jean more gentle.

Expecting her that afternoon, Beckett had set off on his longest walk yet, to find the flower kiosk.

God! It was years since he'd given her flowers.

He turned what he hoped would be the last corner.

Outside Intensive Care three men were speaking rapid Urdu. Beckett recognised Mustaph Ali and slowed his pace even more. With nothing else to do but read and listen to the radio he'd inevitably heard the early news, and seeing Ali the two things connected in his mind. Stopping, hoping it wasn't another Ali family member, and saying that was automatic.

Ali remembered Beckett's voice, but had to struggle past the tube and sagging dressing gown to remember the face. When he did he excitedly passed on his knowledge to the other two men, pumping the inspector's hand with vigour, and half embarrassing him.

'It is not my family, no. It is the son of my friend, Mr Beckett,' Ali said, drawing Khalid forward. 'And it is very bad. I have told him he should leave his home and live in another place. Now you must tell him the same.'

'I can't,' said Beckett. 'We've all got a right to live where we want. But the bloody thugs'll be caught, I can promise that.'

'That is not enough,' said Ali. 'There will be more of them.'

'What about you, Mr Khalid. How is your son?'

'He knows no one,' Khalid grieved. 'Not even his mother. I blame myself. For seven months we have been told we must leave; now my son is sacrificed. This is my stubbornness.'

'I wouldn't call it that,' Beckett said. 'It takes guts to stand up to intimidation.'

Khalid shook his head and spread his hands. 'I must go to Azar; he is my punishment,' he said, and left them.

BY MID-AFTERNOON Copeland's trawl through Malminster had netted four Patriots. They were locked in separate cells, sullenly refusing to talk. Badger was picked up in an amusement arcade at three-thirty, and the bleached white stripe down the centre of his crew-cut made it a simple job for the night attendant at a local launderette to remember him sitting in his jockeys, waiting for the machine to stop.

Barrett was chirpy. All they needed now was Guffey, who had neither the brains, or the means, to get very far, and he gave it as his considered opinion that it wouldn't be long before they had him. Then a Panda driver radioed in from Joe's Caff and pricked his bubble of certainty.

Guffey's looks were unique enough not to be mistaken. If he'd been picked up by a truckie on Canal Road that morning, he could be anywhere in England now.

Gloom replaced elation. Barrett had caught four tiddlers, but the piranha had gone.

NINE

IT WAS NEARLY half-past eight and Morrissey and his wife sat in companionable silence by the fire, their dinner over, the washing-up done. The heavy curtains were open, letting light flow out across the long front lawn. These days Margaret refused to have them closed until both her children were home, a change of habit that, like the friction between himself and Mike, reached back to April and a serial killer's personal vendetta.

Police work and families sometimes clashed; it was one of the hazards of the job, something that had to be lived with. This time Katie, who had suffered the most, had recovered her equilibrium while the rest of them still floundered. Tonight she was out busily rehearsing in the college play.

Mike was out too, supposedly watching a Batman video at a friend's house, but in reality locked in intergalactic combat in a forbidden amusement arcade. The game itself wasn't important, although Mike would have said differently; his real objective, only half recognised, was a levelling of scores with his father. Mike knew most of the tension between them was his fault, but knowing it, and being able to stop the process, grew harder after each skirmish.

By eight-thirty he'd fed the machine all the money he had except for a fifty-pence piece, and he exchanged that on the other side of the roundabout for a bag of chips and a can of cola, which led in turn to the breaking of another of his father's rules, when he had of necessity to walk home instead of catching a bus.

Morrissey, happily unaware of what his son had been up to, watched cherry logs crackle and spurt on the open fire and settled comfortably back in his chair. Evenings of such domestic felicity were rare. Margaret was knitting, one eye on the red yarn and the other keeping track of a television play, her face looked relaxed, placid even, and gave her husband no hint of the inner struggle engaged in to find an unprovocative way in which she could bring up discussion of Claire's coffee morning. She'd been having difficulty deciding how to broach the subject ever since she arrived home. The important thing, she had decided, was to stress that in her own opinion Claire was neither over-imaginative or hysterical.

In the end she had to give up trying for diplomacy and come right out with it, the knitting lying loosely in her lap while she related Claire's theory about Thewlis, doing it in a kind of dogged determination to hold Morrissey's attention, and finished up by telling him firmly that what would be really kind, especially since he'd already said how quiet things were at the office, would be for him to read through Richard's file again.

Kind, maybe, Morrissey thought, except that he knew the damn thing by heart already, and if he read it back to front and sideways on, it wouldn't come out differently. He was chary of saying so however because his wife infringed on the official side of his life so seldom that when she did he tended to listen. When she took up her knitting again, the needles rubbing against each other rhythmically as her fingers moved, her eyes were not on the transfer of stitches but on him.

He said unwillingly, 'I'll talk to her again, but I'm not a miracle man. I can't produce anything that isn't there in the first place.'

'I don't think she'd want you to,' Margaret said. 'I think she just wants the things that are there explained.'

Morrissey sighed. Hadn't he just said he wasn't a miracle man? He was wondering whether to reiterate that when Mike banged into the house, slamming the door behind him with unnecessary violence, provoking quick annoyance, and the resulting sharp exchange between father and son spoiled Margaret's pleasure at her child's safe return.

THE SMALL LEATHER case that Thewlis took with him when he went out on Thursday evenings held a similar effect as a security blanket. It reminded him how far he'd come from the hovel he'd been born in on Cow Lane. Membership of the Masonic Lodge was by invitation, and entailed being either a close friend of a member or holding a position of power that might prove useful. Thewlis wasn't in the first category, no one willingly called themselves a personal friend of his, but a small coterie whose ethics didn't correspond at all with those of the Masonic movement as a whole had decided that to admit Thewlis would be both a good insurance and a way to keep an eye on him.

Thewlis, at first chary, had now taken membership literally to his bosom, enjoying the rites and trappings and the way attendance at Lodge evenings allowed him to wear a respectable face. It was also a place where he could meet unnoticed with the men for whom he sometimes expedited, sometimes slowed, the passage of planning applications through various committee stages.

The day after he'd visited Claire Simms, he talked with them again. No one disagreed when he said Simms' heart problem had surfaced at just the right time, and no one contradicted him when he said it had been a good thing for them, but when he said they still might have a problem with

Simms' private papers—the ones he'd kept at home—a few looks were exchanged that he affected not to see.

When he left, reassured that such papers represented only a minor problem that could easily be taken care of by others rather than him, he didn't ask how. He wasn't even all that interested. But it was comforting, he thought, as he swung his car onto the main road, to have an accommodating policeman on-side looking after their concerns.

MORRISSEY DIDN'T notice Margaret's guilty relief that the dispute with Mike couldn't erupt again at breakfast. The chief inspector had made up his mind to get Claire Simms off his mind once and for all, and left home early so that he could go through the file again in peace, skipping breakfast except for a cup of coffee, and saying he would get something from the canteen.

He went into the police building through the back entrance and down the basement stairs, sniffing fatty fry-up smells with appreciation, but in the end with the memory of Beckett's grey face still in his mind, he settled for poached egg and grilled tomatoes, and had toast in place of fried bread, knowing such sensible eating would inevitably lapse into greasy chip butties when he was forced to eat on the wing again. When he turned from the counter he saw the bulky Lister, alone by a radiator mopping up dregs of cholesterol with a piece of bread.

He took his tray to Lister's table. 'Waste not, want not,' he said as he sat down.

Lister glanced at him. 'Bad habits die hard. What got you in this early? Fallen out with the missus?'

Morrissey said, 'A bit of sniffing around I want to do, not strictly official but necessary for peace of mind.' Lacing his plate with salt and pepper.

'Hah! Let me guess. Simms' wife got at you again.'

'Indirectly.'

'Heard she'd been in once to see you, must be making it a habit.'

'She hasn't been back.'

'What, then?'

The chief inspector ate stolidly. He was beginning to see why Lister's manner would annoy Barrett; every word that came out of his mouth held implied criticism.

'Intuition.'

'Women's stuff!'

'Chief Inspector's stuff,' Morrissey said sharply.

'Duff hares.'

'We'll see. Nothing that worried you about the accident, nothing at all?'

Lister threw up his hands. 'God Almighty! How many more bloody times? Procedure was followed right down the line, car checked, froggies down the weir, witnesses talked to. What more do you want?'

'Did you find out what he was doing, working that late?'

Lister's eyes flickered over Morrissey's face. He said impatiently, 'It wasn't relevant, was it? I needed to know where he'd been, not what he'd been doing. Look, I'll talk to Mrs Simms myself. Get her off your back that way.'

'She isn't on it,' the chief inspector said. 'This is personal curiosity.'

'Nice to know CID have time. Break's over.' Lister heaved his weight off the chair and moved away, leaving an aura of bristling resentment behind him. A man with a serious attitude problem decided Morrissey analytically. Didn't like encroachment on what he saw as his piece of territory.

Back in his office Morrissey re-read every piece of paper with an increasing sense of futility, nothing left undone. Accident reports, forensic reports, post-mortem results. A painstaking survey of the car's mechanical systems. Tyre

checks. Witness statements. All too meticulous to pick holes
in. Cursing with quiet vigour as he closed the cover, because the unease was back.

Barrett came in whistling, said, 'Good morning,' and
riffled through the few preliminary reports on his desk, one
eye on the chief inspector, and looking pleased with himself.

'That good is it?' asked Morrissey dourly.

'I'd say it was just about wrapped up.'

It was a positive statement. Barrett saw no reason for any
pretence at modesty. Guffey might not have been flushed
out of his hiding place, but it was only a matter of time, and
he didn't believe loyalty would be a strong factor, not with
a minimum ten years in jail as the price of silence. Faced
with that, the four banged up in cells would shop their
mothers.

Buoyant in a vanity of perceived success, he couldn't
prevent a grin when he recounted Badger's self-betraying
oversight. It wasn't everyone who'd launder combats and
forget to clean his boots. Seg-soled too. Bagged up and labelled as soon as Barrett had seen the state of them, they
were now in Forensics' loving care.

Morrissey beamed expected approval, gratified Barrett
had performed as expected. 'Shows what you can do when
you put your mind to it,' he said. 'Try and do it more often.'

Going upstairs to brief Osgodby turned out to be a mistake. Morrissey's intention had been to get his visit to Claire
Simms over with when he got out of the chief superintendent's office, but things didn't work out that way. Over-
joyed to hear how things were being tidied up so fast,
Osgodby delegated Morrissey to replace him at that morning's meeting of senior officers. 'Be a lot more useful for
you to talk about the needs of inter-divisional co-operation

than me,' he said blandly. 'Like you're always telling me, it's you down at grass-roots level, cleaning up all the dirt. Nothing important on, had you? Quiet but for this assault business, and Sergeant Barrett's handling that nicely. Free lunch—wine thrown in—what more can you want, John?' He lifted his wrist with a show of innocence. 'Starts in thirty minutes. Just gives us time for a briefing.'

Morrissey fumed with impotence. The last thing he needed was a morning spent listening to how many new rules could be formulated. The more a thing got talked about, the more difficult it became to achieve. Once upon a time, he'd been able to pick up a telephone, ask for whatever information he needed, and get it. Now it was forms and procedure, and having to find the correctly authorised officer, who nine times out of ten had just gone off on tea-break.

It'd be two o'clock, maybe later, before he got away. Impossible to get to the Simms' house now before mid-afternooon.

'If anything comes up...' he said gruffly resentful.

Osgodby smiled widely, his reddish face under the sparse, sandy hair, cherubic. 'I'll be with the CC all morning. Expectation of a messy balls-up in race relations hasn't pleased him; he'll be glad to know you've got it sorted out.' He looked at his watch again. 'Better get a move on,' he said, and, reaching for a blue-starred file, looked happy.

IT WAS EARLY afternoon and the line of washing was almost dry. Claire stood under the rose arch, and lifted her face to the sun, unseasonably warm for late October. The yellow rambler still had heavy, delicately scented flower heads. It would need to be pruned back; something else to add to the list of things she must learn to do herself. She felt a lethargic disinclination to do anything, even think. The temptation to walk away from it all was a persistent force. It was

hard to keep faith with Richard, when at the core of her being all she wanted was to grieve. Why did it matter how he
died? It was enough, surely, that he was dead. She rubbed
her hand restlessly against the knobby wood; maybe it was
a natural human need at a time of bereavement to right
wrongs, but it was damned hard to climb up a mountain
everyone else said didn't exist.

And what if she proved it did?

Shying away from the idea that she might at the same time
prove her husband had been less than shiny bright. Would
she really gain anything by that? Was that the way to keep
faith?

The telephone rang stridently from inside the house and
cut across her thoughts, severing them from things to be
done. She went inside and moved into the cool hall. When
she lifted the receiver a chill, flat, man's voice, said, 'I've
been talking to your pretty little daughter, Rachel. Happy
little child. Very fond of Smarties. Leave things alone, Mrs
Simms, while you still have two children.'

Air rushed fast into her lungs, coming out in a gasp. The
receiver clicked and hummed in her ear. She laid it back on
the rest and stood in silence. Through the window the sky
was surprisingly blue, with raggy bits of white muslin cloud
dragged across it by a light southwest breeze. It was warm
in the hall, the coldness that made her skin shiver in response came from inside herself. She thought of ringing
Morrissey, but instead dragged on her jacket and fled to the
kindergarten, insisting on taking Rachel home. From there
she went to her son's school and concocted some story about
a medical appointment only now remembered. On her way
home, she called at the estate agents on North Street, and
put her house up for sale, then took her children into a quiet
cafe and let them eat chocolate biscuits and drink cola, until she stopped feeling sick.

When she put her key in the front door at four-thirty, she'd missed Morrissey's visit by ten minutes.

VIC DUTTIN hadn't asked what Guffey's final disposal had been; he didn't really want to know, the method didn't matter, but when it was done he'd telephoned Richardson to say the problem had been dealt with and couldn't recur. He hadn't mentioned how much he was out of pocket, that wasn't the way he did business, but Friday's post brought a bonus in a brown padded bag that more than covered it.

Late Friday afternoon Richardson had another, and totally unexpected telephone call, one that brought a new worry; this call wasn't from Duttin, and its content didn't please him at all. Unbridled initiative wasn't something to be encouraged when a badly judged move could waste everything, things were critical enough without amateur dabbling. His response was an acidly snarled: 'Something you thought up yourself, was it? Spur of the moment? Off the cuff? Bloody idiot!' The caller hadn't liked that; Richardson hadn't cared. Thick as two short planks; threatening Claire Simms' children. He'd said that too, with succinct venom, wondering all the time if he ought now to go for safety and call off the Saturday break-ins. It hadn't been easy, finding the right people, setting it all up. But if the Simms house were watched . . .

'I'd know about if it was, wouldn't I?' said the caller. 'So cool your frigging knickers.'

'And if she goes straight to Morrissey?'

'What if she does. What's this bloody myth about Morrissey; he's not the Great White Whale.'

'But I am,' said Richardson silkily. 'One more mistake and you'll know Ahab was lucky.' He slammed down the receiver then, and the idea that he might give Duttin another little job went through his mind.

If he did, it would cost.

Another couple of days, he decided. Wait and see what the widow would do.

TEN

MORRISSEY WAS restless, never a good or comfortable sign. He had been preoccupied all through breakfast, only half hearing what was said by the other members of his family, then snapping with unreasonable irritation when Mike dripped egg and swore mildly. He told himself he'd been right to correct his son, bad language left unchecked escalated into worse, but he knew the reaction had been harsher than was necessary, and the knowledge made him resent all the more Margaret's quick attempt at a salvage operation. It hadn't worked of course, father and son had widened the distance between themselves even further, and Morrissey didn't want to think where the continual head-butting might lead. Remembering Mike's Saturday morning rugger practice, he had gruffly offered his son a lift to school, hoping the boy would take it, but Mike had given him a cool, 'No thanks,' and turned away.

Turning left onto Middlebrook Road, he passed a mother with two children, each child carried a turnip lantern. Nostalgia for simpler days flooded over him.

Autumn had never been his favourite season, not even when the weather stayed mellow instead of blasting in on cold gales. But the restlessness he felt this year was different. He knew in his bones that something was going to happen, and it worried at the back of his mind like a thorn in his thumb. He couldn't get Claire Simms and her sad eyes out of his head. Frustrated at his inability to pinpoint the exact cause of his *angst* he stayed in his office only long enough to ruffle Barrett's feathers before driving out to the Simms house.

When Claire opened the door her son appeared in the hall behind her, the look on his face protective, a seven-year-old trying to fill his father's shoes.

Left alone in a bright sitting-room, Morrissey stood with his hands clasped behind him, looking out at the garden while she made coffee, rehearsing in his mind how he would tell her again the things she'd heard and not believed before. When Claire came back into the room he took the tray from her and set it on the low table, waiting until she had seated herself on the chintz-covered sofa, a child, guardian-angel-like, on each side, before he lowered himself into a wide but low easy chair opposite, his knees sticking up at an ungainly angle as a penalty of his height. He watched as she poured, her hands firm and capable.

Morrissey began to repeat the negative things that had to be said as soon as she sat back against the cushions, but this time he approached it differently, telling her in detail what investigations had been done, and why, and what the results had been. He left nothing out. She listened and looked attentive, but the anger and drive were gone from her eyes and the chief inspector felt her mind was occupied with more pressing things. Before the difficult exercise in diplomacy had finished, the doorbell rang, and Claire excused herself, leaving him to be scrutinised by the children. The hall door closed behind her, cutting him off from whoever might be calling.

Morrissey cleared his throat.

Standing square before him the small girl stared wide-eyed and crammed a biscuit in her mouth.

Claire was back almost at once, wiping chocolate from her daughter's fingers and looking more distant still.

Outside the house a rhythmic hammering, of wood on wood, started up, overriding traffic sounds. Morrissey half-turned in his chair, looking out through the window across the angular lawn. Two men, jacketless, were busy near the gate, hammering a *Hearthstone* HOUSE FOR SALE sign into the dry soil.

He brought his attention back into the room, seeing Claire's set face, the clumsiness with which she re-tied the yellow ribbon in Rachel's hair, and gentled his voice.

'You're moving, then. That surprises me. I'd have thought it the last thing you'd want to do.'

She answered without looking up. 'Off-hand, I can't think of any good reason to stay in Malminster. Not without Richard. He was the only reason I had to be here. His job brought him, and his job killed him. Now I'm going back to roots. That's the traditional way of dealing with family crisis, isn't it?' She finished tying the ribbon and lifted Rachel onto her lap, wrapping her arms around the child, her cheek against the dark hair, eyes hugely melancholy. 'I'm not a Yorkshire woman. It's better if I take the children home to Bolton; they'll have a family there. And if they can't have a father, at least they'll have an uncle and grandfather to do the things Richard would have done if he'd still been around.'

'That, I can understand,' said Morrissey. 'But what puzzles me is, Why just now, so sudden, when I know for a fact it wasn't on your mind two days ago.'

'You mean the coffee mornings? I shouldn't have troubled Margaret; it was thoughtless of me to involve her. I suppose I ought to be glad you don't charge me with wasting police time.'

'Except that isn't what's at issue, is it? It's something else that's worrying you enough to sell up. What is it—gossip, unkindness?'

'You're a very difficult man to please, Chief Inspector. You came to convince me I should accept the way things are. So, all right, I accept it. I lost my husband, but I still have two children, and having them safe is the most important thing on my mind right now.'

Unease multiplied even more in Morrissey's mind. Some inflection of voice warned him the simple statement held more than surface meaning. He said, 'And they'll be safer in Bolton than Malminster? Is that what you're saying?'

From his leaning posture on the windowsill, hands flat down, nose up against the glass, Mark said, 'They're going, Mummy. Will they come back?'

Rachel wriggled from her mother's knee. '*I* want to see.'

'One of them will come if someone wants to look around the house,' Claire said. 'It will be fun, won't it, having new people to meet?'

Turning to face his mother, Mark said stubbornly, 'I don't think so. I shouldn't want anyone else to have my room. And if I don't live here anymore, I'll miss Derek, won't I?'

'He can come on visits to Bolton, if his mum will let him. That would be fun too.'

'But he won't be at my school every day,' Mark pointed out with logic. 'I don't want to go to Grandma's. I want to live here.'

'Take Rachel upstairs and play for a little while,' Claire said quickly. 'I'll talk with you about Grandma's later.'

Mutiny came into her son's eyes, then faded.

'He's an intelligent boy,' Morrissey said when Mark was out of earshot. 'Perhaps you should reconsider. Changing school might be the wrong thing for him right now, even if you think moving would be best.'

'I don't *think*, I *know*,' she came back with an edge of anger. 'I'll come back to Malminster for the inquest, and that will be the end of it.'

The end of it! Morrissey accepted more coffee, and frowned at the dark liquid. He'd come to convince her to let things lie and she was doing just that. Why, then, this urge to contrariness on his part, and feeling that things were out of kilter. Bolton was a good idea. She'd feel a lot better with family around her—get support and some stability back in her life. Except that he recognised in Claire a self-reliant woman, who wouldn't fall easily into the role of refugee.

He said, 'Have you had another unwelcome visitor since you spoke to Margaret? Since Thewlis came?'

'No one, unless you count the milkman, the paperboy, the postman. By and large, people keep their distance when there's been a death. They don't know what to say, you see. Afraid they won't be able to cope with all the extra emotion maybe.'

'Then what? A letter? A telephone call?'

'Making mysteries where there aren't any, Chief Inspector, I thought that fault was mine, not yours.'

'I can't help you if you don't tell me what's going on,' he pointed out reasonably.

'Funny,' she said, 'I somehow got the impression you can't help me if I do.' The slight smile didn't take the sting out of her words, or ease his conscience, and he knew that for that morning at least, she wouldn't confide in him, or tell him anything he didn't already know. She said: 'It was good of you to come, but I'm going to hurry you off now. There's a Halloween party to go to tonight, and I promised we'd go out and buy masks.'

He got to his feet with the restlessness still in his mind, coupled now with irritation at Claire's new unwillingness to trust him. Still smiling faintly, she walked with him to the door and stood politely in the opening as he began to move away. Three strides down the path he turned.

'If you're being intimidated . . .' he began.

'I'm just going home, that's all. It will be better for the children.' Her voice softened. 'I'm sorry, John. Thank Margaret for me.' She closed the door on him.

He started the car and slammed into gear with unusual savagery, speeding through amber lights that would normally have brought him to a stop. Then he felt his stomach pumping acid again, and forced himself to drive the rest of the way more sedately.

When he reached the police yard someone had taken up his parking slot.

Fuming, he occupied the surgeon's empty spot, dropping his keys off with the desk sergeant, and snarling tersely, 'Get that blasted idiot, whoever he is, out of my place. And fast, damn it!'

The sergeant stared after Morrissey's retreating back. The chief inspector in a mood that foul was a rarity.

Upstairs, Morrissey saw the note on his desk, initialled by Osgodby, and tersely brief. *Time I had a briefing . . .*

Hah!

He left the command where it was and went to the canteen, his stomach burning. The light was out on the milk cooler, and the milk itself, while not exactly warm, was a long way from being chilled. He pointed out the fault with aggressive complaint, but the sanguine woman behind the counter wasn't intimidated. Faced with warm milk, or no milk, he drank, and his stomach quieted. The memory of Beckett's bloody vomit sank back into a dark recess.

Hunting for Barrett, the chief inspector found him in one of the interview rooms, giving Badger a hard time. Morrissey beckoned an imperative finger, noting the wary look that crossed the sergeant's face. Recognition that blame for that was his did nothing to improve Morrissey's frame of mind. Black moods might be as uncommon as honest totters, but today he felt himself wavering at the edge of a pitch-pit.

He'd been far too hard on Mike, unforgivably acerbic with Margaret, and not content with that tally, he'd unfairly rattled Barrett's chain. The half-suggestion earlier that morning that luck, and not good detection, had netted the detective sergeant quick results, hadn't gone down well.

Barrett came out into the corridor and closed the interview room door behind him, stiffly formal.

'Sir?' Pulling on his waistcoat.

'Any update?'

'I've had to let two go. Reliable witnesses put them in the snooker hall at the relevant time.' Defensively he tacked on: 'I thought I'd better go by the book. We've still got Badger and Duggan.'

Morrissey forced himself to fairness. 'You're handling things well,' he acknowledged in gritty reparation, 'good enough for it to have been noted and passed on. What about Guffey?'

A little of Barrett's stiffness dissipated. 'We're still looking for him, but Badger's trying to cut a deal. He wants to turn Queen's, but I don't plan on giving him anything. We've enough hard evidence without, like a signed statement from Duggan, saying Badger and Guffey did all the damage while he just watched. Says he thought they were just out to give Azar a fright, and didn't expect it to go that far.'

'You'll let me know when Guffey's pulled in?'

'Yes, sir. You'll want to interview him yourself?'

'It's your case, Neil. The update's for Osgodby. He's sitting in his office instead of playing golf.'

Barrett digested that and relaxed a little more. He wanted to tie up this case on his own. He'd called at the hospital on his way home the previous night, and in Intensive Care had stood silently outside Azar's cubicle, looking in at the boy and the mass of tubes and wires through the observation window. What he saw had sickened him. Azar's face could hardly be recognised as human. The detective sergeant's attitude to the investigation had changed at that moment—it stopped being just something that would add a feather to his cap if he wrapped it up quickly. He thought he was inured against the results of violence, but there, in the clinically clean department, he learned there were exceptions. The savagely beaten flesh, the arm encased in plaster, the tube that came from somewhere beneath the light sheet and fed bloodstained fluid into a sealed glass container, conspired to make his stomach lurch. Memory of spilled blood in the ginnel brought a flash of what the boy's terror must have been in the dark, confined space. His instinct then had been to turn away and refuse to see, and the effort of making himself look again had raised perspiration on his body.

He'd driven home with a hard core of anger inside him.

This morning Morrissey's comment about luck had struck home because it was ninety per cent true; luck had got the results, not intelligence and effort. He watched the chief inspector walk away with mixed feelings. For once praise had failed to raise cocky pride, and it was a new experience.

ELEVEN

AT TWELVE-THIRTY, with the duty solicitor present, Badger made and signed a statement that agreed with that already given by Duggan, except for one thing. According to Badger, *he'd* done most of the watching, while Guffey and Duggan did all the damage. Barrett reflected on the wonders of gang loyalty.

Osgodby's relief was made manifest by the speed with which he telephoned the good news to Ishmal Habib. From the noises Morrissey heard coming from the receiver, Habib was also relieved.

'I'll admit,' the chief superintendent told Morrissey, 'it's had me sweating a bit. I thought you'd made a bad mistake delegating. Given him a lot of help?'

'Minimal.'

'A few words of praise, then?'

'He'd appreciate it,' said Morrissey. 'On his record perhaps, for when he gets put through for inspector.'

'Not as easy as it once was, not with graduate entry. Lets the brass be too picky and choosy. Still, let him know he's done a good job and it's being officially noted; that should make him happy.' Osgodby glanced at his watch and grunted, his mind shifting to other things. He came out from behind his desk, clapping Morrissey on the shoulder, hustling at the same time, pleased he'd put the golf clubs in the boot, impatient now to be off and make the best of the remaining daylight, leaving the chief inspector to give Barrett his due praise.

But when Morrissey went looking for him to do just that, the detective sergeant had gone out in search of Guffey, and there was nothing to do but go home and try to make reparations there. He didn't expect the peace initiative to be easy, and it wasn't. Mike gave him a bleak look and a brief: 'No sweat!'

From Margaret, he got a frosty smile, straight out of the ice-box. Katie, the only one he hadn't upset, wasn't home.

He ate lunch sitting alone at the table, pariah-like, and spent the afternoon a self-exile in the garden. When he finally closed up the greenhouse, the rim of fading sun in the west was hung with black lace. Morrissey noted it as another sign the late spell of good weather was ending. Maybe the lull in crime would end with it. Part of him hoped that would be so; something he could get to grips with might be a help.

From the Marshall's house across the road, the shrieks of a Halloween party brought Claire's children forcibly to mind, the girl too young to fully understand, the boy rebellious at leaving his friends. A feeling of isolation swamped him, and for once the garden had lost its healing power. Heavy with blackness of spirit, he leaned against the apple tree and watched the red sun rim fade.

THE FIRST BURGLARY report came in at nine that night, and by midnight there were six more. Suddenly, it seemed, everyone was busy on both sides of the fence. The spate of break-ins were handled by DCs Smythe and Copeland from division and DS Gosnay, borrowed from Manorfield subdivision. Morrissey didn't hear about them until Sunday morning, when DC Smythe remembered the chief inspector's interest in Claire Simms, and rang him at home.

The receiver still in his hand, buzzing its disengaged signal, he lay for a minute on his back, staring at the bedroom ceiling. Coincidence? Margaret got up and padded to the bathroom. He replaced the receiver on its cradle and put both hands behind his head, listening to the shower, denying a wishful impulse to be in there with her. Official days off were meant to be spent with families, but Margaret had heard him tell Smythe differently.

When he heard her wake Mike, and then her feet on the stairs, Morrissey rolled out of bed and took her place in the bathroom, going down to the kitchen fifteen minutes later, shaved and dressed for work.

'Do you *have* to go in?'

There was resignation in Margaret's voice, but the hand stirring scrambled eggs moved furiously against the pan, telling Morrissey only too clearly that that wasn't the question she really wanted to throw at him. What she wanted to say would run more along the lines of, Why in hell did he have to work today of all days, when for the first time in months her parents were visiting.

It was fatal to make promises, especially weeks in advance. How could he be expected to foresee Beckett's ulcer, much less Barrett's need to stay with the hunt of Guffey. He said: 'I'll try to be home by one,' taking his plate to the table, wondering if Mike were delaying upstairs deliberately to avoid conversation with his father. He transmuted self-guilt into irritation.

Margaret went to the foot of the stairs, crisply authoritative.

'Mike? You're either down in thirty seconds or you can starve.'

'He knows you don't mean it,' Morrissey said dourly when she came back.

'Today I do,' she said, and her lips quirked in satisfaction as she heard Mike on the stairs. The look she exchanged with her son excluded Morrissey, acknowledging as it did the secret signal system between them that let Mike know when he could, and could not, get away with being tardy. It had always been so between mother and son, but it hadn't irked Morrissey until now. He ate silently. Mike slid onto an empty chair

'Morning, Dad.'

'You should come down when you're called,' Morrissey said, the words coming out without any real volition on his part, and he heard the gruff, unfriendly sound of them and felt instant remorse. But it was too late of course, the damage had been done, Mike's face closed up again in hurt. Chewing, swallowing, debating in his mind, the chief inspector wondered why he hadn't just said a cheerful good-morning as he would have done a few months ago. What was it between him and his son that was turning things so sour?

Then he caught Margaret's half-angry look and felt resentful. Did she always have to take the boy's part?

Mike asked, 'How come Katie gets a lie-in if I don't?'

'Because Katie isn't home. She stayed at Fran's last night, that's why. And you can give me a hand getting the house tidy.'

'When isn't it?' asked Mike. 'Honestly, Mum, nothing needs doing.'

'Then doing nothing shouldn't take you long, should it,' Margaret said equably.

Morrissey stopped staring at his empty plate and got up, moving round the table to kiss Margaret's oddly resistant cheek. 'I'll try to make it back before one.'

'I'll set a place then,' Margaret told him evenly. 'Just in case.'

Passing, he put a hand on his son's shoulder; that felt resistant too.

Sighing heavily, Morrissey left them alone. Outside, the temperature had dropped overnight with a change in wind direction, and the sky was pebbled with grey clouds. Driving into Malminster down the Middlebrook Road there was scarcely any traffic. He relaxed a little, recognising there would be nothing to keep him in his office any longer than it took to read through the burglary reports. Even doing the other thing he intended and calling in at the Simms house wouldn't cause that much delay. He should still be home in a bit under three hours.

Made more cheerful now, he parked in his slot and pushed thoughts of family from his mind.

Smythe was waiting, yawning freely. 'I drew the short straw,' he said. 'Didn't seem sense all three of us losing a night. Anyway, they'll be out knocking on doors while I'm asleep, hopefully. Do you want a coffee fetching? If I don't get another I'll drop asleep here.'

'Plenty of milk in,' said Morrissey. 'I'll have a read through these while you're gone.'

He flicked through the burglary reports rapidly, then read them again in depth. Seven break-ins in one night, and nobody home at any of them; it smacked of good information and planning. Halloween parties had a lot to answer for this year. Two houses had alarm systems fitted, not very sophisticated and circumvented neatly. So who among the local tribe would be likely to do that?

Smythe came back. For once the coffee was palatable; unthinking, Morrissey followed a first sip with a great gulp that seared his throat. Eyes watering, he said, 'Come up with anything?'

'Doesn't especially fit anyone local. Neat, clean entry, fast in and out, bypassed two alarm systems.'

'But not the biggest houses,' said Morrissey. 'All middle range. Now why would that interest a villain from outside? Better pickings round the BMW bits.'

'Riskier though, maybe,' offered Smythe, 'or a bit of the old Thatcher opportunism, at play. Only went for small things, and didn't touch electrical gadgets that'd take a bit of carrying.'

'Nothing different about any of them?' asked the chief inspector casually, hoping for his peace of mind the answer would be no.

'I didn't see all of them,' the DC hedged neatly.

'How many?'

'Three.'

'And heard first-hand about the rest. It'll do. Which were your three?'

'Pentland Avenue, Woodman Close, Colbrook Grove.'

'Go on.'

'Well, they'd all been well turned over, cupboards and drawers tipped out, that sort of stuff, but...' Smythe looked at Morrissey uneasily. The chief inspector led Barrett a right dance sometimes, and Smythe didn't fancy getting taken down a peg; neither did he fancy the dangers of stopping mid-sentence. He went on doggedly. 'The Simms house seemed to have come in for a bit of extra attention, like whoever went in was looking for something special. Left it like a paper chase. Mrs Simms said her husband had kept a lot of files at home, work and what-not. I don't know what they were, but they'll take some sorting out.'

All of Morrissey's unease solidified.

'What about the children?'

'They were round at a neighbour's.'

'Mrs Simms?'

'Sort of quiet and resigned. I wasn't sure she'd taken it all in. Different reaction to most.'

'You'd better get on home,' Morrissey said. 'And I'm pleased you used your initiative and got me down here. Job all right, is it? No problems?'

'None,' said Smythe. 'Except we could do with a new typewriter.'

'You can always go back to a pen,' said the chief inspector. 'Go on, then. Get off while the going's good. And tell whoever's on the desk I said to organise a lift.'

'Thanks, sir,' said Smythe, and plodding heavily downstairs thought he might just manage to make it home before his eyes shut.

A few minutes later Morrissey put the reports back on Smythe's desk and went to his car. He expected to find Claire still tidying, and still shocked, but instead there was no one in the house at all. A small side window had been boarded up. From a neighbour he learned Claire had driven away early, with both children and a suitcase. The neighbour didn't know where they had gone, but Morrissey thought Bolton would be a good guess. A depressing sense that he had failed to give help when it was needed took its place alongside all the other guilt in his mind. He drove home, glad that at least he would be there a full hour before he'd promised.

TWELVE

MORRISEEY WAS home ten minutes before his in-laws arrived, and Margaret's relief showed in a smile that for the first time in two days held no reproach and no disappointment. Half-way through Sunday dinner the telephone rang and Morrissey prayed fervently it wouldn't be for him, but when Mike came back from answering it, he knew from the look on his son's face that the prayer had gone unanswered.

'Who is it?'

A shrug as Mike sat down. 'Sergeant Barrett. I told him we were eating, but he says it's urgent.' He got busy again with his knife and fork, not looking at his father. The chief inspector got up with a kind of despair, feeling the ambience evaporate around him. Isolated in the hall he picked up the receiver, and behind him Katie's laugh came from the dining room, his father-in-law's voice, the laugh again.

He said roughly, 'It had better be good, Neil.'

Barrett started edgily, apologising for disrupting the meal. Got at by Mike obviously.

'Just get to the gist of it,' bade Morrissey impatiently.

'Guffey's turned up in a lay-by rubbish skip, looks like he's been dead a couple of days. The crows have been busy.' The chief inspector stared at a small crack in the ceiling, and saw the rest of his Sunday shred itself. 'I thought you'd want to know,' said Barrett when the silence stretched. He was aggrieved too. It wasn't just a GBH anymore, and he expected that what had been until then his case would be whipped out from under his nose.

'On our territory?' said Morrissey with his last shred of hope.

'By fifteen feet.'

Fifteen feet!

'Bloody Sunday.'

'Yes, sir,' in agreement about that at least. 'The lay-by's on Wraghill Lane, first right after the South Kirby turn-off. SOCO team are on their way, but I thought you'd want to let the pathologist know yourself.'

Warmsby wouldn't be pleased to lose his day off either, thought Morrissey grimly. Pathology had its hazards too.

When he got back to the remains of his meal, all talking stopped and attention focussed on him. He said his piece, and saw uncomfortably dropped eyes, but Katie's stayed on his face. 'Poor old Dad,' she said. 'It's rotten being dragged out when you don't want to go.' His burden of guilt felt that much less heavy.

The food on his plate had cooled, but it might be the last he had for God knew how long, and he ate it with a show of enjoyment. Let Margaret have that at least.

Driving fast along the near-deserted A638 a few spots of rain speckled his windscreen, stopping again almost as soon as they'd started. The pebbled sky was now a uniform grey, blank and depressing, across it a late phalanx of birds headed south, wings beating hard. He passed the South Kirby turn-off, slowed, looking for Wraghill Lane, turned right onto a narrow road that twisted and turned, swung round a bend to the left and saw police cones narrowing the road to a single track. The SOCO team had got there before him, and what was left of Guffey had already been hidden behind green canvas screens. A police photographer was busy with a hand-held video camera, getting the whole scene on film. Farther down, where the road straightened, a police car stood on a dirt patch by a farm gate, its clipboard-carrying two-man crew posted to stop and question passing drivers.

Barrett seemed to have thought of everything, which was as it should be if Morrissey hadn't been wasting his time. He waited for cones to be moved, and when they were, pulled in smoothly behind the SOCO van. Barrett appeared as Morrissey got out, his face giving an indication of how unpleasant was the sight to be viewed.

Get it over quickly then. Moving towards the screens at a fast stride.

'Who found him?'

'Poor sod dumping household rubbish; threw up twice so I let him go home. I think he's genuine enough.'

The skip was a dirty sand colour, with Malminster MDC on the side in black lettering, the rim scarred and pockmarked with rust. Morrissey's nostrils twitched protest a couple of yards away. The smell was rich, sweet, acrid; something to be walked away from. He looked over the edge. Guffey was folded into awkward angles like a broken puppet, stained and reeking. The size of him, and the clothes, and the shaved-side hairdo with an inch of stubble on the crown said who he was, but Morrissey thought something more than crows had been at his face. He didn't fancy Warmsby's job. He asked dispassionately, 'Any ideas?'

'Could have been a hit-and-run, could have been deliberate. I'd go more for the second, the average hit-and-runner doesn't hang around to hide the body. Question is, Was the ride he picked up at Joe's Caff the mistake of his life, or did he only go a couple of miles or so and then hitch another?'

Another spatter of rain came and the dry ground absorbed the moisture and waited for more. The white-overalled Scene of Crime Officers busy in the lay-by gave the sky a glance and speeded up, a heavy shower was about the

last thing they needed. More drops came, teasing. Two
SOCOs broke off from what they were doing and went to
the van; screens weren't enough if it rained.

Morrissey watched the portable metal-framed plastic tent
go up over the skip. The whole thing looked like a side-
show. 'Let's get back to the car,' he said. 'It smells better.'

JUST NORTH of Selby, a pub called The Toby Jug had gathered a reputation for good food. It was far enough from
Malminster for the cartel to meet without it being remarked on, while the purely English menu made the meetings something more than a chore. With the exception of
Gerald Mason, whose Parliamentary life had broadened his
gastronomic appreciation, a meal of roast beef and Yorkshire pudding pushed well down by jam roly-poly, was a
culinary treat. Thewlis, known for crapulence, invariably
followed roly-poly with treacle tart, and belched gently for
the rest of the afternoon.

The meetings were irregular and mainly for Gerald Mason's benefit. The MP spent something like one weekend in
four at his Malminster home, and liked to get a progress report that didn't entail making a telephone call.

That particular Sunday, Richardson chewed on other
things besides beef; there were worries that he had to both
pass on, and play down. A certain amount of violence went
with the business of making a fortune. He knew how to organise it and how far it could go. And he knew who to trust
not to let it come back and dirty his doorstep. Vic had done
jobs for him—for what, ten years?—and had not let him
down, not let things slide out of hand like they had this time.
Bloody shambles.

Hopefully it had been tidied up.

He had Vic's word on it.

Hell, he paid enough!

When he'd said he wanted the run-down terraces cleared without fuss, Vic had come up with the racist angle. Let everybody believe it was Asian-baiting. A good idea gone bad. Now they'd have to try something else, take longer, risk losing the lot. Then there was Simms. His eyes slid to Lowry, deep in some kind of joke with Mason. Too many people were doing things on their own.

He said: 'About Simms' replacement,' and three pairs of eyes swivelled to him in unison.

IF MONICA THEWLIS could have had a wish granted, it would have been that her husband spent more Sundays at The Toby Jug, but she had learned to be grateful for small mercies. Left to herself she didn't bother with the ritual Sunday roast. For one thing it wasn't worth the effort, and for another she'd never fancied beef since the mad cow thing. A bowl of tinned soup and a poached egg on toast did her nicely, except when Angeline came, and then she'd make something a bit more special. Jack didn't know about her and Angeline having little lunches, he wouldn't have liked it if he had, didn't want anybody there when he wasn't, not even his daughter. After a little thought she amended that to especially his daughter. Whipping up a packet of instant mousse she felt happy. Angeline had said there was something she had to tell her mother—a secret, and her father wasn't to know.

Monica thought she could guess.

She sent up a small prayer of thanks that Gordon Bridges hadn't turned out to be anything like Jack, in fact—she felt a little flutter in her throat and stopped whisking—she didn't think he even *liked* his father-in-law. She looked at the mousse. Had it thickened enough yet? Angeline had always liked caramel whip and ice cream, although now she called it a comfort food, like the chocolate biscuits Monica liked to nibble during quiet mornings.

She was much too fat! The whip went into the fridge and she licked the whisk. Almost ugly with it. Such a slim thing she'd been before Jack came with all his lies.

Comfort food.

There was a hot gathering behind her eyelids and she threw the balloon whisk forcibly into the sink. How much fatter did she have to be before she was *too* ugly?

She checked on the chicken casserole and the two place settings, and went to sit by the window where she could watch for Angeline. A secret. But if it were a baby, Jack would have to know sooner or later. Not for a while, though. Monica thought about knitting small things in secret; something else that Jack couldn't spoil for her.

THIRTEEN

'WELL THEN.' Believing he had a fair idea of the root cause behind the detective sergeant's long face, Morrissey poked around a little. 'While we're sitting here waiting for Warmsby, have you thought out the next move?'

He'd framed the question with deliberate care, but Barrett still hedged. Innocent though the words might sound, he'd fallen into holes Morrissey had dug for him before, and he was suspicious. Of course this time the chief might be genuinely asking his opinion. He decided noncommittal was his best bet.

'I'm not sure what you mean, sir.'

The *sir*, told Morrissey a lot, bearing in mind that Barrett was deliberately circumspect only when he felt got at. Sighing, the chief inspector went for patience. Of a kind.

'Guffey didn't walk here.'

Barrett stared at nothing in particular. 'No, sir. We know that. He picked up a ride at Joe's Caff, Thursday morning, the counterhand saw him leave. That's all we've got unless SOCO come up with anything.'

'More questions at Joe's then.'

'That's the way I'd go.'

'Open Sundays, is it?'

'Don't know about that, sir.'

Morrissey sighed again. He was wedged with his back to the car door, one elbow resting on the seat back, the other on the steering wheel, and from this uncomfortable-looking position he watched the ritual smoothing of dark moustache, its accompanying downward tweak of waistcoat, and wondered for the umpteenth time what stress markers Barrett had used before he grew the damn thing, and pre his three-piece suit? Patience ended, he said rattily, 'Radio communication's a wonderful thing.' The bit of minor sarcasm went home. Barrett's right hand left the blue pinstripe points.

Morrissey straightened, shifting in his seat, they'd shilly-shallied enough. If things were normal Beckett would be handling this particular case, but Beckett wasn't available and Barrett was the next best thing; the problem would be getting Osgodby to see that. Warmsby arrived in his black Volvo, pulling in with a showy little scud of gravel, and the chief inspector said briskly, 'Neil, it's your investigation until somebody tells you differently, so get on top of it.' Swinging a leg out of the car he applied a judicious spur. 'Unless you don't think you're really up to it, and if that's the case for God's sake say so now and let's not waste time.'

Barrett said, 'I can handle it. Thank you, sir.'

Morrissey got out as another flurry of rain came. He turned up his collar. 'I'll be with Warmsby,' he said, 'so don't take too long, I wouldn't want you to miss anything.' Heading towards the Volvo in long-legged strides, he knew from the sour look the pathologist gave him that here was another Sunday come to grief. *Six days shalt thou labour and on the seventh rest.* All right for some!

Left alone, waiting for Communications to get back and tell him if Joe's Caff opened Sundays, Barrett's mind idly occupied itself in speculation. Something had to lie behind Morrissey's delegation of command. As the chief inspector himself was fond of saying, actions don't happen without motivation.

Maybe promotion to inspector was closer than he'd imagined.

With that happy thought, and confirmation that the Caff was open, he ruined DC Woods' Sunday off too, and was still grinning with the pleasure of it when he rounded the canvas screens and saw Warmsby standing in the skip, kitted up like a spaceman.

Morrissey's eyes flickered over him speculatively and Barrett schooled his face. 'Got it sorted to your satisfaction, then?' asked the chief inspector.

'Place is open Sundays,' said Barrett, 'so I sent Woods along to start enquiries. Shouldn't be that busy in there today, and experience'll do him good.'

'Pleased, was he?'

Barrett's grin came back.

Warmsby climbed down and the reek of decay came with him. When he pulled off the head cover, his face looked hot. 'Hope you're not expecting miracles,' he stated squinting round impatiently. A white-overalled SOCO with a plastic bin-liner speeded up. Grumbling all the while he did it, the pathologist peeled off the rest of his protective covering and dumped it in the sack; the gloves went in last. 'I suppose you're going to ask how long he's been in there; that's what you lot always want to know. Must think I'm God or something. Well, more than twenty-four hours is the best I can offer. There's a bit of maggot activity, usual thing in warm weather. Want a generative check as well, I suppose?'

His eyes lit on Barrett's look of distaste. Peering acidly over his gold-framed spectacles, Warmsby said, 'The life cycle of a maggot can be a very interesting topic. Remind me to discuss it with you sometime.'

Barrett had seen the maggots and his stomach had shown its aversion to corruption; it was bad enough that he'd have to stand there and watch the post-mortem, without being invited to discuss the bloody things. He said stiffly, 'He's been missing three days.'

'Then I'd say that's about right,' said the pathologist. 'And while we're on the subject, don't even ask about holding a PM today; Monday morning will have to be good enough. Ten o'clock. I've got a brand-new granddaughter waiting for me at home.' He waved a dismissive hand in the skip's direction. 'Bag and shift him whenever you want.'

'But you can hazard us a cause of death,' Barrett said, and instantly regretted it. Morrissey wouldn't have asked, not when it was blatantly obvious without.

Warmsby blinked a little, snapped, 'Hedgehog syndrome,' and left them to it.

THEWLIS ALWAYS got home at four, expecting Monica to have made him a pot of tea and one of her fancy cakes with icing on. She'd made the cake early this morning, before Angeline came, an orange flower cake, with ground almonds that made it moist and sweet flavoured, and because at that time she had reason to think she was going to hear the best news in the world, it had been less of a drudge than usual. When her daughter drove away at half-past three, Monica took the cake out of its tin and wished it was poisoned.

Not even knowing she'd been right about the baby made up for what else Angeline had said. She tried to concentrate on her coming grandchild, hugging the warm thought close, but it kept slipping away. It would be born miles away, *miles and miles and miles and miles*. She washed up the lunch things and put them away, cleaned already clean work surfaces, keeping her hands busy. At five minutes to four she filled the kettle and set it to boil, laid the tray that he ate from torpid in the sitting-room. At four o'clock precisely she heard his car and saw her hands begin to shake.

He was *vile!*

FOURTEEN

MALMINSTER'S CHIEF Planning Officer, Malcolm Lowry, had known ever since Simms' car went off the bridge, that however fortuitous—to use Thewlis' word—that accident might have seemed at the time, the end result had been to replace a known problem, with an unknown. Simms' sudden discovery of conscience might have posed all sorts of problems, but at least they'd been voiced, and a little bit of fatherly talking to, coupled with upping the ante, could have smoothed things over. Now somebody else had to do Simms' job, and Lowry hoped to God he'd put up the right name as a likely candidate. One bad fright was enough, as Richardson has taken pains to point out at The Toby Jug yesterday. Too many things were going wrong, and he didn't appreciate the feeling of living on tenterhooks.

If it hadn't been for a standing agreement with the union, he wouldn't even have had room to manoeuvre over Simms' replacement. Lucky it had been NALGO's insistence, not the Local Authority's, that vacancies had to be advertised internally, before outside applications were sought; it meant fingers couldn't point back at him. Of course the union's intent had been to minimise redundancies, but this time he'd be manipulating the agreement to meet his ends, not theirs. It would have been near impossible without it to justify rejection of a qualified and experienced applicant from another authority in favour of someone who, while qualified, had no real experience at a senior level.

Even with it, the appointment he'd have to push for wouldn't go through without a few toes being trodden on.

Restless he took a look out of the fifth-floor window. The traffic flow had eased a little, but the feeder road south was still busy enough to leave tail-backs at the traffic lights. With a high view he could follow its snaking turn left onto the bypass that took it away from the congested town centre, and then the sweep right that fed the flow into the bridge traffic. Simms would have followed the same route. His hands became fists thrust deep into trouser pockets.

Fortuitous!

Something in the inflection when Thewlis said it set Lowry's teeth on edge.

The next-door office was identical to this one in every way except size; same supposedly soothing green carpet tiles, same warm beige flat-painted walls, same pseudo-teak bulk-bought office fittings. What the *hell* had Simms been doing in there alone, until close on midnight the night he died?

Lowry swung round from the window. *Get on with it before any more doubts crept out of the woodwork.*

He crossed the corridor—burnt umber carpet tiles and almond walls with stylised architectural drawings—and put his head round the door of the main planning office. His eyes dismissed everybody in there except one. 'A minute of your time,' he said, 'now, in my office,' and, leaving the door open behind him, went back to his desk.

Not knowing whether she'd been summoned for reprimand or praise, Debra Lewis schooled her face to accept either, and was still caught unawares.

The Chief Planning Officer had anticipated her look of surprise, the negative head shake when he suggested she apply for Simms' job, and he followed up the suggestion with just the right hint of disappointment. 'Of course, if you yourself don't feel you could handle the job, then obviously I've made a mistake.'

'Oh, no,' Debra corrected quickly, 'it isn't that. I'm sure I could handle it, there isn't a problem there. It's just that I hadn't thought I'd be in the running. I mean Charlie Rundle has a lot more seniority.'

Lowry slowly raised hands and eyebrows, a calculatedly artless gesture. His voice became confidential, suggesting by tone she was already as good as his second-in-command. 'If seniority, Debra, were the only consideration, then of course you'd be quite right, but we have to look at other things like a first-class degree and a lot of potential, both of which you have to offer. And where Rundle's concerned, well, quite frankly, I don't want to say too much but there is such a thing as being in one place too long. Not that I'm implying Charlie doesn't fit in here, you understand, don't run away with that idea, but it might be a good thing careerwise if he applied outside.'

He let himself lean back then, exuding an air of humane authority, and watched, waiting to see how effective his words would be.

Debra waited too, testing her own reactions, eyeing the Chief Planning Officer a little less overtly than he eyed her. Fifty-ish face benevolently austere, shiny dome compensated for by a springy growth of side-whiskers and a moustache, Lowry had the look of that certain type of politician who never gives a straight answer but always gets re-elected.

Charlie Rundle hated his guts!

She silenced the prick of conscience that said the job should be Charlie's. Whoever got it, it wouldn't just go on Lowry's say-so. The final choice would be made, as always, by a selection panel, and they'd be a lot more likely to appoint Charlie than her. Of course they would.

Lowry was still looking at her expecting some kind of reply, so she made the right appreciatory noises and accepted the application form he'd set before her, creasing the A4 paper neatly into more manageable size.

When she went back into the big office she met Charlie's jaundiced eye, and the thought came that perhaps Lowry's patronage stemmed less from admiration of her being a first-class honours graduate and rather more from a hope that inexperience would render her pliable. Angry at the very idea that that might be the case, she crammed the blank form into an envelope and dropped it in her shoulder bag.

She met Charlie's eyes again; they were really very nice. His face became friendlier and she looked away, an office affair would really screw things up. With that at the front of her mind, she consigned him to No-No Land and got back to work.

OSGODBY HUMMED and hawed a bit, sucked his teeth, steepled his fingers, and avoided looking at Morrissey until he'd decided on his position.

Guffey wasn't someone who'd be missed except by his mother—if he'd ever had one. Nonetheless, the Khalid affair was now a murder investigation, and murder investigations in the chief superintendent's book shouldn't be handled by anyone less than inspector. He told Morrissey that, setting his hands square on the desk, the wiry, sand-coloured hairs on their backs more plentiful than those on his scalp. The chief inspector reminded him that Barrett had already that year passed his Nationals, and probably when the results came through the follow-up assessment as well.

Which meant that in all but name, he was an inspector looking for a post. Morrissey then added gently that taking into account how short they were with Beckett in hospital, an increase of establishment to two inspectors wouldn't be a bad thing.

Osgodby started sucking on his teeth again.

'Barrett's following the same line I'd take myself,' pursued Morrissey, who knew the strength of that argument. 'I'd be loath not to wait and see what develops. Time enough to step in later if it comes necessary.'

'This sort of leaving it to somebody else isn't like you, John. I've not known you to want to delegate before. It worries me.'

Morrissey, whose unease about he knew not what had now reached mammoth proportions, didn't intend to offer any sort of explanation. Hunches could be wrong as well as right.

He said, 'I'll keep an overview.'

'What about this transport cafe, any chance of a clear identification there?' asked the chief superintendent, clutching at straws.

'It's still being looked into. A possibility, that's all.' Morrissey added, 'I thought I'd look in on the post-mortem. Be interesting to see if Warmsby turns up anything unusual.'

Picking up on the deliberately misleading nuance, Osgodby said: 'Ah, I see what you're up to now, playing it close to your chest again, seen something other eyes have missed. Is that it? Another hunch. In that case I'll trust in it enough to leave things as they are.' Suddenly cheerful, he waved a hand at the door. 'Go on then, get off, have it solved by tea-time and you can buy me a drink.'

Morrissey grinned. 'I'll keep you posted,' he said, glad Osgodby's talents didn't run to reading minds.

FIFTEEN

WHEN MONICA THEWLIS encased herself in Vicks vapour rub and sniffed at the pepper pot, streaming eyes, pungent odour, and forceful sneezes had served to keep her husband well away from her. That had been an extremist measure on Sunday night, when desperate needs had demanded desperate remedies. Since then gratitude that her panicking mind had come up with something that worked so well had calmed her a little, although how long the charade could be kept up remained to be seen: two days, three—then what? All Monica knew was that revulsion against her husband had increased to the point where she couldn't bear the sight, let alone the feel of him. She'd spent the night in Angeline's old room with the door closed, listening to Thewlis' snores penetrating the wall between them; noisy reminders that separation was a temporary thing. Knowing that had kept her awake half the night, panicking again. Escape she must, but without income and no savings—how *could* she have saved when every penny of house-keeping always had to be accounted for, when fifty pence lost or forgotten brought on a rage.

'Walk out,' Angeline had said. 'Mum, do it now, walk out on the bastard. You've had enough!'

Walk out with nothing though.

Angeline! Marriage had been kind to her at least; Gordon was a good man, kind-hearted too. He'd said Monica mustn't worry, money wasn't a problem. The thought of not worrying brought a bitter smile; easier said than done. Impossible not to worry when it wasn't fair to even *think* about making herself dependent on Gordon, not when she knew he'd need every penny he owned to open up a new business in another town.

But she had to leave Jack—Jack the bastard. Oh *God* it was a terrible thing to wish, but why couldn't he just die and leave her? When morning eased dull-grey and damp through the window, she heard her husband get out of bed and stayed where she was, coughing and sneezing with desperate realism until the front door banged behind him, and his car moved out into the lane; only then did Monica feel safe enough to push the duvet aside and run a bath as hot as she could bear, lying in it submerged up to her neck and brimming with self-hatred, loathing her puffy body and ashamed of what she had become, because of him.

A thumbnail dragged hard down the inside of her thigh left a long, vertical red line that stung; parallel, she etched another, and another. Criss-crossing them with short horizontals made a grid pattern that she studied with detachment, her breasts hanging heavy against her rib-cage, uncorsetted folds of stomach spreading widely as she bent her head. When she got out of the bath the weals were thick and raised, and still smarting sore: carefully she dried herself. Heat had turned her skin bright pink and her head felt fuzzy with it, as bad as if she really did have a cold, and she couldn't remember why she had wanted to mutilate herself. She let the towel slip to the floor and rummaged in the bathroom cabinet for a salve, the cool white cream felt pleasant against the heat of her skin, and when the soreness subsided she dressed herself, and cleaned the bath with consummate care. Jack was very particular about the bath being clean; big and unbalanced just before Angeline was born, she'd skimped, once, on a tide mark—never since. No one ever forgot one of Jack's lessons.

But he'd never hit Angeline and she'd been glad about that—until yesterday.

Fuzzy-headed again, Monica leaned against the bath. How could she not have known!

Mid-morning, watering the half dozen plants on the kitchen windowsill, she noticed spider-mite, and went to the garage to get an insect spray; easy to find since Jack practised what he preached where tidiness was concerned. The white bug-gun stood on a shelf next to a bottle of paraquat filched from the Parks Department; on a shelf above, anti-freeze, oil and Quick-Start rubbed shoulders with a near-empty whisky bottle—Jack's warm-up kit for cold mornings.

Paraquat.

Her thigh was really painful now.

Paraquat.

She took the bug-gun back to the kitchen, spraying each plant with slow care, because her mind was occupied with other things.

SOMETIME DURING the night rain had begun to come down in earnest, and the dry ground had sated itself to the point where it would take no more. Over the back entrance to the police building leaves, or an old bird's nest, had blocked the guttering, sending a steady cascade onto the second step; Morrissey eyed it sourly, he'd been got at by it once already that day, on his way in. He edged sideways but was still too big a target to miss. Cruising round the hospital car-park he met with a variation of the same problem, all the vacant parking slots lay under heavily dripping trees. Settling for that nearest to the mortuary, he wondered why he had wanted the Indian summer to end.

Not for this!

The post-mortem was already begun. Warmsby took a beady eye from what he was doing and noted the chief inspector's presence. Barrett, who would have preferred to be anywhere other than next to Guffey's sliced-open corpse, moved away from his prime position. An unseen miasma drifted along with him.

'I didn't think you'd be coming, sir. Something new happened, has it?' The question carried a thread of hope, his physical presence needed elsewhere formed the peak of desire.

'Nothing. Relax, and enjoy it.' That last was a deliberate and unkind addition. The colour and dampness of Barrett's skin were clear indicators that enjoyment had no place in things. Shrugging into a spare green gown, Morrissey repented. 'Never pleasant things, post-mortems.' He went to peer at Warmsby's handiwork.

A few seconds later Barrett drifted back, only slightly mollified. Guffey's partly crushed ribcage lay open. A pair of toothed dissecting forceps in one hand, a scalpel in the other, the pathologist said breezily, 'Lying on his back when the wheel got him, poor sod. Question is, What finished him off? He picked a couple of bone splinters out of the pleura, dropped them in a kidney dish, found a third, took that out too, a fourth, deeply embedded, needed teasing, all made small rattling noises as they hit the bottom of the metal receptacle.

'Crush injuries wasn't it—that killed him I mean,' said Barrett. 'Wouldn't have been alive after that, would he?'

'Wasn't alive before it,' said Warmsby, 'what blood there is has mostly oozed, not squirted, so...' He concentrated, lifted a portion of pleura in his forceps, swung the mutilated ribcage back in position. *'Gotcha,'* he said in triumph. Barrett peered, forgetting his nausea briefly, but not knowing what to look for.

'There,' said Warmsby kindly, indicating one skin abrasion out of many, pulling the skin edges to show the neatness of cut. 'And'—putting the ribcage aside again—'here,' feeding a slender probe neatly through a matching slit in the lung membrane. Gently, and with infinite care, he let the probe find its own path. 'And if I'm right . . .' The tip came out close to the heart, crossed between the two organs and entered the left ventrical. 'Very neat. A thin stiletto-type blade, inserted at an angle between the seventh and eighth ribs, death would be a matter of seconds.'

'Sod it,' said Barrett under his breath.

Warmsby had sharp ears.

'Sod it,' he agreed cheerfully. 'Upset the applecart, haven't I?' With neat precision he sliced down through the trachea, and with small, neat strokes of the scalpel, carefully dissected lungs and heart from anchorage in the chest cavity.

Barrett met Morrissey's eyes. Being anything more than second string on a fiddle after this would be well nigh impossible. He looked at the mortuary attendant's impassive face above the big stainless-steel bowl; the discoloured organs squelched as Warmsby dropped them inside, a blackish-brown splash leapt upward. The detective sergeant's stomach clenched and his legs shook. 'Excuse me,' he muttered thickly, and went out at the very best speed they would take him.

Warmsby rinsed his gloved hands, and the water coloured darkly. 'Be interesting to see what he'd do,' he said reflectively, 'if we got a really bad one.'

SIXTEEN

BARRETT GOT back to the office an hour after Morrissey, still peaky-pale, with the smell of the post-mortem room trapped at the back of his nostrils, and his taste-buds actively aware of the aftermath of nausea. The whole thing gave him a sense of personal failure; the chief inspector hadn't turned a hair watching Warmsby's grisly work, just stood there doing his chunk of granite act, and if he, Barrett, said anything about it he could guarantee what reply he'd get, he'd heard it often enough. *'That's why I'm Chief Inspector, while you're only Sergeant.'* It wasn't the words that niggled, but a sensed truth behind them. Yesterday he'd been thinking how *Inspector Barrett* had a natural ring to it, now it seemed as unlikely as winning the pools.

He wavered in front of Morrissey's desk: 'This new angle on Guffey's killing...'

'Tea and a bacon butty apiece,' cut in Morrissey. 'Empty stomachs aren't conducive to constructive thinking. Stick your head around and see who's in next door.'

A bubble of gas surfaced and rumbled at the mention of food. 'I don't think, sir...' said Barrett distantly.

Morrissey pushed out of his chair.

'I'll do it myself then,' he said. 'Just this once.'

Stiffly, the detective sergeant headed for his desk. When the chief inspector came back Barrett had the window part open, and, disregarding the chill fingers of rain blown in through the gap, was sucking in deep breaths of damp air.

'Take your time,' said Morrissey kindly. 'Nothing like fresh air for whipping up an appetite.'

MARK COULD BE obstinate, and he'd been that way this morning, climbing into the car and needing to be lifted out bodily, then having to be held in his grandmother's firm hands so he couldn't get back in again. With chin thrust out and lips set firm, he'd looked enough like his father to make Claire's throat constrict. Would he change as he grew, or would the likeness stay with him? She didn't know which to hope for, both were painful to contemplate, and she forced her mind into calmer waters, soothing, cajoling.

To her own ears, when she explained that she had to go back to Malminster alone, that the children would be staying with Grandma, her voice stayed level and determined, but her mother caught on to the note of desperation, and while still not fully understanding why Claire had brought the children to Bolton—especially at a time when she herself (had she been in the same position) wouldn't have wanted either of them out of her sight—she lent her own weight to her daughter's need, and Claire returned to Malminster alone but plagued by guilt. Rachel's face had been untroubled, but Mark's had been filled with panic as he stood stiffly waving goodbye. How could he know that tomorrow, or the next day, he wouldn't wake up and be told as he had about his father, that he wouldn't ever see her again? To read that in his eyes and still leave him there had been agony.

When she parked in the drive of her home the white estate agent's sign stood like a tacit admission of surrender, but that was all to the good, the enemy would see it as such too, it would signal she had become compliant when she had not!

Inside the house, the sheer magnitude of effort she would have to expend to restore order, was very nearly too much for her to face. No drawer or cupboard however small and innocent had escaped having its contents spilled partly or fully onto the floor. Claire's jewellery had gone. That hurt! Not because of its cash value, heaven knew none of it would fetch much second-hand, but because Richard had given it to her it couldn't be replaced. Silver-plated flatwear given as a wedding present had gone, and so had the only really valuable thing she owned—a Georgian silver candlestick given to her by her godmother. That could never be replaced either. The only spot of brightness was that the house hadn't been vandalised; obscene graffiti sprayed on the walls and mindless destruction was something she couldn't have coped with right then. Perhaps when anger subsided she would actually feel grateful! She sat back on her heels and thought about that. Maybe she didn't want it to subside, anger stopped self-pity—and, dear God!—if that ever crept in she'd be lost!

MORRISSEY'S super-cholesterol butty cure had worked well enough for Barrett's skin to have lost its look of terminal illness. The detective sergeant was grateful, but it was a gratitude still overlaid with resentment that only his stomach had suffered. He let the thought of Guffey into his mind, testing the waters as it were, and when the labyrinthine depths of his being stayed silent said, 'This Guffey business. The question uppermost in my mind at the moment is, was he a specific target? I mean, it seems to be a choice between that and having a psycho loose. That's unless he'd been thriftier than anybody guessed, saved up for a quick get-away and flashed a wad—I suppose him thinking he could handle anybody on two legs he'd be thick enough to do that.'

'Robbery, then, is that what you're saying?'

'It's a possibility. Depends. There's the Khalid business, Guffey'd likely boast about that, and if it got back—well, it'd be a neat bit of vengeance. I'd rather it be that or robbery. I don't fancy hunting a loony.'

'Nothing from the transport cafe?'

'Iffy. Two witnesses agree about Guffey picking up a ride in a tipper truck, but nobody's come up with a name, not surprising though, that, when you think the custom's mostly long-distance truckies. I mean, I've had to get one call out to Strathclyde and you can't get much farther away than that.'

'Wait till the channel tunnel opens,' said the chief inspector with gloomy foreboding, able, much against his will, to envisage a future where hiding places for villains were multiplied to the nth degree. Barrett, who until then had thought only in terms of quick access to the continent, the odd weekend in France to impress a girlfriend and no worry about a rough sea crossing, felt a bit of Morrissey's pessimism rub off. Why was it that progress always brought penalties along?

Smythe came in and cut through the gloom, his tie loosened and top shirt button undone, the whole effect looking as if he needed to buy a larger collar size. So what! thought Barrett resentfully, body-building wouldn't help solve any crimes. He flexed his own shoulders experimentally. Smythe said, 'Thinking about Guffey and the lift he picked up; this came in Thursday and got filed away.' He put a stolen vehicle report on Morrissey's desk. Morrissey gave it to Barrett. 'It's a tipper truck that went missing from a Bradford builder's yard and turned up again just outside Garforth about mid-day. Could be a connection, do you think?'

'What happened to it after that?' said Morrissey. 'Any follow-up?'

'I can find out if I check with Leeds, sir. It turned up in their area.'

'Do it then,' said Barrett. 'You're asking about damage, fingerprints, anything found in the tyre treads, get a Fax through fast and bring the results to me.' Smythe looked doubtful. 'To me,' the detective sergeant repeated, 'this is my case until you're told differently.' Morrissey swallowed a smile.

'Yes, well—I'll get right on it then,' said the DC.

Barrett watched the door close and gave himself a mental pat on the back. He'd handled that well! He looked at Morrissey for confirmation. The chief inspector said blandly: 'It'd be handy to know how much mileage it clocked up between leaving Bradford and turning up at Garforth, don't you think?'

'Right,' said Barrett, ruffled again, and went after Smythe. Morrissey went back to his paperwork; at least that was getting less.

CLAIRE HAD STARTED in the kitchen, since that was the centre of things, until the kitchen was cleared up and clean, she couldn't even make a cup of tea. At two it was done, and she was able to put the kettle on. At half-past she made a start in the bedroom. Here, all the drawers had been turned out, and the wardrobe, and the little windowless boxroom in the corner where all kinds of oddments were kept—including a lot of Richard's papers, now strewn in impossible chaos across the bedroom floor. She gathered them into a pile and put them in a corner of the boxroom until she could bring herself to throw them away. What was the point of keeping things that would never have any use? Anyway, they were all old and unlooked at even by Richard. Current work was in his briefcase.

She stopped what she was doing. She'd been given back Richard's clothing, his wristwatch, his wallet and his wedding ring—even his key-case and loose change from his pocket. But his briefcase—no. Why hadn't she thought of it before?

Because, damn it, with her husband dead what importance did a briefcase have? Why *should* she have thought about it? Maybe he'd left it in his office; maybe it had been washed out of the car. *Maybe someone hadn't wanted her to have it.*

Claire folded her arms across her chest, elbows touching, hands gripping their opposite shoulders, and stared out through the bedroom window. The street was so quiet in the daytime, she was almost the only woman who didn't hold down a job as well as keep house. Richard hadn't wanted her to work, not while the children were still young. No, don't blame Richard, *she* hadn't wanted to let someone else have all the joy of watching them grow and develop while she pounded a typewriter in some too-bright office. That would all have to change now, too.

She lifted the telephone extension and dialed, waiting to be put through to Morrissey, it seemed a long time before his voice came on the line. Carefully, without trying to make it seem more than a casual query, she asked about the briefcase.

AS THE CHIEF inspector went in search of Smythe he felt disquiet rising up again like a hungry ghost. Now he had a briefcase to add to a lengthening list of things that bothered him.

Smythe and Barrett were both in Communications; Smythe by the Fax machine, Barrett leaning on a desk, both studiously looking at their shoes. A disagreement then, decided the chief inspector. Smythe should have stuck with a tendency towards acne; a spotty DC didn't threaten Barrett's self-image. Close on the heels of that thought came another—that it wouldn't do Barrett any harm to shed the moustache and waistcoat and let his hair down. He fixed his attention on Smythe. 'The Halloween burglaries, anything happening?'

Barrett relaxed, the break-ins weren't his problem.

'We're—um, not involved, sir,' said Smythe. 'It's been left with DS Gosnay and the uniforms.'

'Whose idea?'

'Um.' A finger pointing through the ceiling. 'Said it wasn't something you should waste your time with, sir.'

'Did he now? Well I'd be a fool to say senior officers could ever be wrong. You've got no feedback then?'

'Er—not exactly.'

'And what does "not exactly" mean?' asked Morrissey, patience thinning fast. 'Not something you can sit on a fence about, is it? You've either got it or you haven't.'

'I—um, er . . .'

'For God's sake!' Morrissey exploded. The Fax machine gibbered.

'I have this snout . . .'

'Informer,' Morrissey corrected.

'Informer. I looked him up last night, on the way home, thinking it'd give me a good start this morning; anyway, word is, none of the Malminster wrong-doers had a look in, it was an outside lot, tailor-made for the job.'

'How tailor-made?'

Smythe spread his hands. 'Sorry, sir.'

'Brought in from where, by who?'

'I don't know that either, sir.'

'But you'll have passed on what you *do* have to Gosnay?'

'I told you what I heard, but he's got his own ideas on where he wants to look.'

The Fax machine quieted, Barrett came, silently collected its output, and retreated to his own office. The chief inspector watched him go and thought about team-work. Did it exist? Anywhere? He sighed. 'Detective Sergeant Gosnay's using his prerogative then, isn't he? Doesn't stop you keeping an ear open while you're on with other things. If you pick up anything new bring it to me.'

'Anything I should ask about in particular, sir?'

'Use your initiative,' said Morrissey. 'You seem to be doing quite well on it so far.'

Smythe perked up, maybe drawing the short straw for office sitting had worked to his advantage after all.

SEVENTEEN

MORRISEEY MADE his interest in the Halloween break-ins known to Terry Gosnay. Gosnay was put out at having to communicate his comings and goings on what was essentially a nice little time-waster to a senior officer as ballsingly straight as Morrissey. Nobody really expected to pull a result out of house burglaries these days; it was all a public relations exercise. He debated whether to pass that theory on to the chief inspector, decided it wouldn't net him anything but more aggravation, and said he'd keep him informed—and so he would, putting up dummy hares was just part of looking busy. When the phone buzzed emptily in his ear, he looked at it gloomily. Outside team! Who the hell'd go to that amount of bother for penny pickings?

Barrett's confusion about Morrissey was growing minute by minute; he'd listened to one end of the conversation with Gosnay, and ended up wondering why half a dozen robberies were more interesting than a major crime. Barrett liked nothing better than that everything stayed on an even plateau; enough ups and downs in his personal life without the same thing creeping in at work. For some worrying reason unknown to the detective sergeant, Morrissey was acting out of character, and the more Barrett swung between wild self-confidence in his own ability and a deep depression that he didn't know what to do next, the more the worry grew.

Take this Fax about the tipper truck, for example, all Leeds had done to it was dust for fingerprints, now it was *him* that had to decide whether it was worth pulling off the road and into the police garage for a full top-to-toe. Like

Smythe had said, right kind of truck and the times—missing sometime before eight A.M., dumped around noon—fitted. Oh shit! He'd have to risk it coming to nothing and get it done. Depression deepened. It'd be out on site somewhere, fresh mud in its treads. Forensic'd love him! He stopped chewing on a ballpoint and got on with telephoning. In the middle of it all, Morrissey got up from his desk, gave Barrett a thumbs-up, and went off to do things of his own.

FOR A PLANNING department that raised difficulties about the environmental cohesiveness of simple domestic additions, such as minuscule conservatories, the relatively new building which housed it pointed to a blind spot. Six stories high, it presented a dark façade of dark-tinted windows interspersed with black Perspex cladding, rising like some glassy monster from a welter of low red-brick buildings, some of which, like the old decaying Ritz cinema, not closed and covered in fly-posters, presented environmental hazards of their own. All this went through Morrissey's mind as he parked in a visitor's slot, and made his way to the splendidly carpeted entrance lobby.

Ten per cent of Malminster's citizens had avoided paying poll-tax; last week the local paper had been crying out about the number of schools in need of repair, but somehow there was always enough money for extravagant showpieces. Disgruntled, Morrissey waited for the softly purring lift, and when it came that was carpeted too.

On the fifth floor he was faced by a reception desk high enough to deter frustrated visitors from reaching over and throttling the bright young thing behind it. He stated his business; it achieved nothing.

'You can't see Mr Lowry without an appointment,' she said with the kind of sing-song delivery that only comes with repeated usage. 'And he'll be busy all afternoon. Sorr-ee, shall I try to fit you in tomorrow?'

'No,' said Morrissey a-sizzle with barely contained wrath, 'you can fit me in now. Let him know Chief Inspector Morrissey is out here and getting stroppier by the second.'

'I'll tell him,' she said without noticeable variation in tone, 'but it won't do any good. If he's busy he's busy.' With one eye on him, she picked out Lowry's number on the internal telephone and said into the mouthpiece: 'There's a Chief Inspector Morrissey to see you, Mr Lowry. I've told him it's impossible, but he's being very difficult. What do you want me to do about him?'

Do about him! Morrissey scowled.

'Really?' said the girl, with arching eyebrows. 'Yes, I'll tell him.' She put the receiver down, ignored Morrissey's frosty look, and said brightly, 'If you'd like to sit down over there, Mr Lowry will be out to talk to you in a minute.' Her hand waved to a conversation group of low chairs and a table in the farthest corner. Morrissey didn't move.

'Right here will do me fine,' he told her shortly, and folded his arms; the scowl was just getting through when Lowry came and apologised for keeping him waiting. The chief inspector grunted; more appeasement than that was due. He walked down the cool almond corridor, eyes flicking over the architectural drawings as he passed, refusing to be drawn out about the purpose of his visit until he was ready to come to that himself. In Lowry's office he eyed the visitor's chair with disdain, and after prowling to the window and staring down at the traffic, came straight to the point and asked about Simms' briefcase.

Lowry looked surprised, and to Morrissey's practised eye relieved, which must mean he'd been expecting worse. He said: 'Briefcase? Well, yes, obviously I know he had one. Don't we all? But it isn't here, Chief Inspector, and if that's why you've come I'm afraid it's been a wasted trip. If he'd left it in his office I'd have seen it.'

'Yes,' agreed Morrissey. 'You would, wouldn't you, and if you had seen it, you would naturally have returned it to the widow.'

'Of course. There would have been no reason to keep it.'

'That's what I thought,' said the chief inspector. 'Not as though he was working on anything top-secret, but then we come to another question. Why would Mr Simms be working so late the night he died?'

Lowry's head tilted forward confidentially. 'You know, I've asked myself that many times—a very conscientious man, Richard; always had to be on top of everything. But to my knowledge he hadn't stayed in his office until that time on any previous occasion.'

'How would you have known if he had?'

'There'd have been a note in the night security book.'

'Which you always check.'

'Which I always check.'

'Then I'll say thank you for your trouble and let you get on with your work,' said Morrissey, moving to the door. 'But if the briefcase does turn up...'

'I'll let you know at once.' All smiles now, Lowry walked him back down the corridor and waited with him in the lobby until the lift came. 'Anything else at all, Chief Inspector—don't hesitate.'

'I won't,' said Morrissey loudly, with a look in the bright young thing's direction. The bright young thing pretended she hadn't heard.

As he reversed from the parking slot and drove slowly out of the car-park to join the main road traffic, Morrissey was wondering what possible question Lowry had been afraid he might be asked.

EIGHTEEN

MODERN TECHNOLOGY had a habit of creeping in where it was least welcome, and the computer terminal on the chief inspector's desk was, to him, visible proof of that. He hadn't wanted it when it was installed two years ago, and an intimate knowledge of its workings still left him unconvinced that he couldn't manage just as well without it. He granted, grudgingly, that it let him tap into other information systems, call up files without having to search through brown manilla forests, but on a deeper and more esoteric level, there was something infinitely more satisfying to be got from reading through sheets of paper than could ever be garnered from a flickering screen—not that Morrissey ever allowed that particular prejudice to stop him from exploiting the mainframe memory when it suited his purpose. And it suited his purpose when he got back from talking with Lowry—he didn't want any little ripples of speculation about how many times he'd borrowed the Simms file recently travelling upstairs to reach Osgodby's ears. Not when he didn't have a good explanation, he didn't!

He'd given the neat tabulation of objects recovered from the car, the weir, and Simms' body more than one cursory glance before, but until now without specific interest in anything except an absence of toxic substances; now he had the list in front of him again, and he stared at the screen morosely. Any inventory painstaking enough to include an uneaten sandwich in a Marks & Spencer wrapper, would be unlikely to have missed out on a briefcase. Impasse then. Not in Simms' car, not in his office, and not in his home, so where the blazes was it—in the mud at the bottom of the weir?

Not feasible. The chief inspector knew that as soon as the thought came, the memory echo of Lister's indignant, 'We sent froggies down,' close on its heels. One thing could be guaranteed, police frogmen were a damn sight too efficient to overlook anything as bulky as a briefcase, mud or no mud.

Morrissey let the listing go back to its electronic limbo and switched off, exasperated with everything, including himself, leaning back in his chair, hands behind his head, staring at nothing in particular. Things that weren't where they should be invariably turned up where they shouldn't be—in someone else's illegal possession—and he shouldn't even be thinking about finding out whose. Unsurprisingly, knowing that did nothing but irritate.

The wall clock said it was almost three, and Claire Simms was alone in a devastated house trying to put it to rights. Guilt hovered like a personalised rain cloud and he had no umbrella of excuses. A woman he knew, even if only slightly, had asked for help and he'd sent her away—would still send her away given the same evidence and the same circumstances—and he didn't have a problem with that. What he did have a problem with was a pervading sense of something missed when he'd nothing solid to pin it to.

THE BRIGHT YOUNG thing had observed how Lowry watched Morrissey's progress to the ground floor, his eyes not leaving the illuminated squares set over the lift doors until the ground-level light remained constant. When he finally turned and came back past the desk she automatically switched on a smile, stowing away his unusual behaviour as food for future gossip. Lowry didn't even notice the smile— or the bright young thing herself, come to that—he had other, more worrying thoughts on his mind. When the line-engaged signal came up on the switchboard, the bright young thing silenced the bleep and thought about listening in. She was reaching out to do just that when a broad-shouldered trainee from accounts danced in and took her mind off it with talk of a local rave. By the time they'd settled on where to meet, the line was disengaged again, and Lowry had shared his worries.

When he left his office to go into that next door the chief planning officer was sweating freely, mopping at his face with a green cotton handkerchief. All that had to be done was sit tight, nothing had changed hands, nothing was down on paper, and the only profit-taker so far had been Simms. He'd take one more diligent look through the now-unoccupied office, make sure there was nothing in there a Sunday school teacher could find fault with and then, as Richardson had just said, lie low and let the dust settle. What did it matter if this land deal fell through, there'd be others, not as richly profitable but sometimes less was more.

Lowry took his time sifting through papers he'd been through once already. No good waiting for waves to be made; if HM Auditors descended unannounced, he didn't want anything left lying around to provoke difficult questions. It wasn't just his job at stake, it was everything, including his freedom. Especially his freedom. Sod this perpetual sweating, his handkerchief reeked of it!

There were Simms' personal belongings, a small box of them, little things, pens and a desk lighter, a folding umbrella, unused by the look of it, a photograph of Simms with his wife and children in a black leather frame. The widow should have them; it couldn't be put off forever. Yes, they ought to go back. He carried them into his office, conscience clear. Nothing he'd done or caused to be done had contributed to what happened, Richard's death was un-

timely, unpleasant and—except to Thewlis—something to
be regretted. A clear conscience, yes; no reason to avoid a
meeting. He changed his brightly coloured tie for one more
sombre, kept on hand for occasions demanding less flam-
boyance, and went down five floors to the car-park, forgetting to tell the bright young thing where he was going.

Claire opened the door to him dishevelled, tired and, unknown to her, tear-stained. She let him in simply because
there was no automatic feeling of revulsion; he was Richard's boss, met with occasionally and complained about as
bosses always are. She took him first into the living-room,
forgetting it was still chaotic, said briefly: 'Burglary,' and
led him away into the kitchen instead, setting the kettle to
boil with automatic hospitality. Then she let herself hear
why he had come. Out of the box, higgledy-piggledy on the
table, the small pile of belongings looked pitiful, tearing at
her more than anything else had done.

Her legs were jelly.

She flopped on a chair and picked up the photograph,
suddenly overwhelmed with fresh grief.

Lowry stood uneasily, cursing himself for not anticipat-
ing what might happen. Awkwardly he mumbled plati-
tudes. Claire's mind heard and refused to comprehend.
After a few minutes, when she stayed silent and made no
response, he told himself it had been a mistake to come,
shifted, blundered excuses, and let himself out through the
kitchen door.

It was an unwanted shock, as he rounded the corner of the
house, to see Chief Inspector Morrissey striding up the drive
towards him with a face cold as granite.

INSPECTOR BECKETT, fully ambulant, and bored out of his
mind, had taken to wandering the hospital corridors in
search of excitement, and the fact that he'd had a singular

lack of success finding any didn't act as a deterrent. What he *had* come to realise, fed a steady diet of cops and robbers via the ward television, was just how badly fact compared with fiction. Real life could be a terrible let-down—no murdered housemen or stolen blood-banks for him; the most demanding thing he'd been asked to do was count the ward cutlery. He was itching—literally as well as figuratively—to rid himself of the drain poking out of his wound, so he could get out of the place. Not that he would have been in anything like as much of a hurry if Jean hadn't already agreed to come home and look after him—never mind if she said it was a trial period; he'd learned his lesson.

Ever since the day he'd recognised Mustaph Ali outside Intensive Care, and stopped to talk—the same day he'd been escorted at his then slow shuffle to see Azar—his daily schedule always took him past that department. Up until now the daily bulletin had never varied, Azar was stable. Abdhul Khalid had a way of pronouncing the word 'stable' as if it were some magic mantra that repeated often enough would work a miracle, but he, Beckett, knew all the magic and miracles lay centred in the life-support machine. Let them take that away and stable would be the last word they'd use.

Over the last few days, as his strength returned, the policeman in Beckett had been reasserting itself, and with it his instinct for things not right. The first time he'd talked to Abdhul Khalid the man had grieved, 'For seven months we have been told we must leave, now my son is sacrificed.'

At the time, still sore, and with a Ryles tube in his stomach, the significance of that hadn't registered with Beckett, but it did now. Khalid had either got the length of time wrong, or there'd been some sort of intimidation going on a lot longer than the police had known about. He went in through the doors and purposefully asked his question. It had to be repeated. Khalid finally understood, but looked baffled that Beckett should ask.

'Seven months, yes.'

'And nobody thought to mention how long it had been going on, not even when it escalated. Why was that, Mr Khalid, why didn't we know?'

Khalid spread his hands because the answer was simple.

'It was that no one asked us, Mr Beckett.'

MONICA THEWLIS had no idea how long she'd been sitting on the kitchen chair before the telephone began to ring, and it stopped just as she put her hand out to lift the receiver. If it had been Jack, he'd be wanting to know why it hadn't been answered. Panic came, then she remembered her supposed heavy cold. If she said she'd been asleep in bed, he'd accept that—he liked her out of the way when she had an infection; germs were a terror to him. The inside of her thigh throbbed sore and hot. A painful memory of sitting in the bath tearing at her skin. The next memory was of spidermite on the windowsill plants. She remembered spraying them but couldn't remember putting the insecticide back on its shelf.

Looking for it in the kitchen took a little time. Her head had felt fuzzy; she remembered that now too. When she failed to find the bug-gun she went to the garage; a place for everything and everything in its place, emphasised painfully when she forgot. Jack would see straight away if it wasn't there. But it was there, innocently next to the paraquat.

The paraquat.

Her eyes went to the whisky bottle. She remembered—something. Two deep lines creased her forehead. Had she actually done it? No, no, of course not. But suppose... fuzzy head, fuzzy thoughts, mightn't she have...?

No!

Shouldn't she, just in case...? Her hand moved to the whisky bottle and withdrew. If it wasn't there when Jack came home, he'd kill her. She knew he would. Fear *of* him outweighed fear for him. She closed the garage door and went back to the house. Monica concentrated but the only word she could latch on to was 'divorce.'

'Divorce?' Panicking again. 'Not you and Gordon, not with the baby coming, and...'

'No, Mum. Mum, you've got to listen. Gordon says...' —a pause there, Monica could sense Angie feeling for the right words, then going on in a rush again—'Gordon says you could divorce Dad, it'd be really easy, and then he couldn't stop you doing anything you wanted to do, *and* he'd have to pay you alimony, Mum. You could come live with us without worrying about not having any money, and he wouldn't have any right to come and find you. Are you listening to me, Mum? You'd be rid of him.'

Rid of him! 'Yes, Angeline, I'm listening.' Divorce him for what? Bruises he'd swear he didn't know about. She'd tried once when Angeline was small; the solicitor had sent her away and told her not to be silly. Of course there hadn't been Legal Aid then and she'd had no money. Money really mattered where solicitors were concerned. A woman, a dog, and a walnut tree—the more you beat 'em the better they be. She'd heard that said, time and again, in those early years, not anymore though.

Angeline was still talking.

'Sorry, love, tell me again, I wasn't concentrating.'

'A mistress, Mum. Those nights he doesn't get home until after twelve, he's with her. Gordon says he'll get a private detective, then there'll be photographs, and a witness. Mum, just pack a bag and come to us.'

'It's the first place he'd look. Think what trouble he'd cause Gordon.'

'Then we'll find somewhere safe, instead, until it's over.'

'Love, what with yesterday, and now this . . . I can't think properly.' But she *was* thinking, she was thinking divorce, over and over again. The word wrote itself large in her mind. 'Who is it, Angie?'

Silence.

'Angie?'

Unwillingly. 'She's called Lilian Carver.'

'What is she, young, middle-aged . . . what?' The fuzzy edges left her mind.

'Gordon says about thirty-five.'

'And lives where? Where does she live, Angie?'

'Woodbine Terrace. Mum . . . you're not to try to see her. You mustn't. It'd spoil things.'

'I don't want to see her. Say thank you to Gordon for me, love.'

'You sound funny, Mum.'

'Bit of a cold.'

'I'll ring you tomorrow.'

'That'll be nice, love,' said Monica, and put the phone down absently. He'd be there tonight. Home first, expecting a cooked tea, then out again. Her mind floated back to the whisky bottle, light as a balloon.

She was almost sure she hadn't.

Almost.

NINETEEN

GOD! BUT she could have done without Lowry's visit.
Splashing her face repeatedly with cold water, anger fast and
clear as the gush from the tap. Oh *shit,* Richard! Who gave
you the damn right to die, who gave you the damn right to
leave us in this sodding *mess!* Drying her face and going
back to the kitchen to brew a pot of tea. Agonised at being
caught with her emotional pants down. And there was
Morrissey, wary of so much freshly released emotion, sitting like a graven image. Well, she was wary too. Did he
think she liked to hang her grief out in public? That wasn't
the English tradition, was it? Stiff upper lip—*nil desperan-
dum* and all that bloody rot! She set cups on the table, and
a plate of biscuits. Observing minor formalities of hospitality helped, tea lessened tension, for her if not for him. Richard's belongings were on the table still, Morrissey idly
fiddling with the pens. Claire grabbed the box and angrily
swept the table clear; the umbrella teetered and fell on the
floor.

Damn it.

Morrissey bent in retrieval, set it in the box with the other
things, but didn't release his hold of a pen, elegant black
with gold banding, turning it over in his fingers. 'I suppose
Richard got a lot of this kind of thing; courtesy gifts from
firms the Council do business with.'

'I don't know.' Shaking her head. How did he expect her
to know?

'No, I don't suppose you would. Nice pen, though.'

'Have it.'

'Kind of you, but that isn't what I was thinking about.' He set it aside, not disposed to tell her where his thoughts had been, knowing that in any case the pen wasn't expensive enough to constitute a bribe, but not a cheap, freebee gimmick either, not with Waterman embossed in its side. He ate a biscuit and without thinking took another. Why did *C. S. Richardson, Property Developers and Consultants,* give away such luxury knick-knacks? And if that was the sort of casual hand-out a minor Council employee got, what kind of freebee might someone higher up come away with? Someone like Lowry for instance, and what for? Sweeteners for the future?

'Did you find the briefcase?'

The chief inspector brought his mind back to the purpose of his visit. He hadn't gone there to drink tea, nor to speculate on the value of perks either. He shifted his weight a little, said on a confidential note, 'Now that's something of a mystery, because if you tell me the briefcase isn't here, and it hasn't been left in the office, and it wasn't in the car, I'm at a loss. I hoped you might have ideas on where else I should look.'

'I don't.' Shrugging her shoulders because the briefcase didn't seem important now. But that couldn't be right, could it? It had been important three hours ago. Frowning at herself, 'It could have gone in the burglary. I can't prove it didn't. It just seemed unlikely at the time.'

'Because he never left it at home, you mean—always had it with him?'

'Yes.'

'Not likely he'd have changed his habit then, too big a coincidence for it to have happened on that one day.'

'*Yes!*' Relief in her voice.

'And that's why you told me about it.'

'You said to tell you if anything odd happened.'

'That I did. So, I'd better get on and find out who has it, because someone must.' Morrissey moved his chair back a little but didn't get up from it quite yet. 'Where are the children, Mrs Simms? Not here, I can see that. One of the neighbours has them, perhaps?'

A shake of her head. 'I took them home to my mother's in Bolton, Sunday morning.' Now he'd want to know why.

'Because of the break-in, I expect.'

'Partly.'

'Something else, then?'

To tell or not to tell. What a blessed relief it would be to shift a bit of the burden onto his broad shoulders—not that he could *do* anything. First, though, conjure back the voice—chill, flat; broad vowels. If she told Morrissey why she'd wanted her children out of Malminster, he'd ask about that voice. What it had sounded like. Was it young or old? Frowning again, hands round her cup and gripping hard— if it shattered she'd slice her fingers open. Morrissey saw that too, and took the cup from her. She didn't resist its going, just marvelled at how much his voice changed as it gentled the truth from her.

BARRETT DIDN'T feel he'd made much progress, but despite that a lot of man-hours had gone into the tracking down and questioning of drivers who had been in Joe's Caff early Thursday morning, and all the hours it seemed, wasted, unless you counted three drivers who gave accurate enough descriptions of Guffey to confirm they'd actually seen him there. A pity they hadn't been looking at the right time and noticed who'd given him a lift.

Catching up on paperwork while he waited for results, the detective sergeant tried looking on the bright side; there were still ten drivers to go, and it only needed one...

He hadn't told anybody about the tipper truck yet; it hadn't all been plain sailing there either. To begin with, there'd been a bit of dispute about which flaming truck had actually gone missing. The site foreman said one thing; the police report, another. In every other case Barrett could think of he'd have taken the police version as kosher, but this time things were complicated beyond belief by consecutive registration numbers. D 825 HWY, and D 826 HWY, both on tipper trucks, and both trucks on the same site. Coated in mud it was hard to tell one from the other. D 826 HWY had been reported stolen, D 825 HWY had been reported found. What was he supposed to do?

Faced with Solomon's choice he'd played safe and now both trucks were in the police garage, and the building contractor was threatening all kinds of action to get them back. If Forensics found nothing on either vehicle he'd be nailed to the wall.

Three minutes short of four-thirty a message came upstairs that Badger wanted to talk to him again. Pessimism said it would be a waste of time. Clattering down three flights, turning right along the stump of corridor, left at the end and along a longer stretch, past the briefing room and communications, catching an antiseptic whiff from the medical room and turning right again through the double doors of the charge room, thinking all along how he was wasting his time, then listening to the custody sergeant's sour directions. 'I've shoved him in room one, and I'll tell *you* now he's a right whiney little bugger today; must want you to write a letter to his mum.' Out through the far set of double doors to hear Badger, pale and spotty in the interview room, tell him: 'He thought he'd get paid for it like, Guffey did, like what he did the first time. Dunno how much he got, a bit I expect, 'specially since he kept the lot what with Skeggy and Beano gettin' flattened an' all.' Then whining. 'S'right, is it? What you told me about Guffey being dead like, I mean s'right, in' it, 'cos he'll frigging 'ave me if it's not straight.'

'It's straight,' Barrett said shortly, digesting Badger's rush of words and seeing how the investigation might suddenly double in complexity, disgruntled that it couldn't stay simple. 'Who paid Guffey, and for what piece of nastiness?'

'Them frigging Pakkis, that's what, weren't it,' said the other, surly now, grubby middle finger scab picking among the acne. 'We was supposed to give 'em a bit of aggro so's they'd clear out. Only it got called off didn't it, 'cos there was a bit of a cock-up.'

Barrett had to struggle with Badger's simple concept. A bit of a cock-up—seven dead. Eight if Azar didn't make it. Short-fused at the best of times, wanting to explode, but holding back because he was investigating officer and there might be more to come. Surprising himself that he could do that.

'Who paid the price?'

'Dunno.'

'Think a bit harder.'

'Wouldn't do no good, Guffey didn't never let on about that side of things. When do I get me boots back? These bloody things is too small,' he complained, scowling at his feet. Boots gone, bottle gone, Barrett thought. Black plimsolls didn't make good weapons.

'After the trial. Not that you'll be needing them then for a bit.' Pleased to get that in and hear the whine come back.

'But I'm helping now, aren't I? Turning Queen's. You tell the court that and they'll go easy.'

'Help a bit more then. Who paid?'

'I don't bleedin' know, whad' ja want—me hand on a Bible?'

'You can have it on a stack,' Barrett said nastily, 'and it won't convince me. Think a bit harder.'

'S'truth.' The whine reached a higher pitch. 'I need lookin' after, them frigging Pakkis'll slit me next.'

'What do you mean—slit?'

'S'how he went, in' it? one of them bleedin' long knives.'

'Who told you that?'

'Don't matter.'

'Who?'

'I heard one of your lot gabbing.'

Nice one! Barrett thought. Somebody had a loose mouth.

'S'right, in' it?' Badger said.

'I can't tell you that. Who paid Guffey?'

Silence.

Barrett shrugged. 'Suit yourself. We'll need all that you've said in another statement. I'll get your solicitor to come down,' he said, moving towards the door.

'But you'll put a word in?'

'Shouldn't think so. Pity you can't give me a name; might be worth something then. As it is now, it's all old ground. Think about it,' Barrett said noncommittally and opened the door.

Badger squeaked. 'Joe's Caff.'

'What about Joe's Caff?'

'S'where he did business, in' it; that an' a squat.'

'Where's the squat?'

'Down the wharf.'

'Where down the wharf?'

'Past that swanked-up bit. I can show you.'

'You can tell me,' said Barrett firmly, sensing he was onto something at last, and sent for a map.

BARRETT WOULD have recognised the chief inspector's frame of mind and headed in the opposite direction, because Morrissey in a mood of self-censure was a man to be avoided, and the mood was deep upon him. There were too many things, one piling up on another, to be easily dismissed now as imagination. He should have listened to instinct. Enough to lose a young husband without all that had followed; house burglarised, child threatened, and now to be cooped up in there alone, having through no fault of her own to re-create order from chaos. It was too much, even for a woman as strong and independently minded as Claire. No doubt in Morrissey's mind about that with his new perspective on things; but not so easy to acknowledge that if nothing was seen to be done soon, she'd crack.

More than likely Gibson would be at home by now, his slicing and cutting finished for another day. Courtesy then to ring him there before asking Warmsby to take a look, and Osgodby to tell before he took that step anyway.

Gibson tonight then, Osgodby tomorrow.

And a word with Bill Newton before that.

When he radioed in there was a message from Inspector Beckett. The WPC's voice sounded vaguely apologetic. 'He said could you drop in at the hospital, sir, and to tell you it's business not a hand-holding job.'

Unmistakably Beckett.

Waiting to be patched through to Newton, Morrissey speculated on the kind of business Beckett wanted to discuss. Too young to think about early retirement—not a sounding out about that, then. And nothing to do with Jean either—that wouldn't be business. What then? Some case he'd been working on before the ulcer got him? More likely. Non-urgent hopefully, since CID had shot from idle to overstretched in under a week.

Newton's voice boomed.

Morrissey dismissed speculation and brought his mind back to his own problems, phrasing his wants with care, unwilling to raise too much interest on Newton's part. Enough at that point if he could be persuaded to answer the chief inspector's questions without wanting to start up hares of his own.

'On me way home though, aren't I,' said the fraud squad officer breezily. 'Promised the wife a fish 'n chip supper tonight for her birthday. Where are you now?'

Morrissey told him.

'Right; well if I turn round we should end up at the Chancellors about the same time. Last one in pays.'

'If it's halves,' agreed Morrissey.

'Always were a skinflint,' Newton said.

Impatient, half a mile from the Simms house, waiting at the T-junction to make a right turn across rush-hour traffic, the chief inspector didn't doubt it would be him who paid.

TWENTY

THEWLIS DIDN'T bother going home, didn't even bother to tell his wife he wouldn't be. Instead he came out of the Town Hall into the heavy drizzle alone, and picked up Lilian Carver ten minutes later down a side street behind a row of dingy shops. 'Nice this,' she said as she got into his car. 'Aren't I lucky?' Thewlis grunted, and drove her to a Beef-eater just outside Batley. No free lunches and no free dinners either. He amused himself by working out how he'd extract payment for her meal.

Monica Thewlis had cooked high-tea from long habit, and the HP Sauce bottle was on the table. Coated in Vicks again, she watched the clock hands move around and smelled the thick pork sausages drying up. At seven-thirty she turned off the oven and knew he'd not be home now until after midnight.

It wasn't the first time she'd wasted effort.

Upstairs in the bathroom, she put more salve on her thigh and tried to wash some of the strong Vicks smell away, nervous at the idea of going out when it meant using the Fiesta. He'd check the mileage and want to know where she'd been. Thinking about that made her sit in her coat on the bed. Supposing Angeline was wrong? Supposing Jack came home and she was out? Her heart gained a beat, pounded faster, gained another beat. She could say she'd been to the doctor's; he wouldn't check up on that. Take some deep breaths, in...out, in...out, feeling the beat slow. Gloves on quickly before she changed her mind, get the car keys, leave the lights on and lock the door.

It was ages since she'd driven in the dark, and it disoriented her. Slowly, like a learner, she hugged the white line, and didn't change out of third gear until she reached the sodium lighting on the main road.

Woodbine Terrace was a narrow, bumpy little road on the south side of Malminster, with houses on one side, and a playing field on the other, not even in a good part of town. Monica sat in the car and waited, quite uncertain what she should do. A love nest. No, that couldn't be the right name for it, not where Jack was concerned, love wasn't in his vocabulary. A sex nest, that was better. Did *she* know, or had she only seen the honey jar yet, and not the vinegar bottle?

With the car lights out it was dark, the street lamps were well distanced and didn't throw much illumination, and the scraggy hedgerow across the road looked darkly sinister. She didn't really want to get out of the Fiesta at all, but Jack's car stood outside a house a bit farther up the road where the downstairs window was streaming light out across the garden. Moving towards it she thought. Supposing he comes out? Heart in mouth again. Halfway along the front path the light went out and left her in darkness. While she stood there, hesitating, the bedroom light went on in its place and Lilian Carver stood squarely before the window, naked, her arms reaching up to close the drapes. Thewlis, still dressed, came behind her, his big hands reaching around, kneading the heavy breasts. Lilian couldn't see the expression on his face but Monica could and felt her mouth slacken and widen into a wide 'O'. Then the curtains closed, some blue, heavy material that let out only the barest glimmer of light.

Blinking, unable now to see at all, hands spread blindly, and turning on the path, her heel slid into a hollow, throwing her foot sideways. With the intervening hedges and tall trees cutting off light from the street standards, she was sightless in the darkness, feeling continuously ahead one foot at a time, testing for the black pit that seemed to be there waiting for her to step into it. The darkly damp night pressed like a physical weight. Then the gate appeared dimly and she lurched for it with gladness and stumbled again. Driving home the thought of divorce crept into her mind again, and for the first time it had a flavour of certainty that she savoured like a captive savours freedom. To be free, to see the back of him, was a tantalising possibility, taking on solidity as she drove. Tomorrow, her mind decided, tomorrow she would tell Gordon to do whatever he thought best. Tomorrow he'd find her somewhere safe until it was all over, just as Angeline had promised.

BILL NEWTON was fat, no other word for it. Put him in uniform and he'd be the archetypical jolly policeman. He knew that; it was an image he'd accepted and learned to live with. He didn't mind being thought a buffoon by strangers. It put them off guard and made them careless. Who'd look for a sharp brain inside a man mountain with owl glasses. He and Morrissey had been friends a long time, respecting each other's expertise without rancour, and by rights Newton should have ranked chief inspector himself, but to be that in his own particular speciality would have kept him desk-bound too much, and that wouldn't have suited anybody's interests, least of all his own. He didn't fancy sitting on his bum all day teaching up-comers what to do. He liked to be out and about where his far from handsome nose could sniff the scent of fraud a mile away. It was his reason for getting up on a morning. That and to get away from his wife harping on about diets and heart attacks until he could have had one from the sheer frustration of listening to her.

He'd taken tenancy of a corner table, rump happy on the bench seat, a pint of bitter downed before Morrissey got there. Seeing the chief inspector, his voice filled the space between them, Falstaff without a stage. 'Hail the weary traveller, come rest your ancient bones. Came the long way round, did you? The beer'll be flat.'

'I suppose you were just up the road,' said Morrissey, carrying two halves over.

He set the darker brew before Newton, who said, 'What's that you're drinking, pigeon wee?'

'What else?' Morrissey agreed equably, sitting opposite. 'Pat's birthday, then?'

'Too true it is. I should be home, prettying myself up. You've never seen her with her stop-watch have you, foot tapping, war-paint on, rollers out—no, of course you haven't—but it's a sight to behold; so get on with what you want sharpish, so I can get her down the chippy.'

'Graft in planning departments.'

'Oh!' Eyes brightening with interest. 'What's going on in our unfair city that I don't know about and should?'

'Pretend it's hypothetical,' said Morrissey.

'In a flea's arse. Think I should sniff around then?'

'I'd take it as a favour if you didn't. Not yet.'

'Might scare the customers away, is that it?' A surprisingly slim finger laid at the side of his nose. 'Say no more—except I get first bite.'

'If anything jumps in the net.'

'Right, well. Little fish get paid for speeding up planning applications, but you're not after small fry, are you? Fat barracudas get to feed off contractors eager for some lucrative Council construction work, and speculators looking for cheap land deals. That'd mean somebody high up on the Council planning committee, colluding with somebody in architect's or planning.' Leaning forward, breathing beery enough to give Morrissey a peck of guilt—Pat would not be pleased... 'Going down the right road, Am I? Good. Now, for it to work, the briber has to know who to bribe, and that person has to be not only susceptible to an offer, but in the right position to steer decisions through committee and manage to make it look like the committee knew what they were doing—and the bigger the profit the bigger the fish.'

'Now tell me where you'd look for evidence.'

Newton concentrated on his beer.

'Thought it was hypothetical.'

'If I didn't need to know I wouldn't be asking.'

Newton sighed, shifting, seeing the time.

'It'd mean ploughing back through months of planning committee meetings, and looking how often the same contractor's name comes up for lucrative work, and how many parcels of Council land are undersold, or how many buildings have been packaged cheap. Them's the three most likely misdealings you'll find—and good luck to you, I'm going home to the missus.' He came out from his seat, moving quickly despite the bulk of him.

The chief inspector said, 'Enjoy the chippy.'

'Don't be bloody daft, I'd never see morning, trying that on. I've got to squire her to some posh restaurant, other side of Leeds, and that's me piggy-bank gone again. See you, John,' he said, clapping a hand on Morrissey's shoulder. 'Stay sober!' jostling a young woman, passing as he turned. Both apologised, she dark-haired, intelligent-looking, simmering as she did so, not because of him but from a heated exchange with the red-haired man at the bar. Morrissey had seen the argument develop while he talked. Lovers' quarrel? The barman, wiping a glass, knowing all about it. Newton and the girl vanished through the door, both in a hurry, a couple of weary-looking men in tired suits came in.

The red-haired man got another Pils, looking at Morrissey speculatively. He brought his glass to the table, sliding into Newton's empty seat. Morrissey finished his beer, made to get up. 'What did you talk to Lowry about?' No preamble, just the question. The chief inspector settled again.

'Why would it be your business?'

'I work in the sodding place.'

'And . . . ?'

'Lowry's raked out Simms' office twice since he snuffed. Went through it again after you left.'

'Looking for what?'

A shrug. 'You tell me. Want another?' Nodding at the empty glass. 'Or would that constitute a bribe?' Seeing Morrissey's eyebrows twitching up and offering a compact hand, accepted and tested. 'Charlie Rundle.'

'Morrissey, Chie . . .'

'I know. I got it off Lucretia—all comings and goings noted and filed for future gossip.'

'Lucretia?' Then knowing who'd earned the soubriquet before Rundle clarified. The bright young thing!

'Pet name. You'd have met her coming in. Karen Dobbs, by baptism, Lucretia by nature.' Nodding at the glass again. 'Can I get you one, then?' Accepting police refusal for just that and no more, taking a good long swallow out of his glass and saying, 'There'll be nothing there now that shouldn't be. Clean as a virgin's whistle.'

'Wasn't always, though; that's what you're hinting at. What would I have found before?'

'Depends what you wanted to find. Look, the town's divided up into as many slices as there's planning officers—one slice each, that's how it works. Simms had a chunk of the north side.'

'Which chunk?'

'The Industrial Estate's bang square in the middle of it. You saw the girl I was with; you were watching. Well, that's Deb, and Lowry wants to give her Simms' patch.'

'What's wrong with that?'

'I've said enough.' Drinking off the Pils. 'The rest's up to you.'

Nothing bred resentment faster than somebody else's success. It was something Morrissey had reflected on at other times without understanding the mechanism. He didn't think that it was part of Charlie Rundle's problem, but it had to be brought up. He said: 'Debra's important to you, is she?'

'You could say that.'

'And it's not sour grapes; not a promotion you'd fancy for yourself.'

A look of distaste; then understanding.

'Not if you dangled it in diamonds. Lowry offered it because she's too naïve to know a Jabberwock when she sees one.'

'"The jaws that bite, the claws that catch." Nasty piece of work as I remember. You'd know him, though.'

'Oh, yes,' agreed Rundle. 'I know the sod.'

TWENTY-ONE

BIG-BREASTED, generous-mouthed Lilian Carver called herself a therapist. Which she was, in a way. Nobody could say the services she provided weren't therapeutic. She kept her client list small, but reaped enough financial reward from it to keep her well clothed, well fed, and to deposit in her bank a big enough nest-egg to look after her retirement years. What more could a successful businesswoman want? The secret, Lilian believed, lay in being choosy; choosy and discreet. Clients by recommendation—strictly no casuals.

Lilian had also discovered a sideline that fitted in well with the idea of herself as therapist: dispensing herbal potents and potions, brewed, infused, and decocted right there in her own back kitchen, specially refitted, all shining white and clinical to impress the impressionable. It was an investment not subject to gravity's sagging, wrinkling effect, a sort of insurance policy against hard times. Browsing on a second-hand bookstall, she'd found an old and handsome volume of *Culpepper's Complete Herbal,* and carried it home with a sense of found treasure, to stand with brown-spotted pages ever open on the kitchen work-surface. Above it, on the wall, hung a couple of certificates, Lilian's finishing touch, grabbed in a fast exit from a herbalist's shop and looked on sometimes with a sense of vague regret, because, poor old sod!, she'd provided services for him too.

Never expected him to go like that.

Never expected a client like Jack Thewlis, either.

Little extras he'd asked for; the kind of thing wives didn't like to provide. Short on finesse, but she'd thought she could teach him, given time. Her first mistake. Now he wanted other things. Things Lilian didn't want to do either. Here. Now. Tonight. God, but she pitied his wife!

Bastard. No. Can't move.

Ugly white ape!

Think of something else. Thoughts tumbling over themselves. Methodist Sunday School when she was small. Sin was a pleasure, pleasure was a sin. Billy Barnes in the graveyard pulling down her knickers. Still a pleasure sometimes. Not with bastard Jack, though; not with him. *Relax, relax.* Poor bloody wife, wouldn't want to be his wife, never, never, never.

No...no...no...

Oh God! she was choking on him.

Thewlis; sweating, arching, empowered and pleasured, heard the whimper and buried her face in his flesh, felt her buck and pressed harder, finally heaving off her, saying nothing. Showering, drying off, wondering what she got up to with the rest of them. Going back to her, horny again.

Except that her head had fallen sideways, face half hidden in chestnut hair, Lilian lay exactly as he'd left her. Wake her then, make her sing for her supper, his hands active, slap, slap, before he saw her sightless, empty eyes.

MONICA THEWLIS had gone to bed with a peppered handkerchief under the pillow and Vicks pungent on her skin again. When Thewlis came in, the bang of the front door woke her, and she heard him heavy-footed, up the stairs, past her door, and into the bathroom. What time was it? peering at the luminous hands on the clock.

Half-past two.

Listening to the sound of him splashing in the bath; the water emptying, his feet padding into the big bedroom. Minutes going by and Monica beginning to drowse, then his feet going back again past the door and down the stairs. The sliding thud of the back-door bolt.

What was he doing going out the back at this time?

Get up and look through the rear bedroom window; curiosity getting the better of caution.

Watching Thewlis's actions with puzzlement.

Whyever did he want to light the incinerator at this time of night?

TWENTY-TWO

MIKE THE HUMAN whirlwind, hardly seen in passing, in to dump his school-bag, bolt his meal, and out again.

'What about homework?'

'Do it later,' he replied, waving back, half-way down the drive.

Up to her elbows in warm sudsy water, the night dark outside the kitchen window, and the long garden nothing but twisting shadows, Margaret was alone in the house, not exactly bemoaning her lot, but not exactly in raptures with it either. Katie was out somewhere with Ian Hicks, off nights now and both of them back to mooning over each other. Margaret, gently glad for her daughter, but a little jealous too, because she and Morrissey had been like that once—full of each other, plenty to say and plans to make. No time left for talking now in Morrissey's life, but plenty in her own.

Silly of her, then, to bother waiting her own meal for a husband who came and went to nobody's timetable but his own. And having waited, had watched him eat fast and silently, and leave the house again before she had even drunk her coffee. Discontentment nagged; half her life to live yet and nothing much to fill it with. The empty nest syndrome come before the fledglings had actually flown. A year ago she hadn't even entertained such thoughts. But now... Realising she'd just washed and rinsed the same cup three times, slamming it in the drainer.... Tired old propaganda doing the rounds, on television, in the papers, women's magazines saturated with it, putting families back on pedestals and women in the kitchens, no word about when the job ran out, and no redundancy benefits! Margaret didn't despise domestic bliss—on the contrary would have welcomed a return to it—but the last six months had been bedeviled with arguments, and she couldn't see where they'd all end. Only Katie, in love for the first time, had sailed through apparently oblivious. And Jean Beckett worse off still, swamped with guilt, liking her little flat and independence, but thinking about giving it up to move back in with a cantankerous husband, blaming herself because his ability to take care of himself was so abysmally lacking that he'd put himself in hospital. Promises to change were fine; reality usually something less! How was *she* to know if Beckett could stop taking his job frustrations home with him? In fact, why had Jean come to *her* for advice in the first place? Emptying the water, wiping the sink down, answering the telephone, her hands still wet.

'I don't know when he'll be home, Neil. He didn't tell me. Try again later if you like. Katie's fine. I'm fine too. Mike's at the cinema. Sounding out of sorts? No, I'm fine, Neil. Everything's fine. Ring back later. Really rather busy now.' Hanging up the telephone, cutting conversation.

Unfriendly.

Not like her at all.

THE LIGHTS of the hospital illuminated the car-park almost to its farthest limits, reflecting on the wet tarmac and revealing miniature rainbows where oil or petrol had dripped and left a residue. Morrissey had no fond memories of the place but knew his way around, hurrying down rabbit-warren corridors without getting lost. Almost not being let onto the ward until he got massively official, and still stone-faced as he neared Beckett's bed. Then he saw what the inspector was reading and grinned wolfishly. 'Not mine,' denied Beckett, shutting *Penthouse*. 'That lad's, over there;

probably how he got acne. Gets to a point here you'll read anything in this bloody place. Thanks for coming. How's Margaret?'

'Fine.' He supposed she was. Realised then, he'd come out without telling her where he was going or why. Groaned and shook his head. Had to explain the groan to Beckett, and listen to a homily in return—from an expert on breaking up a marriage. Saw how flesh had left Beckett's cheeks, and heard him out, thinking, there but for the grace of God ... Saw navy blue, starched and disapproving, bearing down on them, and got back to why he was there at all. Forebore from saying it was Barrett who should have been told. Easy enough to pass on what promised to be an additional complication tomorrow morning. Left Beckett convinced he was sorely missed in CID.

Quarter to nine and not even on official overtime; Margaret had full right to be annoyed with him. Seeing Gibson entering the Path Lab, not knowing if finding him there was a blessing or a curse; dithering, husband at war with policeman, husband finally losing. Gibson, bent over the centrifugal machine, surprised when the chief inspector walked in.

'Haunting the place?' Gibson enquired.

'Visiting.' Morrissey watched the machine spin. 'Didn't expect you to be here. Not this late.'

'Married to the job.' Cynical; then seeing the chief inspector's face, moderating it. 'On call.' Tapping on the machine casing. 'Joy-rider's Dracula juice, drop of what's left on it. Needs grouping and cross-matching. Death wish, all of 'em, that's my opinion, don't know about yours.'

'Brainless,' said Morrissey trenchantly, not wanting to get involved in sociological discussion. 'Can you spare five minutes?'

'If you can talk while I work.'

'Simms' post-mortem.'

Gibson squinted sideways. 'I thought you'd be back.'

'I thought about asking Warmsby to take a look, but I wanted to talk to you first.'

'Tact from a policeman—what's the world coming to? What do you expect him to find that I didn't?'

'No idea. Something to bring on a heart attack, and not leave obvious signs.'

'You've read too many Agatha Christies.'

'Meaning there's no such drug?'

'I didn't say that; I'm simply exercising my pique. It'd need blood and tissue analysis to find out if he'd been got at.'

'You didn't do any, though?'

'Kit up this sodding hole with a bit of modern equipment, and I'll run a do-it-while-U-wait service. I've asked three times for a chromatography machine. Underfunding, that's the answer I get back. So, I can cope with simple substances, not complicated chemical pick-'n-mix.' Tone thoroughly disgruntled. 'Of course, it might *be* a simple substance. Either way, it'll have to be Forensics' baby now. I took the necessary samples. But get Warmsby to do it all over again, by all means; nothing like going to an expert. Anything else before you go?'

'Took them before the inquest?'

'Took them after you started sniffing round. I know you too well Morrissey. Mention "interested curiosity" and I get worried. Go home and be nice to your wife.'

Good advice, but it could be a bit late.

Driving home, working out how to ease back into good grace, Morrissey could have cut the last six months from his life without any pain; rooted up the lot. Compost material. Hard to believe domestic life had run on such smooth ground before that; bumps and pot-holes everywhere since, and he hit every bloody one. Parking, fiddling with his door key, and putting off the moment. Letting himself in and calling Margaret's name. Ignoring the lack of reply, determined—this time—to make peace. But when he went into the living-room where she sat knitting, and bent over the back of her chair, his kiss-and-make-up attempt just missed. Leaning to pick up her ball of wool, she said calmly: 'Neil rang twice. I told him I'd ask you to ring him back.'

'Sod, Neil!' he said savagely, and went upstairs.

TWENTY-THREE

BREAKFAST WAS a silent affair, everyone keeping their heads down afraid of sparking more dissent. Katie trying twice to get some kind of conversation going, but getting monosyllabic answers and finally deciding the rewards weren't worth the effort that had to be expended. Lapsing into daydreams of her own instead. Morrissey ate fast, knowing he was the block, bolting his food so he could get out of the house and let their tongues free, knowing he'd get indigestion later. Resenting the conversation he would miss. Happy families!

The car being awkward too, coughing before it started, and doing that only after plugs and carburetta had been doused with damp-start. Intent on time saving, he turned north instead of south, calling in at the planning office on his way to work. Pointless doing the same distance twice, but forgetting that not all offices made an early start.

The bright young thing was there, though, on guard again, heavy-eyed today but still obstructive, ready to work out her frustrations because of what a disappointment the broad-shouldered trainee from accounts had turned out to be! Chirruping at him, 'No good thinking about seeing Mr Lowry, if that's what you've come for. He'll be in a meeting at the Town Hall all morning. Sorr-*ee*.' And smirking.

'But he's got a deputy, has to have, so get him, whoever he is,' Morrissey snapped, thorny with frustrations of his own. 'I take it the whole place doesn't close down if Lowry's not here.'

'We-ll, Mr Simms was Deputy CPO, but he died. Very sad. There isn't anybody that's in charge right now; everybody's sort of equal, if you see what I mean. Until they make a new appointment, that is. Don't know when that'll be.'

'Then find somebody; otherwise I walk through that door and sort it out for myself.'

'You can't do that, not without permission.'

'Try me,' invited the chief inspector, aggravated beyond patience. The bright young thing's mouth set in a wavy line. Pity the husband who got her for a wife, Morrissey thought sourly, and started for the inner door.

'I'll see who's here,' she said, backing down in the face of insurrection. ''Course with us being on flex-time there's not many come in before nine.' Busy with the switchboard. Morrissey folded his arms. 'Nobody's picking up, sorr-ee, I think there's only me here yet.'

'I'll go in and look then.' Suiting action to words.

'No!' a high squeak. 'No, I'll go.' Running round the counter, pushing past, through the door marked *Private*.

Coming back with Debra Lewis, who gave him one of her widely frank smiles, and repeated what the bright young thing had already said about Lowry and his whereabouts, but then adding, 'If it's just information you're after and not Mr Lowry himself, I might be able to help.'

'You might at that, if we can go somewhere private to talk,' Morrissey agreed, letting himself be charmed and thinking how much better it would be for someone with her personality to be manning reception. Or perhaps the un-welcoming effect was desirable from Lowry's stance; hard for complainants to get past. What had Rundle called her?—Lucretia! Poison in every pore.

'Mmm, why not. Come in the office and see how the less privileged work.'

'Less privileged than who?' asked the chief inspector as he trod the cool corridor for the second time. 'Or was that just a figure of speech?'

She laughed. 'Fifty-fifty, I suppose, but it's an open-plan office and sometimes a bit of personal space would be nice. In here.' Going through first and holding the door.

A brightly massive room, with windows on two sides, an open working area that looked less so because planning chests and head-height drawing boards cluttered up the space left empty by other, more prosaic paraphernalia of a busy office.

'So which is your bit of shared space then?'

'I'm over there,' waving a hand, its direction general rather than specific, but a brown shoulder-bag part open on one desk said that was where she meant. 'What exactly is it you want to know from me? Nothing that's going to get me the sack, I hope.'

'Nothing secret. I believe I've been told you've got Malminster divided off, one section for each planning officer. Would that be right?'

'It certainly would. Makes life easier all round.'

'Why would that be?'

'No trodden toes. This way every planning officer looks after his own section. It'd be chaos otherwise.'

'You must have a town map then, marked off, showing which section's which.'

'Over there, on the wall.' Showing him, one finger tracing it out. 'Mr Lowry deals with this circular bit in the middle, and the other sections radiate off.'

'Slices of cake.'

'Looks a bit like that, doesn't it? That's mine, on the south side. The grot spot.' Her finger rested roughly on police headquarters, but he knew that wasn't what she meant. That section took in other things too, like the red-light area, tucked away in the top corner where it joined the central section.

'Put names on the other slices for me.'

Listening, watching her finger move from segment to segment, missing one out. Putting his own finger on that.

'You missed this.'

'Ah, not really. Nobody has that. It *was* Richard Simms' section, but, er, well things are a bit in abeyance for a while. Unless something urgent comes up. I couldn't believe what happened to him, you know? I mean, one day he's here, and the next ... Pffft. A heart attack. It's ridiculous.'

'Stress? Must have been overworked certainly. He was on his way home from here when he died; that's a long working day. Too long.'

'I don't think he'd ever worked that late before, must have been sorting something out. Can't have helped him, I suppose, getting interrupted, probably made him later still.'

'You were here?' Surprised, antennae waving.

'No! I'm not that dedicated. I'd left my car around the back, I do that a lot when I'm going to see a film or something, saves looking for parking spots in town and, anyway, it's safer.'

'What makes you think Simms had an interruption then?'

'We-ll, I'm only guessing because I saw his car here, on the other side of the car-park; but he could have gone into town somewhere and just left it there like I did.'

'Whose car—Lowry's?'

'No. The Chairman of the Planning Committee.'

'Thewlis?'

'That's right.'

'But the night security man said there'd only been Simms in the building. Could somebody else have got up to the fifth floor without being seen by him?'

She grinned. 'Have you met the night security man?'

'No.' *Not yet.*

'We call him Coffee Joe, because he lives on the instant stuff. He's a nice little man but scared of the dark.'

Morrissey said slowly, 'So if he did hear anything...'

'...he'd lock his office door and sit tight,' she finished for him. 'Anything else I can help you with?'

'I don't think so, but you have been helpful. Thank you, Miss Lewis.' Only half noticing the smile this time, because his thoughts were with other things, like the sprawling shape of the Industrial Estate lying almost central within Simms' section of the town map. Preoccupied, he didn't even give the bright young thing a glance as he went out.

Driving fast as a grey morning's traffic would allow, taking the road Simms must have taken until the bridge roundabout, then taking the third exit, nipping through back streets to the police building, mind busy.

Barrett sat behind a desk full of paper, sorting out the pieces, juggling in his mind with the bit of information from Beckett that he'd gathered in last night when Morrissey finally returned his calls, playing around with it much as the chief inspector had played with Badger's new statement, up a ladder this time, down a snake hole the next; looked up and started to say something.

Morrissey hadn't time. Dumping his briefcase just inside the door, raincoat on top, he stabbed a sharp finger heavenward and said: 'Later,' taking the next flight of stairs three at a time not two, cursing when Osgodby wasn't in his office. A lavatory flushed across the corridor and he waited.

Patience was a virtue: Rubbish! Patience wasted time.

The door of the Ladies opened and let out a typist, straightening her skirt, pinking a little when she saw Morrissey, because everybody has their own fantasy and he was hers. The chief inspector oblivious, not even smiling, but admiring all the same, as she long-legged it back to her office.

Another flush and another wait.

Osgodby came out of the Gents, rubbing his hands together, less than thrilled to find Morrissey waiting.

'Keep it short and sweet, John; there's a ten o'clock meeting. Current case is it? New developments? Thought it would break pretty fast, trusted your judgement, you see. Better tell me then; but brief, make it brief.' Stamping into his office and collecting papers, re-filling his pen, busy all the time, his way of cutting things short.

Morrissey, unintimidated, wanting priority, decided the meeting whatever it was had to be less urgent than this. Knowing from long experience how to convince Osgodby of that in few words, and using them, formal as an executioner. 'I have firm reason to suspect that Malcolm Lowry, Chief Planning Officer, and Jack Thewlis, Chairman of the Planning Committee, together with other—as yet unknown—associates, may be implicated in public authority corruption, and I believe the activities involved to be directly linked to Detective Barrett's current investigation, and to the deaths associated with the fire-bombing of a terrace house some weeks ago. I also have grounds to suspect that the death of a planning officer ten days ago is closely related.' Watching the chief superintendent's movements slow and stop.

His head down, fingertips resting on the desk, Osgodby worked out the ramifications of what Morrissey had said, sinking down into his desk chair, cracking his fingers in worry, whistling air again, snapping back when he answered because sometimes Morrissey and his hunches were a curse.

'You'd better be right on this, you know. Don't come with accusations that won't stick. What's been done about it so

far, and why in thunder haven't I been briefed until now?'
Exchanging angst for thunder. 'Dammit, Chief Inspector, I
resent being dropped on out of the blue, especially with
things like this. Set it out. Tell me what you've got.'

Morrissey set it out with care, piece by piece, none of
them fitting—quite—but close enough to show a pattern.
Badger's new statement, Beckett's bit of information,
Simms' changed behaviour just prior to his death. His
briefcase. The warning to his widow not to talk to Morrissey. Charlie Rundle and Debra Lewis. Thewlis's car where
it shouldn't have been. And Guffey made permanently
quiet.

Osgodby heard him out. A hornet's nest.

'Better tell me what you're planning to do, then,' he said,
feeling shock waves, and wondering where they would stop.

TWENTY-FOUR

YEARS OF habit were hard to break. Having escaped the chore for two mornings, Monica Thewlis had got up and cooked her husband's breakfast. Why she didn't know, but it was waiting for him when he came downstairs—two eggs fried until the whites curled up brown at the edges, the yolks still puddly soft as he liked them, a piece of fried bread, and a slice of ham, mild cured and for free from Millam's butcher shop, in payment of past favours. Was there anyone in Malminster who *didn't* owe Jack? She avoided looking at him as she set the plate down, didn't join him at the table, went instead to the sink and began the daily ritual of cleaning. Finished that and filled the washing-up bowl with suds waiting for his greasy plate. Washed her own cup and saucer, scrubbed and rinsed the bread board listening all the while for the scrape of knife and fork to end, and when it did fetching his plate back to the sink, dunking it in the soapy water, still not having looked at him but knowing his eyes were watching her.

No. Not this morning, not ever, never again.

Chair legs scraped. Her skin crawled as he came behind her, saying, 'Better eh, bugs gone,' his body rubbing across her buttocks, hardening, hands splayed on her wide hips. 'A piggy-back then.'

'No!' Twisting sideways sharply.

'NO NOES TO ME.' A thump in the ribs, showing who was master, his hands lifting her dress: her hands still in the water, feeling the sharp carver she'd sliced ham with and tak-

ing its handle and turning, *pushing* him away, lifting the
knife. His eyes focussing on it, shocked.

Monica's voice beating its way out of her. *'I'm not an
animal!* Leave me alone!'

Thewlis, near purple as he spluttered, 'You'll pay for that,
oh yes, you'll pay all right, woman. When I say *fuck*, you'll
fuck. Put that bloody knife down.'

'No!' The blade steady, and her wondering in amaze-
ment why she wasn't shaking; she *always* shook when Jack
was angry.

BARRETT AND Morrissey were in close conference. Barrett
with a sinking feeling that he was swimming out of his
depth, telling himself he'd always known the whole thing
would slip out of his hands and back into the chief inspector's. Face glummer by the second. Corruption! Local big-
wigs tangled up with Guffey and the Asians and God knew
what else. Delicate toes to be trampled on, heads to roll if
Morrissey had got it wrong, and his probably the first to go.

And if a whisper got out to the Press there'd be hell to
pay. Shifting in his chair. His mother hadn't wanted him to
be a policeman; maybe he should have listened. Wishing
vaguely that he had. Staring into silence as Morrissey looked
expectant, waiting for input. Input! His brain coming up
finally with a neat sidestep.

'What would you like me to do then, sir?' Distracted by
the new WPC coming in with a little pile of papers for him.
Looking at her appreciatively, not bad, nice name, too,
Rosie Quinn, might be possibilities there, his mind straying
down other warmer and gentler paths, but brought back to
Morrissey with a thump, neat sidestep negated.

'What I'd like, *if* there's anything in your head but boobs
and legs, is ideas. From you!'

'Then, with respect, sir, I think we should approach it from two directions. Me chasing the Guffey–Asian angle, and you coming round the other side from the Simms death–corruption route. More chance of getting somebody rattled that way, I'd think; squeeze 'em in the middle and see who pops.' Responding out of panic more than thought, but from Morrissey's look of satisfaction, getting it right, and having got it right pursuing it just that little further. 'I was thinking about this intimidation business, especially the Asians that got scared off. Might be interesting to find out who bought up the houses; it could tie in with what you're after.'

'It could indeed. I'm impressed, Neil. How are you getting on with Woods?'

Like climbing uphill backwards, not saying that to Morrissey though, sticking with diplomacy instead, not wanting the chief to know he was having trouble exerting authority.

'He seems to know what he's about.'

'I'll need to borrow him back for a day. Manage all right without him, can you?'

Like losing a boil on his bum! Swallowing a grin of pleasure. 'Can't see why not, I'd rather sort out the intimidation business myself anyway. Don't want clumsy new feet stirring up dust.' Then in a surge of curiosity, asking, 'What is it he'll be doing exactly?'

Morrissey, knowing exactly where Barrett and Woods stood in relation to each other, let himself come visibly down on the sergeant's side, sharing a grin of conspiracy. 'Planning Committee minutes. I reckon going back two or three years should quieten him down considerably.'

'Might even take him more than one day?'

'As long as it takes,' Morrissey said. 'As long as it takes, Neil. Likes desk-work, does he?'

'Hates it. He'll be bored shitless.' And both of them, in tune for once, laughing like big kids.

IT WAS FUNNY how fast the weather had changed, warm and sunny a week ago, and now typical grey November weather. A drizzle so fine it looked like mist. The yellowed leaves on the laburnum were hanging like limp fragments of summer. Monica Thewlis could see them through the bedroom window, made nearly colourless by the moisture heavy air.

Her wedding day had been in November.

She watched grey water beads form and run, leaving wet paths on the outside of the glass. Behind her on the bed her suitcase was packed and she had a cup of tea in her hand with two chocolate biscuits in the saucer; comfort food again—no other comfort that Monica had ever been aware of, not since she changed her name from Crowther. When *he* was gone out of her life she'd change it back, take her father's name again, make up for not having taken his advice.

The thought made her feel happy. She'd change other things too—her hair for one, touching it with her hand. It'd be grey now, if it wasn't for Jack insisting it stayed its too youthful blonde. From time to time she had the brassy tints toned down, hoping he wouldn't notice, but he always did. She wished she could be there, invisible, when he came home and found the house empty, the kettle cold, and no hot food in the oven. Oh, yes! Nibbling on a biscuit and watching through the window for her daughter's car—she would dearly love to see his face.

A car came swooping round the high-hedged bend, big and blue, definitely not Angie's, although it had stopped at the bottom of the drive. She wouldn't open the door to him, whoever he was, oh no. Watching the tall man come up the front steps. One of Jack's friends. Remembering her defiant stand that morning and feeling a frisson of fear because Jack had all kinds of friends, and some of them were less than pleasant. No—hearing the bell play that stupid tune and feeling glad she would never hear it again—she wouldn't open the door, she'd drink her tea instead and stay out of sight, and in the end he'd go away. See if he didn't.

THE BRIGHT young thing, still smarting because Debra Lewis wouldn't tell her what Morrissey had wanted, waited until nine-thirty and then rang Lowry just before the planning meeting got under way. 'I don't know what the chief inspector wanted,' she said in her best loyal-servant voice, 'but he was getting really nasty, so I let him talk to Debra. Why Debra? Because there wasn't anyone else here but me.' Smiling when he made exactly the request she expected. 'Yes, of course, Mr Lowry, I'll put you through to Debra right away.' And in making the connection, left her own line open and listened avidly to what was said, disappointed when Lowry hung up because it hadn't been very interesting after all.

TWENTY-FIVE

ROOK'S LANE was one of those indeterminate places that can't quite decide whether to be a through road or an interesting digression. It was narrow enough to need passing places every so far, bulging out into the hedgerow in sudden swellings as it ran between high hedges of hawthorn that hid the pastureland behind. Funny, how five minutes out of town and you were back to fields again. Driving along, wondering how long it would take for vegetation to get back to where it was before cities were built if one day disaster struck and wiped out all the builders. The sort of science fiction scenario Mike would come up with. Something in common with his son.

The houses, when he came to them, were out of place on the lane, looking a bit as if some giant's hand had plucked them from an urban setting and planted them where domestic dwellings weren't supposed to grow. Nothing, behind or in front but agricultural land. Three houses, four-bedroomed, stone-built and double-fronted with nice neat lawns, nothing much changed since the Edwardian builders set them there, expecting the town to expand in a direction it hadn't as yet chosen to go. Rather dreary-looking, really, Morrissey decided, as if the architect had expanded a doll's house design and then given it over-large windows and a door not quite to scale. There were two semi-circular steps to the front door of Thewlis's house and when he went up them and rang the bell the chimes played the first few bars of 'The Red Flag.' He guessed, rightly, that would be

Thewlis's touch, a hint of Labour solidarity in a more Conservative setting.

No one came to answer the door, but he had a strong sense that the house was not empty; an uneasiness that said he was being observed. He looked up at the bay windows of the two front bedrooms, but both were heavily netted and he couldn't see beyond the terylene lace. The ground-floor windows were netted too, but on these the curtains rose in the centre and left a gap that a Nosey Parker could peer through if he wished. Morrissey wished, and bent himself almost double to suit the wish to the deed. The room he saw was high-ceilinged and over-furnished, with a tasselled three-piece suite in maroon and good moquette. Dust would never be allowed to settle in a room like that. He did a circuit of the house and came back to the front unrewarded, the impression of a doll's house reinforced, houses so completely tidy worried him. Glancing back as he retreated carwards, sure he was watched. Not by Thewlis, though; Thewlis was too brash to hide away, and the old green Fiesta wasn't flash enough for him to drive, but his wife was a different matter. Remembering what Claire Simms had said about bruises. Was that why she didn't come to the door, afraid he'd see what went on?

She wouldn't be the first woman to hide herself away because of it. Sighing. Not his business. Not yet.

Turning his car, going back the way he'd come, braking into a passing place to let a black Citroën through, the woman driver hunched forward, going too fast and not even noticing he was there.

LOWRY WAS sweating again, perspiration damp on his forehead. What did Morrissey want to look at the planning map for? No reason for it, none at all, not unless he suspected something; suspected what, for God's sake? That damn briefcase, the nub of it all. Hurrying down the off-shoot of corridor, seeing Thewlis about to disappear inside number two committee room. 'Jack! A minute, before we go in.' Putting on a bit more speed.

Thewlis turned back, irritated.

'Malcolm. Can't it wait? I've another damn meeting at eleven. Can't be that important, can it?'

'Morrissey's been in again, early on, looking at the planning map. Obviously thinks he's on to something. I'm out of this land deal, Jack. It isn't worth it.'

'Worth it?' Roaring, then remembering the open door and banging it shut. 'Don't talk about bloody worth it! You're in until t'rest of us drop out. Hear me?' Shoving his face up to Lowry's, intimidating from a lesser height. 'And wipe your bloody face. You're sweating like a hog.' Barging through the committee room door, taking his place at the top of the long table, and leaving Lowry to follow, handkerchief mopping.

Morrissey!

Half-way through the meeting Thewlis heard the name again, spoken carefully into his ear by a clerk. 'Tell him he'll have to wait,' Thewlis said dismissively, and turned back to the table. Five minutes later the clerk was back, quiet words not reaching past Thewlis's ear but Lowry looking jumpy all the same.

'I'm sorry, sir, Chief Inspector Morrissey says he'll have to ask you to come out now. It's important.'

'Tell him five minutes, then,' turning back to the table for the second time, his mind fixing on Lilian Carver. No, he'd tidied up nicely there; it wouldn't be that. Make him wait a little bit longer then, best not to seem too obliging. Not knowing that the chief inspector, who hated waiting, was getting sharper by the minute. By the time Thewlis came into the ante-room Morrissey's mind was honed nicely, and the

Planning Committee Chairman's aggressive approach didn't help. No preamble, no polite skirting; Thewlis letting Morrissey know his place.

'Well, then, get on with it. What's to say that's that important I've to be fetched out of committee? And it had better be bloody good, I'm a busy man.'

'As was Richard Simms. I'd like to know just what business you had with him in his office the night he died.'

Thewlis hadn't expected that. It showed in his eyes. Morrissey saw the surprise and was gratified, recognising the answer he got for what it was, flannel laid over confusion.

'I don't remember if I was in the planning offices that day. I'd have to check the diary. Nasty business, of course it was, not anticipated though, not by anyone. Like I told his widow, anything we can do to help, she'd only got to say. Is that all you wanted then?'

Nothing in Morrissey's eyes but grey slate. 'Your car was seen standing in planning department's car-park at ten-thirty the night Simms died, and I have reason to believe you were in his office at that time. I should like to know what business you had there.'

'And I should like to know what business you have to come here asking me damn silly questions! I'll have something to say about this, I won't be harassed. Simms had a heart attack. Whether I saw him that night or not makes no difference, and it's none of your blasted business.' Waving an arm, red in the face. 'That's the end of it, Chief Inspector. I've got more important things to see to.'

'I won't keep you much longer,' Morrissey said stonily, 'but these questions have to be asked when there are grounds to doubt a cause of death.' Expecting that to stop Thewlis in his tracks, and pleased when it did. 'As possibly the last person to see Mr Simms alive you were witness to his state of mind.'

Thewlis, facing him again, showed a flicker in the near-black eyes at the let-out clause. 'You're suggesting it was suicide?' Morrissey stood solid, saying nothing, waiting for the other man to work out which move to make to be least damning. 'A bit depressed, yes,' Thewlis said finally. 'Now you've said it, yes, he was. Shouldn't have been there, a lot too late to be working. Finished with me now?'

'Almost. I'd still like to know why you were there.'

'I saw his bloody light was on, driving home. Night-watchman's useless.'

'You went up to see why he was there?'

'I went up to see who was there.'

'What was he working on?'

'No idea. I told him to pack up and get on home.'

'And left at what time?'

'Must have been quarter to eleven. Where's this all leading to?'

'Where was his briefcase, on the desk or by his chair?'

'Did he have a briefcase? If he did I didn't see it. Does it matter?' Shifting. 'I've got a committee waiting, cut it short, Chief Inspector.'

'The briefcase matters,' Morrissey said, 'because he always had it with him. Simms and his briefcase were an inseparable couple. So he should have had it with him in his office that night, and it should have been in his car when he went home, but it wasn't, and I'd be more than interested to know what he'd been working on so late, Mr Thewlis, because it made his briefcase worth stealing.'

'Rubbish! He worked for the Council, not bloody M15.'

'His death still leaves a lot of questions to answer.'

'What questions? Suicide, you said it yourself.'

'Did I now?' asked Morrissey gently. 'I don't remember saying that. I said: *"Grounds to doubt a cause of death."* You were the one who said suicide, but I don't believe that,

Mr Thewlis, not for a minute, and I don't think you do either.' Watching Thewlis struggle with his anger, wondering if this was the face his wife saw, and adding the final straw. 'I should get back to the meeting now if I were you. Wouldn't do to let anything slip past when you weren't looking.'

Walking away, hearing the chairman's voice behind him bellicose with rage: 'I'll have your bloody balls for this, Morrissey. Your bloody BALLS!' and feeling satisfied to have done what he had set out to do—to rattle the man enough to make him careless.

'IS THIS IT, Mum, one worn out suitcase for thirty lousy years.' Disgust in her voice, but not meant for her mother whose condition wasn't much better than that of the suitcase. What Angeline felt for her was a depth of aching pity, deeper than ever now that new life had stirred in her own body. She slammed the boot on the old brown leather and wrapped her arms round her mother, hugging fiercely, sharing pain, disgust reserved for a man she would willingly consign to hot flames in Hell. Ashamed to call him father. Bastard of bastards! A sickeningly familiar frisson of fright in thinking about him. Hustling her mother into the black Citroen, eager to get away.

Monica asking: 'Where are we going, somewhere Jack won't look?' Thinking how he'd be in a rage, because possessions were everything to him. Panicking as the tall hedgerows went by. 'Angie, take me back. I can't leave him. I can't. He'll kill me for it!' Not a bit reassured by Angeline's hand squeezing her own.

TWENTY-SIX

MORRISSEY WENT home for lunch, wanting to find Margaret there alone, hoping that with just the two of them she might respond to yet another peace attempt, rehearsing it in his mind and knowing he was clumsy with such things. Stopping to buy flowers and then wondering if that was a good thing to do, so desperate was he now to break out of the noncommunicative cycle they were in. Wanting more than anything else he could imagine to be greeted with that affectionate brand of domestic solicitude he missed; building a picture of it as he drove. Telling himself this wasn't the first bad patch in their marriage, but knowing it was lasting longer than any other had done. And then letting himself into the house and finding it empty.

He made a pot of tea, and a sandwich with a wedge of cheese, lonely at the table. Ate a piece of apple pie, and went away uncomforted, flowers in the sink the only evidence he'd been there at all. Detoured on his way back, driving along the access road past the ginnel and down between the terraced rows, counting empty homes, skirting a removal van busily emptying another, parking finally near the row of garages and getting out of the car to scowl at the wasteland and wonder what its attraction would be for a speculator. He remembered the cramped and ugly buildings, streets of them, that had once been there, as he trod a thready path through scrubby rubble and patchy weeds and got his trouser bottoms soaked.

Traffic flowed endlessly along the motorway, car after car, doubling and trebling at peak times. He'd driven down it

himself often enough, without noticing the wide triangle of
land except as a patch of green from the corner of his eye,
but standing on it now, near its centre, watching the flow of
vehicles, counting heads, gave him new ideas on its potential worth, and he played around with them in his mind
while the drizzle turned into a hard, fine rain. The whole
parcel of land right up to the access road—most of Council
land—to be undersold at some future date, its sale steered
round the right committees by someone who knew the short
cuts, bought up cheap at the ratepayers' expense and sold on
at astronomical profit to a developer keen on building a
newer and bigger Meadowhall; a gleaming shopping and
entertainment complex combined, creaming custom for
miles around. He could see it taking shape in his mind,
glass-domed avenues and fast-food plazas. Enough money
to be made there for all kinds of risks to be taken.

Murder had been done for a lot less.

Back at police headquarters, his clothes steaming gently
in the office heat, he sent Smythe out asking questions; a
policeman to chase up policemen, and some working on
nights, having to be got out of bed. Morrissey's instructions were simple. No police officer involved in the recov-
ery of Simms' car must be missed, and there was only one
question to be asked: Had any of them seen the missing
briefcase.

RICHARDSON'S SCALE of values placed money above all else.
It was the only source of power he knew, and he believed
that kind of power to be absolute. Almost the only sin he
recognised was the wasting of it, and the pain of how much
had been lost in Malminster through mistakes and incom-
petence was near physical.

Since just before midday his telephone had been like a
hotline with a state of war imminent. First Lowry, panick-

ing at Morrissey's nosing around Planning. Then Thewlis ranting about being dragged out of a bloody committee meeting; rampant egomania and a damn sight worse than panic. And now two from his snout.

He liked that word snout; it amused him to reverse the usual system of things. Money bought anything, and people easiest of all. It was just a matter of finding the right price; the right sequence of buttons to press. It would be interesting at some future time to find Morrissey's buttons, but right now the important thing was to throw him off scent. Nothing unlawful in buying up houses, or in altruistically providing alternative homes, and nothing illegal either in buying land from the Council—not when the sales were sanctioned by all the right committees. No, whatever Morrissey might suspect, he himself was in the clear, so let the chief inspector prove otherwise.

Which was precisely what Morrissey planned, he and Barrett together, conspirators for once, mulling over how to cause maximum worry with minimum effort.

'He hasn't tried any cover-up,' said Barrett, 'which shows he's pretty sure of himself, not surprising, I suppose, given who he is.'

Osgodby had said much the same thing, but with a lot more vehemence; enough of it for Morrissey to remember the words, even if not to be worried by them. The chief superintendent had been worried, though; all the signs were there, whistling air, frantic tattoo, voice like a hanging judge, mournful in its task. 'You'd better be damn certain of your facts, John. He's not a man to get on the wrong side of, not a local little-big-man like Thewlis. Sam Richardson pulls weight right across Yorkshire; he's put his mark on every big town in the county. So I'm warning you, if you're not a hundred per cent sure, don't cross him. There's more than one career on the line and he's got powerful friends.'

Who wouldn't want to know him if the chips were down.

Morrissey hadn't said that because he didn't need to. Osgodby knew as well as he how powerful friends became fast-fading shadowmen in the light of adverse publicity. If Richardson was brought down there'd be a hell of a lot of red faces, and anybody riding his coat-tails would let go in a hurry.

'You'd have thought he'd try to cover his tracks a bit, though,' said Barrett, still pursuing the same thought. 'Make more sense to buy up the Asians' houses with a shell company instead of doing it out in the open like that, as if he didn't expect anybody to notice.'

'He's a gambler, and gamblers always take one risk too many,' said the chief inspector, thinking that in the end it would probably be Bill Newton and the Fraud Squad who delivered the coup de grâce. That didn't matter much, not when the tally so far was nine dead. Sitting across from Barrett, planning the next day's strategy, he wondered just how many Malminster pockets had been filled.

DETECTIVE CONSTABLE Woods was less than happy; the chair he'd been allotted was ancient, made from hard moulded plastic with a shape that bore no relationship at all to the human body, but which threatened to add callouses to that part of himself he treasured above all other. He had a feeling he was less than welcome in the chief executive's department, and that the police request to examine Council minutes was seen as tantamount to an accusation of treason. He also suspected, wrongly, that Barrett had exercised more than a little say in his present discomfort, and by three-thirty that afternoon he had decided it wouldn't hurt to be a little more circumspect with the jumped-up prick.

Turned out of the Town Hall just before five, and sent on his way by an overweight sparrow with grey roots, he had nothing to report back with but a wasted day and a sore bum. And by then Smythe was back too, with a pile of 'noes' and one very iffy 'maybe,' that he didn't even bother to mention, because it was so obviously a mistake.

THEWLIS WENT through the house—stormed through it—looking for Monica, the pricks and problems collected during the day added to anger festering since that morning's confrontation. To be shown a knife by her, fat lumpish hen. No one did that to Jack Thewlis; no one, not a man born yet that'd face him down. Thinking how he'd make her rue it, the pleasure of fist sinking into fat flesh. My God! but she'd beg before he'd done with her this time. Banging out of the house to look in the garage and seeing the elderly car still there. Where the hell was she then? Gone crying to Angeline? Incensed by that, going back in and finding the telephone number, hearing Angeline's voice and demanding harshly: 'Put your mother on!'

'She isn't here.'

'Then where the hell is she?' Shouting down the line, blood boiling up inside him. 'Don't bloody lie to me, girl; there's nowhere else for her. Nowhere. Now you hear me. Fetch her, or I'll come round and give you a bit of what she's due to.'

Gordon's voice, angry as his own, inflaming him even more. 'Through me first then, Jack, and don't threaten Angie. She's my wife and I'll not have it.'

'Oh I'll go through you all right, if that's how you want it. What's bloody matter then, going soft? Can't handle your woman? Put Monica on and keep your sodding nose out.'

'She's not here'

'Bloody liar!'

Gordon's slammed receiver explosive in his ear, Thewlis staring at his own instrument in disbelief, lurching to get his bottle of Johnny Walker. By *fuck* he'd make her pay for that, cradling the bottle, tossing down a full half glass and pouring in the same amount again, drinking that more slowly sitting in front of the cold hearth and planning how he'd do it.

MORRISSEY LET himself in for the second time that day, seeing the bronze chrysanthemums he had left in the kitchen sink bright in a white china vase on the hall table. Some strange, fragmented music came from upstairs, signalling his son's presence; it followed him into the kitchen where Margaret was chopping cabbage. Her hand paused its downward movement briefly. 'The flowers were nice. Did you find something to eat?' Chopping again before he had time to reply. He wanted to wrap his arms around her and say he loved her, wanted to say that everything would be all right if she loved him; but he couldn't make himself do that, and compromised by leaning towards her, hopefully.

Briefly, but he thought with affection, she met his lips with hers. A small step forward in the cold war.

TWENTY-SEVEN

MORRISSEY'S VISIT wasn't exactly unexpected, and Richardson wasn't particularly worried when it came. Expensively tanned, dapper in a chalk stripe suit, he didn't bother to get up from behind his desk but simply showed his teeth in what could have been either smile or grimace. Either way, thought the chief inspector, the teeth would have looked good on a shark, and there was something about the pale gooseberry eyes that gave visual confirmation to Morrissey's instincts. When Richardson spoke it was an expressionless lip-service to formality. 'Do sit down, Chief Inspector. Can I have my secretary get you a cup of coffee, or would you care for something stronger? I can offer a particularly fine malt.'

'I'm sure you can, sir, but no thank you. I don't want to take up too much of your time.'

'I couldn't allow you to; I'm a busy man. What exactly is it you want?'

'I'm making inquiries into the death of a man called Richard Simms. I believe you knew him. Perhaps you'd like to tell me how well.'

'I don't remember that I knew him at all. Simms... No, I—ah, the young planning officer. Yes, I read about it in the paper. Sad, very sad, and you're quite right, Chief Inspector, I met him several times. Simply in the course of business; not socially.'

'What business, Mr Richardson?'

'Don't fence, Chief Inspector. You know what business. Property and land development. Which by its very nature means planning applications are submitted almost continuously. Simms dealt with some of them, efficiently as I remember.'

'And he was suitably rewarded?'

'I presume his salary was adequate.'

'I was thinking of extra gratuities—tangible thanks for speeding things up perhaps. No doubt it helps when applications move along quickly?'

'Oiling the wheels? Such things aren't legal, Chief Inspector, and I wouldn't be foolish enough to involve myself. Occasionally an overzealous employee gets carried away; but if I find out, knuckles are rapped. Is that what you want to know?'

'That's pretty much what I expected you to tell me. I believe you've been buying up property behind the Industrial Estate, terrace houses that have come empty. Can you tell me what plans you have for them?'

'No, I can't. Refurbishment possibly; it hasn't been decided. It's hardly a prime site for new development, not with noise from the Industrial Estate.'

'Not a good investment, then?'

'It wouldn't seem so on the surface, but things change.' Shifting a little, but only to ease his position. 'What does that have to do with Simms?'

'The houses stand in what was Simms' section of town, and something in that section was causing him worry. He'd been working on it until almost midnight the day he died.'

'I wish I could help you, Chief Inspector, but I can't. I haven't authorised submission of any planning applications for those properties, and I doubt he even knew about them.' Spreading his palms, the shark's teeth coming into play again, he remarked: 'Frankly, I don't see where your interest lies.'

'I find unexplained deaths are always interesting, especially when they coincide with other things.' Seeing he'd pricked Richardson's curiosity with that, he got abruptly to his feet. 'Thank you for your time.'

'No problem. Anytime, don't hesitate. Next time try the malt. What did Simms' death coincide with? Just from curiosity.'

'Other police interests. But I'm sure you'll find out what they were in good time.' Showing his own teeth then, and leaving Richardson to think on it. Rendezvousing with Barrett round the corner out of sight, not getting out of his car but giving the detective sergeant a thumbs-up and watching Barrett's car move away from the kerb, another visitor for Richardson, and this time not expected.

When his secretary told him the police were there again, Richardson irritably thought it was Morrissey back and said brusquely, 'Send him in, then,' and surprised when Barrett came through the door. 'You're too late,' he said, 'the chief inspector's already left.'

'Really, sir?' said Barrett. 'You're having a busy morning then. I'm investigating the death of Gerald Lee Harpin, commonly known as Guffey. The chief inspector is working on a quite different case, although funnily enough he does expect the two to converge at some point.' Picking up an onyx cigarette box and putting it down again. 'Nice that, very nice.' Richardson lifted the lid. 'No, thank you, sir, I don't smoke. Other bad habits, though. Haven't we all? But not that. To get back to Guffey, sir. He seems to have been involved in harassing residents of a group of terrace properties behind the Industrial Estate. I hear you too have a particular interest in those properties, sir, and I have good reason to believe Guffey's death is linked to his activities there. Did you know him, sir, before his death?' Wandering to the side wall and looking at a Lowry, squinting at its matchstick men. 'Original is it, sir, that's nice too, fits in well, best I can do is a calendar. Did you say you knew Guffey?'

'No, I did not, and yes it's an original. I've had it a long time. How did this—Guffey—die?' Watching the detective sergeant's movements and weighing them with care.

'Run down by a truck, it seems. Nasty. But we've got the vehicle, and it won't be too long before we have the driver. What I'd like to ask you, sir, is, Are those old houses worth more than they seem, because somebody paid Guffey to get the tenants out?'

'They're worth a pittance, Detective Sergeant. Someone's been spinning you a yarn.'

'Oh, I don't think so, sir. We have a witness to the payment, and it does look as if Guffey might have been killed to shut him up.' Stroking a finger on rich red-brown wood. 'Genuine mahogany is it, sir? Nice, but then...' opening his arms encompassing the room, '...it's all nice, isn't it? Can you tell me, sir, what do you intend to do with the terrace properties? Shall you put them on the market again, or are there other plans for them? It's something I have to ask. But I know a man as keenly civic-minded as yourself will want to see an end to racial harassment.'

'That's the crux of it, then, racial harassment?' Richardson's eyes half closed, thinking.

'I don't know, sir. Perhaps you can tell me what else it could be. If it isn't people, it has to be property, but you'd know more about that than me, wouldn't you, sir? If you see what I mean. Property being your speciality.' Seeing Richardson's lips thin out. 'I'm living in one of your conversions myself, sir, and very nice it is too. The old warehouse on the wharf; small flat but a great view. Don't know about doing up the terraces, though. What do you think

about it, sir, would that type of property be worth paying
out harassment money for?'

'How the hell would I know?' Richardson exploded.
'That's enough, Detective Sergeant. If you want any more
information on those properties, see my legal advisors. I've
given more than enough of this morning's time to the police. If you wouldn't mind cutting it short, I've an appointment to keep.'

'That's all right, sir,' said Barrett cheerfully. 'I'll come
back another time, when you're not so busy and you've had
time to think.' Picking up a table lighter and looking at the
hallmark. 'Nice patina silver gets when it's handled a lot,
but then you'd know more about that than me too, sir.'
Putting it down and heading for the door, turning at the last
second. 'Tomorrow morning then, sir, if you can spare the
time.' Rapping gentle knuckles on the door. 'That's solid,
too. I appreciate good wood. Don't get much of it in flat-
packs, but then you get what you can afford, don't you, sir?
About ten, shall we say?'

'I can spare ten minutes at eleven.'

'Should be long enough, sir,' agreed Barrett and went out,
closing the door with the respect such wood deserved, a grin
spreading over his face in the empty lift on his way to the
ground floor. Richardson didn't know if he was coming or
going after all that. He told the same thing to Morrissey
when he got back to the office. 'Maybe I'll take up a new
interest, sir,' he said. 'Join amateur dramatics. I think I'd
be quite good at it.'

'You've been careful, though, not made any open sug-
gestions, nothing that could be seen as entrapment.'

'Not a thing,' denied Barrett, pleased with himself. 'All I
did was admire his pretty things; anything else is all in his
own little mind. Reckon he'll offer something good, then?

I could fancy a Porsche; make a change from keeping up payments on the Escort.'

'Don't even think about it.'

'Oh, I can think; sir, never yet got my hand slapped for thinking,' he said, his eyes on Rosie Quinn coming in with more reports; she, not looking at him, faintly pink.

'Got over WPC Yarby, then?' Morrissey asked behind her retreating back. 'Fickle?'

'I'd call it knowing when to give up myself,' said Barrett, who still yearned but no longer let it show.

TWENTY-EIGHT

WHILE BARRETT had been having his tête-à-tête with Richardson, Morrissey—still looking for the briefcase—had been talking to Inspector 'Froggy' Willis, about the chances of it being in the weir. Willis wasn't all that encouraging. 'Can't imagine how we'd miss it,' he said. 'The basin isn't that big. 'Course, if it bounced out when the doors sprang and landed in the canal proper, we'd not have found it. Might have shifted lower down by now too. All depends if it floated a bit. Important enough to go back in for, is it?'

'I shan't know that unless I have it,' Morrissey said. 'Not for certain, but I'm guessing yes.'

'I thought it was natural causes.'

'Things change. It's turned iffy.'

'But you wouldn't want to push a second search because you think upstairs won't wear it, but if we happened to be doing any practise work... Sly, Morrissey, sly.'

'I'd call it sensible politics,' the chief inspector said mildly. 'Where do you reckon a briefcase would have got by now, supposing it had gone in the canal?'

'By the old warehouses probably, stuck in a pram or a supermarket trolley. I'll let the lads have a look for it, Morrissey, but I don't like risking 'em tangling up in junk without good reason. It isn't worth it. What's the percentage of it not being a natural?'

'High.' Resting his hopes on Forensics sending a report to confirm that, if they didn't... well, leave that till it happened.

Willis said, 'Sometime this afternoon, then, unless there's a call out. Stay dry.'

Rain-drops grey and heavy as mercury fell and burst outside the window. Not this weather, Morrissey thought as he hung up. Not without a wetsuit!

MONICA THEWLIS vacillated between relief and fear, jumping at every knock on the door, feeling her stomach churn when the telephone rang. It didn't matter how many times Angeline and Gordon tried to tell her she was safe; she still couldn't persuade herself it was so. Jack didn't let go easily, and he never forgave.

'You're not going to be on your own, Mum,' Angeline coaxed, 'not for a minute. There'll always be me or Gordon here. Just one more day and it's you and me and two weeks on Corfu. It'll be warm there. We can shop for new clothes for you, and get your hair done the way you'd like. You'll love it!'

It all sounded lovely, and it was very good of Gordon to spend all that money. She tried picturing the aeroplane they would fly on, thought about relaxing in a chair under a blue sky and knowing that Jack couldn't possibly come round the corner in the next five minutes and take her back home. But try as she might, she couldn't make the pictures stay firm in her mind; they always dissolved away in her husband's angry face. Clenching her hands so her daughter and son-in-law shouldn't see them twitch and shake, she went upstairs to her bedroom, sitting on a chair near the window, staring out through the terylene net, watching the street and wondering when he would come.

WHATEVER HE MIGHT have said to Morrissey, Willis didn't expect to locate anything small and dark as a briefcase among the murky canal clutter. Other things maybe: dead dogs well anchored, rusting bikes, bits of cars. The canal had been turned into Malminster's waste-bin. Come to that, so had Stye Beck, nice little spot when he was a kid, frog-spawn and tiddlers, water clear right to the bottom, reminiscing, canal mud thinning out and moving up to meet him in little clouds, enough shopping trolleys to start a business with, and something else floating in pallid luminescence, him and his co-diver, both with the same thought, veering off together, not a dog this time but anchored like one, arched as if her body was trying to get to the surface without the neck that kept it down, rump up, hair like seaweed round her face. Treading water, waiting for a marker, Willis knew he'd found a lot more than Morrissey wanted.

TWENTY-NINE

MALMINSTER was an old town. It had paid Danegeld to the Vikings, sent Yeomen to Agincourt, and bled with Richard on Bosworth Field; a white marble monument marked the dead of two world wars, heavy with names. Square in the town centre stood the Parish Church of St. Anselm, a Puginesque celebration of Victorian Gothic, saved from being slowly shaken to bits by passing traffic when the area around it became pedestrianised. The precinct was now a focal point for civic activities; Morris dancers jigged and jangled, Animal Rights supporters collected signatures, and any number of organisations from the Samaritans to the Territorial Army freely set up mobile trailers and canvassed support. Today, when Claire crossed the herringbone-patterned paving, the police had set up a mobile information unit, attracting no one out of the pouring rain except an occasional time-killer like herself. she'd come out regardless of the weather because silence and solitude were fragmenting her resolve, and with the house pristine again she had nothing to do except miss her children. And Richard. It would pass, she knew it would pass, but in the meantime she alternated between numbness and agony. She climbed the trailer steps, past a middle-aged sergeant cramped behind a minuscule table, and began a slow circuit of the display, reading leaflets, looking at photographs, her umbrella leaving a serpentine trail of dampness as she went. Someone else came in and she glanced idly and looked away when she saw the blue uniform, picking up a leaflet on opportunities for women, and beginning to read it. A low conversation began. Claire took no notice, picked up a booklet on road safety and leafed through that. The newcomer left and all was quiet again. Then he came back, heavy-footed up the three wooden steps, leaning in through the door, his voice distinct. 'If I send Lessing down at four—that's early enough, is it?'

'Plenty.'

The doorway emptied again, the dark blue uniform gone but not the voice. That resonated in Claire's head. She put down the booklet and leaned on the bench, suddenly sick.

'You all right, love? Want a cup of tea?'

That voice was all right, firm, reassuring.

'No!' Saying it too quickly and too loud as the sergeant began to get up. Modifying it a little. 'Thank you, I'm fine, I just need some air.' Moving back along the umbrella trail and out onto the precinct fast as she could. To her right a police car was moving off the precinct area into the traffic flow. Claire turned away from it, first walking, then running, into the anonymity of the brightly lit shops.

'Looks like you're going to have to put the Simms business on one side,' said Osgodby, privately relishing respite from fear of falling bricks. 'Unless you'd rather I handled this while you carry on poking around on the off-chance. We can do that if you like. Might not be a bad idea to get some hands-on experience; get out from the desk job a bit.' Flexing his fingers, hearing the knuckles crack, knowing the chief inspector would slice him in half first, but not being insulted by it. It was horses for courses, and Osgodby didn't balk at admitting his strength was in administration.

Morrissey said sourly, 'Richardson and Thewlis'll still be there when I'm ready for them; they'll not be going anywhere.' Knowing if he brought Bill Newton in now instead of later, they could still be squeezed from both sides;

knowing too if it hadn't been for his prompting, Willis and his team wouldn't have been in the canal in the first place. Serve him right then to get more than he'd bargained for. Belatedly recognising that as a kind of self-flagellation, and stalking out of the building feeling angrier still, taking Smythe, with his highlighted designer haircut and two-tone shoes, who looked no substitute for Barrett and his pragmatism, but drove efficiently just the same, and knew when to stay quiet, taking the car along the cracked concrete frontage of the old warehouses and stopping behind the blue police van, not especially wanting to see a body that had been fished out of the water, but welcoming a change from minor crime.

Up on the road bridge a small crowd of watchers mobbed the parapet; some dry under umbrellas, the rest getting wet without seeming to care. Amazing where they all came from. Bad news travelled with the speed of bush telegraph. Morrissey's eyes scanned the faces, wondering if any one of them belonged to more than a voyeur. The rain came heavier than ever, drenching in its intensity, splatting against the sheet of tarpaulin, and running off in rivulets.

Which was the head and which the feet?

Squatting he raised the corner farthest from the bridge, catching a rank stench before he saw the woman's head and the greenish glow of putrescence. Smythe, hunkered at his side, looked unmistakably glad to get up and move away.

The SOCOs slammed out of their van with a green plastic tent, eyeing Morrissey with a kind of weary resignation. Having the tent up in minutes, practice making perfect. With the best of the peepshow gone, boredom thinned out faces on the bridge. Morrissey would have liked to shift the lot. Saw a camera and turned his back on it.

Willis, warmer and dryer inside his wetsuit than Morrissey had been for two days, said, 'If you hadn't bent rules, you'd be in your nice warm office instead of getting a soaking. Dreadful thought isn't it? Because she'd still be down there. Police surgeon's been—didn't do much. Took a look, confirmed she's dead, and buggered off.'

'Just like that.'

'Practically. Can't blame him, he had a maternity case on the boil.' Willis's gaze shifted, watching the photographer's car edge close to the buildings. 'I hope we've got one with a strong stomach. Haven't had a good look yet, have you?'

'Not yet,' said Morrissey, gruffly, knowing he'd get to see more than he wanted when Warmsby came. Weighing up the chances it would be a suicide; hoping it was, so he could concentrate his energies elsewhere. Willis didn't let it rest there, though.

'Short-weighted rope round her neck,' he said, measuring with his hands. 'Best hope she wasn't alive when she got dropped in.'

The chief inspector grunted. Fishing out a few bodies didn't make Willis an expert on cause, not by a long shot; not saying that, though, preferring silence because he owed a favour.

'Go on,' said Willis. 'Say it, I shan't mind. How the hell do I know it's shoved and not jumped. That's what you're thinking. Right?'

'Right.'

'Come on, then. I've something that'll right interest you. Thought I'd put it in the van out of harm's way,' said Willis, stepping round the photographer, leaving him to the SOCOs. Morrissey fell into step, and Smythe stayed where he was, not a hundred per cent sure whether to do that or follow on, wishing the rain would stop. 'I cut the rope in half,' Willis said, loping along, squeaking a bit when rubber met rubber. 'Easier to get her up.' Opening the van doors and letting Morrissey see. 'That's what anchored her.'

Morrissey swore.

'Right one, then, is it?' said Willis. 'Thought it might be.'

Couldn't be any other. Exactly as Claire Simms had described it; initials in the top right corner. *RS*. Sodden black leather. 'That's it,' the chief inspector said heavily, and hoped for Claire's sake that Willis was right about how long the woman had been in the canal.

THEWLIS HAD no meetings that afternoon, and didn't go into his paid job with the NUM. Instead, he went back to his home and brooded, the bottle of Johnny Walker in his hand a new one. He carried it round the house with him, drinking straight from the bottle, a long deep draught of it in the bedroom before he set it down and pulled open the wardrobe, yanking out Monica's clothes and ripping them, dropping them on the carpet, before he fumbled with his fly and urinated on the lot of them, leaving the sodden pile there for her to clear up when she came back. Muttering to himself. Bloody cow! She'd be back all right—grovelling. On her fucking knees to him. By God! he'd put her through it first. Drinking again, cradling the bottle. He'd go to Lilian. Take it out on Lilian—easy Lilian. Sitting on the bed, remembering he couldn't go to Lilian, not anymore. Taking the bottle back downstairs and sprawling in front of the blank TV, drinking and working out how to get Monica on her own, separate her from Gordon and Angeline; sure that she was there, with them, because who else would take the silly cow in?

THIRTY

'WHITE FEMALE, aged between thirty and forty, well nourished, hair reddish-brown, height five feet five inches, own teeth—peering closer—missing left upper molar, crowned lower right incisor, six mercury fillings.' Straightening up, his next comment solely for Morrissey. 'Some dentist should recognise that.' Breaking off to take wax impressions, taking care with them. 'Wife wanted to buy a house here once, said she liked it. I told her no; I'd rather live someplace that didn't provide most of my work.'

Warmsby, the habitual post-mortem humourist, wasn't joking this time, just getting on grimly with what had to be done. The stench of body gasses was so bad that not even a dettol-soaked mask could prevent its lodging in the sinuses and clinging sourly rancid in the throat, and today above all days he could have done without it. He was not at his best. He had eaten too much of the wrong food at a dinner party he hadn't wanted to attend, and his digestion had played ducks and drakes ever since. Closer to heaving than he had been since his student days, he brusquely dismissed Morrissey's great worry, that the woman's death might have anteceded that of Simms, with: 'Not a chance, you're looking at days, not weeks; there'd be adipocere if it were weeks.' Glancing up, an impatient owl, begrudging having to explain but doing it all the same. 'Fatty stuff to you. Three or four days dead, possibly less. And that'—jabbing his scalpel at frilled skin edges and fragmented flesh—'that isn't decomposition, it's scavenging fish. Hungry little buggers always nibble easy bits first—ears, lips, fingers, toes; genitals when it's a naked body.' Turning back to his work. 'Worm eats corpse, duck eats worm, man eats duck. I fancy cremation myself; I don't know about you,' he continued, cutting into lung tissue, then saying on a long sigh: 'Not drowned, Chief Inspector, so you can start looking for who put her in.' And having said it, feeling an unkind satisfaction in knowing that when his work had ended, Morrissey would still be chasing clues.

HILDA GARFITT had moved into the house on Woodbine Terrace the day she married Tom, a fitfully sunny spring day in 1950, with a wind that lifted skirts and blew away hats, and she had never had any urge to move away. Not so her neighbours. Upwardly mobile was the expression used these days. She knew it well. Found herself sometimes wondering if she and Tom hadn't been a bit too placid about the whole thing; not that there was any point in even thinking about it now, not with Tom retired and herself with arthritis.

When Lilian moved in next door it had taken Hilda quite a while to let herself get friendly; she knew what direction Lilian's money-making skills lay in, and she didn't like that kind of thing going on next to her. It had worried her quite a bit that some stray male might come to the wrong house; but that had never happened, and prejudice gave way first to tolerance and then to liking, because when you came right down to it, it took all kinds to make a world, and it was all very discreet. Then Lilian had started her little herbal dispensary and that was quite respectable. She'd helped ease Hilda's arthritis a lot, and Mrs Pearce at number twenty-nine was forever going on about how she'd got rid of her dyspepsia. All in all, Lilian had become an asset. She and Hilda had a little system going between them; Tuesdays, Thursdays, and Saturdays Lilian came round to Hilda's for

a cup of coffee; Mondays, Wednesdays, and Fridays Hilda
had coffee next door. They never missed, except for holi-
days; that was why Hilda was getting so worried. It was all
very well for Tom to sit there saying she was making a fuss
over nothing—typical man's view, that, turn a blind eye—
but why would Lilian go off without saying anything?

'Tom,' Hilda said with sudden determination. 'Tom, I'm
going down to the police station, and it's not a bit of good
you saying no, because I shan't take any notice.'

'You'd better hang on and let me get into my shoes then,'
said Tom, knowing when not to waste his breath. 'There's
no point in bussing it when we've got a car, not when it's
peeing down.' Stamping into the hall.

Hilda buttoned her Mac and tidied the neat grey perm,
restoring Tom to his rightful place on the pedestal of her
affection. He came back, zipping up his parka. 'They'll not
take a bit of notice,' he said deflatingly. 'What they'll say is,
Lilian's a grown woman and why don't you mind your own
business.'

'No, they won't. Not when I tell them the front door's
unlocked.'

'Then why don't you lock the damn thing. You've got a
key.'

'I have locked it,' said Hilda complacently, 'but that
doesn't change it being open in the first place, does it? Come
on then if we're going, I don't want to have to miss "Em-
merdale Farm" on account of you dawdled. We'll call in at
Stanton's on the way back, I could just fancy a fish-and-chip
supper.'

Especially since she wouldn't have to cook it!

THEWLIS DROVE the car with extreme care, knowing he was
over the limit and sweating from the effort of concentration, driving twice past the house where Gordon and Ange-

line lived, seeing lights bright behind the curtains, picturing Monica sitting comfortably, thinking she was safe.

The front hub-cap hit the kerb. He overcorrected and the Sierra careened over the centre line, getting a horn blast from an oncoming bus. Thewlis swore and pulled back to his own side, turning again when the road was clear and making another sortie, not passing the house this time but parking on an ill-lit side-street almost opposite and settling down to watch. In the near dark, with his car lights off and the need for concentration gone, the whisky's soporific effect increased. Thewlis had a lot of difficulty staying awake. Winding down the side window brought in a blast of needle-sharp rain, icy on his skin, spattering across the steering wheel. Cursing both Monica and the elements in equal parts he jerked it shut. At six, just before Gordon came home, the yard lights went out and ten minutes later he was asleep, snoring stertorously, his breath slowly steaming up the car windows.

CLAIRE SAID, in a calm voice that quavered only once to reveal panic, 'Margaret, I promised myself I wouldn't involve you again, but this is only a message. Can you pass it on for me? I've been trying to find John, but he's out and they won't tell me where.' Then gabbling on, 'Oh, this is so silly, he won't believe it anyway. He'll put it down to imagination again. No, forget about it. Just tell him I'm going back to my children. I can't stand being alone here. Yes. Just tell him that, will you?'

Margaret said sharply, 'Claire? What is it, for heaven's sake? Of course he won't put it down to imagination, whatever it is. He's been spending a lot of time sifting through Richard's death. He hasn't been satisfied about it for a while now. Whatever else has happened, he needs to know about it. Trust him. He's a very trustworthy man,' she remarked, realising as she said it that her husband was exactly that. For some reason the thought created a sense of shock, as though she'd dug up a new discovery and not an old belief. 'Tell me what it is, Claire,' she coaxed when the line stayed silent. 'He can't help if he doesn't know the problem, can he?'

'Just tell him if he needs me I'll be with my parents in Bolton; I'll give you the address. It's 17, Friar's Close, Denholme Road. And tell him . . . tell him I heard . . . no, I recognised . . . a man's voice today, in the exhibition van on the precinct, and it belonged to a policeman who came in about three o'clock to find out what time the van closed. I . . . Margaret . . . I don't know who to trust anymore. Tell him that too.'

'What voice?' demanded Margaret. 'Will he know?'

'Oh yes, he'll know! It was a telephone call. A man making threats about what he'd do to Rachel if I talked to John again.'

'Talked to him about what, about Richard?'

'Yes. Oh sod it, Margaret. I was scared out of my head. I felt so alone; there was no one I could tell, no one to unload onto. Then the damned house got broken into, so I just packed up the kids, took them to Bolton, and came back without them.'

Margaret knew that kind of fear intimately.

'I wish I'd known,' she said. 'I would at least have tried to help. Can you tell me anything else about the man you saw today, what he looked like? Tall, short, thin, fat?' Feeling anger similar to that she knew Morrissey would feel if there was a rotten apple around.

'I don't know. I panicked. I'm ashamed to say that but I did. I just saw the back of him. Stocky, I think, but I don't really know. He'd come in a patrol car. I saw it drive off the precinct towards North Street. I have to go now, Margaret. It's a long drive.'

'Yes, of course you must. The sooner you start the better, if you feel you really have to go tonight; but there's a spare bed here, if it's only company you need.'

'I need my family,' said Claire, 'but thanks. Bye.'

The receiver clicked and buzzed. 'Bye,' said Margaret to the empty line. 'Take care.' Wishing she'd known about it all before now, knowing from painful experience what it felt like to have a beloved child in danger, wishing too that Morrissey could talk to her about such things instead of having to keep it all jammed up inside himself.

Perhaps that was the worst thing about being a police wife, not being allowed to share problems before they grew big enough to swamp a marriage with their silence. Had he ever talked about his work? Frowning, going back to the letter she was writing when the telephone rang, and remembering that yes, back in the beginning when he was a young constable and it had been nearly all parking tickets and lost dogs, he'd come home full of it all. Now, only rarely did she get to peep into his mind. She suspected it was partly a wish to protect her from hurtful things, but she neither wanted or appreciated that kind of protection from him. What she wanted was an end to the loneliness she was beginning to feel even when he was there.

Jean Beckett said it would have been easier to put up with her husband's moods and tempers if he'd let her share in the reasons for them, had likened it to living in a semi-silent world where the only communication left between them had lapsed to a level of meals and bed, with constant sniping in between.

Margaret didn't want that to happen to her and Morrissey. Would do almost anything to prevent it.

She sat at the small writing table in the sitting-room, looking out across the wet garden, making no effort to pick up her pen again, her mind occupied with the man she had loved for so long. She could barely remember what her life had been like without him there, trying to fathom just what it was that separated them now. So many people found him frightening, were intimidated by his presence. But she knew how gentle he really was, knew how much the constant bickering with Mike must hurt. That stone face of his that intimidated wrong-doers could light up a room when he lapsed into laughter.

The slanting rain and rising wind was stripping leaves from the chestnut, scattering them over the lawn, bowing the few clumps of Michaelmas daisies that were still blooming. He'd shaped all that from what had been a veritable wilderness. No, no he hadn't; they'd done it together, the way such things should be done. Remembering blisters and backache, feeling the old tide of love for him flow warm in her veins. Deciding then that Mike had to be talked to, not by his father but by her, the problem shaken out and looked at, patched up and mended before everything fell to bits.

Leaning back, her whole mind was on Morrissey. A trustworthy man—that's what she had told Claire—and he was. It was time Mike remembered it too.

WHEN THEWLIS woke, he was cramped and cold and it was after midnight. There were no lights at all now in his daughter's house. His mouth tasted like foul flannel and his head pounded heavily. All the car windows were impenetrable with condensation and he had to wipe them before he could start up the engine and drive home. Not until he'd turned out onto the road and picked up speed did he discover from the noise and bumpiness that some practical joker had let his tyres down while he slept. Banging up and down on the foot pump in the pouring rain, livid with frustrated fury, if he could have got his hands on Monica at that point he would have killed her.

THIRTY-ONE

WOODS, SENT out armed with a stack of photocopied dental charts and a list of local dentists, felt as relieved as a sixth former let out of detention. Two sodding days callousing his bum, and he still didn't understand the logic of it. Pushing open the door of O'Donnell & Webster on Queen Street and seeing three glum faces on his right and a crisp white overall on his left, smelling the usual dentist smell and hearing a high-pitched whine from somewhere behind a closed door, grinning because he wasn't going to make a fourth glum face, not today, and thinking to himself that this was the first time he'd ever walked into one of the damn places without a sudden urge to shit. Flashing his identity card and getting instant attention, thinking this was the best-looking redhead he'd seen in years until he saw the wedding ring and fixed his mind on why he was really there. 'A question of identification,' he said sombrely, handing her a chart. 'Reddish-brown hair, medium height, about thirty-five. Probably a good-looking woman.'

'Probably?'

'Hard to tell sometimes, when there's facial injuries, if you know what I mean.'

'No, I don't, and I don't think I want to,' she answered, making a face and giving a shudder; long, slim, bronzy-tipped fingers busy writing down what he'd said. 'Road accident, was it then?'

'Not a road accident. No, nothing like. This is a murder investigation. It'd be a help if that chart could be looked at fairly quickly.'

'*Murder?* How? When?' Avid and repulsed at the same time, her voice went two decibels higher. 'Who?'

'Who, is what I'm trying to establish, isn't it, love. Can I just have your name, for the records,' he said, opening his notebook.

'Karen Elizabeth James,' she answered, leaning forward now, as curiosity overcame distaste. 'When was it?' she demanded eagerly. 'I mean it hasn't been on the news or anything, has it? Why's it being kept quiet?'

'Yes, it has been on the news—this morning,' Woods replied, his eyes occupied with the way her forward movement had sent her breasts into prominent relief. 'And it's not being kept quiet, so give us a ring at this number if the chart's one of yours, will you?' Scribbling his name, noticing the once glum faces weren't glum anymore, hearing voices chirrup in speculation as he shut the door behind him and moved on. Sharma's on Peel Street next. Might get the whole lot done by dinner-time if he got a move on, impress with efficiency and make up for two wasted days.

Feeling a few spots of rain, he stepped out briskly, hoping it wouldn't come tippling down again, letting his imagination play with the possibility that he could go back to Morrissey with a name, turning up his coat collar and nipping into a newsagent's doorway dodging a sudden squall, remembering his horoscope that morning had warned about dampened enthusiasm and thinking maybe there was something in that sort of rubbish after all.

RUNG AT HOME the previous night and given a sketchy outline of things, Bill Newton had his bulk in Morrissey's office by eight-thirty the next morning, his coming noticed and commented on by diverse people. When he left a little after ten, well briefed and a joint strategy decided on, he was moving fast and surprisingly lightly, although fast wasn't the way he liked to do things. Given any choice in the matter, and able to approach from an angle less pressing in its urgency than homicide, he would have much rather set up a leisurely investigation, the kind of gentle sleuthing that let him keep his hand well hidden until he had rock-steady grounds for shaking out Malminster's public figures, dirty washing and all. But he didn't have that sort of choice. Whatever approach he took now, it would have to be done in a hurry, before Morrissey's murder hunt made all the rabbits run.

Newton didn't fancy being left with an empty bag.

Trying to decide as he drove the big Volvo, ancient but comfortable and in sore need of a de-coke, which magistrate would be most likely to append an unquestioning signature to the search-and-seize warrants he would need, and knowing that since finesse was out of the question he'd have to make do with a sledgehammer instead.

BARRETT'S INVESTIGATION seemed to be grinding to a halt. It wasn't much good having the tipper truck that crushed Guffey if there weren't any clues left to its driver. Fingerprints all over the bloody thing—inside and out—and everybody on the building site having to be checked. A waste of time—Barrett knew that already. Saw how the thing had been set up, recognising he was looking for a professional not just an opportunist, seeing a kind of black humour in the way Guffey had innocently hitched a ride to his own death.

Not that the detective sergeant felt any particular sorrow for him. No, he couldn't pretend to do that. On the scales of retribution Guffey hadn't got more than he was owed. Idly wondering how much cash had changed hands in the doing of it.

At eleven he presented himself at Richardson's office and got no further than the dark-haired secretary's desk. 'If you *did* have an appointment he must have forgotten about you,' she said, unsmilingly. 'There's no message. I suppose you're absolutely sure he said today? Yes? Well, all I can suggest is you tell me what it was about and I'll find somebody to help.'

'Where is he, then—out of town?'

'I can't discuss his movements. Sorry.'

'But you can tell me when he'll be back, can't you? I mean you'd have to know that to make a fresh appointment.'

'I wasn't going to make one. Mr Richardson didn't say how long he'd be away.'

'Well that's not good enough,' Barrett said sharply. 'He has to have left his address, emergencies and such, and I want it. I'm not making a social call; it's police business.'

'It's also my job,' said the secretary, 'and I wouldn't keep it very long if I ignored instructions. Sorry, Mr Barrett, but I need to pay the rent.'

'Detective Sergeant.'

'Detective Sergeant,' she corrected. 'And I still can't help you. Maybe if you try in a couple of days.'

'I suppose he's not in there hiding?' Scowling at Richardson's door. 'I wouldn't put it past him,' suiting action to thought and barging in to find the big office empty.

'Satisfied?' she said coldly, reaching past him to shut the door again. 'A shame you've had a wasted journey, but there it is. When he rings, I'll ask him to get in touch.'

'Do that!' Barrett snapped, stalking away with as much dignity as he had left, wondering if Richardson had seen through the act and set up a goose-chase deliberately.

Impossible he could have got wind of Newton's interest and made an early run for safety.

But if he had been tipped off...

Going back and facing the unexpressive face again, deciding she was a dragon-in-the-making. 'When did he actually go?' he asked. 'Can't be any state secrets in that.'

'Early this morning. Something came up unexpectedly, and please don't ask what because I don't know.'

'How?' said Barrett.

'How?'

'How did the something come up? Visitor? Phone call? Letter?'

'Phone call. He left half an hour later.'

'What time would that be?'

'Half-past nine.'

'And you wouldn't know who the call was from?'

'No I wouldn't'—icing out again—'it went through on the private line, and before you ask it can't be listened to.'

'I wasn't going to ask that,' Barrett lied. 'Not the sort of question I'd put to a girl of your integrity. You've been a great help without even knowing it. Thanks!' Pulling out his most charming smile and leaving her worrying about what she'd said to earn it. Switching his mind back to Guffey and deciding to have one more try at Joe's Caff before he gave up hoping for a good witness.

The rich and greasy smell of fried food reached out to greet him before he'd done much more than get out of his car, twitching at his olfactory nerve and starting up a flow of saliva. Thoughts of cholesterol overload and blocked arteries got elbowed to one side by memories of crisp chips and browned, succulent bangers crowding round mushrooms and a thick pork chop. Getting nearer the door and thinking he could kill two birds with one stone; fill up on food and information at the same time, knowing the food wouldn't be a disappointment even if the other was. Finding himself recognised by Rick and May behind the counter with looks that said one more question out of him would bring out the worst in them, and ordering his food first, sitting up at the counter to eat, not mentioning Guffey until the second pot of tea, then saying casually: 'Pity we didn't get anything useful on Guffey. We found the lorry, you know. Stolen. Nothing in it to say who'd nicked it. Shame. I mean, Guffey might have been nowt but a scum-bag, but who's going to go next. That's what you've got to look at. Could be any innocent kid picking up a lift.'

'We 'adn't thought about that,' said May, stopped in mid-reach. ''Ad we, Rick? Don't think Joe 'ad neither. Might be one of them perversioners what's all up and down an' all over the blooming place now.'

'I wasn't here,' said Rick without turning round from the chipper, 'so I wouldn't know, would I?'

May said, 'Not got nowhere then, shame that. 'Ave a few more chips? Go on, you're still a growing lad.' Watching Barrett blink as he got them. 'Barney 'ad his lad with 'im that morning. 'Alf-term you see. Always brings 'im in. Comes early, stops an hour or so—so's young Kev can get 'is numbers.'

'What numbers?' queried Barrett, trying to cope with the new influx of chips, wanting to duff but not daring, listening to what May said but not making any connections yet.

'Registered numbers, on lorries an' what-not.'

'We've got the lorry,' Barrett said. 'We don't need the number.'

'No, not on a lorry, on the other chap's.'

'Other chap's?' Totally confused now.

'Feller he were talking to afore he cadged a lift.' Explaining patiently, seeing Barrett frown. 'You weren't told, were you? I told it to that young chap 'at come in t'first time. Guffey were talking to another man, afore he got a lift.

Dark glasses, leather jacket. Not a lorryman. Kev might've got 'is number though, collected it like, with the lorries.'

Pushing the plate away, on his feet and reaching for his notebook, thinking it might have been worth pushing the extra chips down for after all.

THIRTY-TWO

THE RAIN had stopped and the wind had shifted round to an easterly, strengthening as it changed. Leaves were everywhere now, sodden and treacherous, the trees stripped bare. On the precinct a couple of Council work-carts were out, clearing up, and Monica and Angeline were shopping; Monica nervous, Angeline certain nothing could go wrong.

At the side of the canal Morrissey and Smythe huddled, hands in pockets, doing nothing in particular except stare at the water and poke through debris. Smythe couldn't work out why the two of them were there at all, with nothing to see, less to do, and what his gran called a pneumonia wind whistling round his arse. Keeping his back to it and wondering if the DCI was going off a bit.

'We after anything in particular?' he queried when his ears had gone numb, and got a flat look and no reply. The divers were still bringing up rubbish, and he half envied them—only half though. 'It's just if I knew what we were looking for, it'd make it easier for me to find,' he said, realising too late the sarcasm of it and waiting for the inevitable.

'What weighted her down?' Morrissey asked, flinty-edged.

'A briefcase, sir.'

'The one you went looking for. Right?'

'Right, sir.'

'Ever wondered what happened to its original contents?'

'Papers would have floated, sir, so it'd have to be heavier stuff, like books, to sink.'

'Your cognisance amazes me.'

'Yes, sir. But whichever it was he might have wanted them, whoever had it, if they were important enough to nick in the first place.'

'Indeed he might. But when the hell did it happen?'

'The theft, sir?'

'Of course the theft, Smythe. That's what we've been talking about.' Turning and striding back to the car, Smythe following, troubled by what something he'd left unsaid before, still thinking it insignificant. Settling himself behind the wheel but not turning on the ignition.

'Well out with it, then,' Morrissey barked. 'Whatever it is, I don't fancy sitting here all day.'

Smythe started the engine. 'Sorry, sir, miles away then.' Shunting with care, turning the car, putting off the telling for later. 'Where to?'

Where to indeed with everything in limbo waiting on Forensics! Driven to impatience with too many random threads to follow, and bad-tempered with it, wondering if Barrett were back and if Newton had got his warrants, mind and destination both decided for him by a stomach that rumbled and sent a burst of fire. 'Back to the office,' the chief inspector snapped. 'It's time we had something to eat.' Hoping that by then somebody, somewhere, might have noticed a good-looking woman had gone missing.

BECKETT'S DRAINAGE tube was out; there was nothing left of his operation but a scar and a dressing. He felt cock-a-hoop that he'd been given a definite date to go home, and sat in the day room, a beatific smile on his face for all comers, thinking that when he went he wouldn't be wifeless anymore, it really would be home and not an empty house, his mind fixing itself safely in the early years of his marriage before everything went wrong, expecting that when he told her the news, Jean would feel as pleased as he did. Having no idea that his wife's mind wouldn't fix on anything but the foul moods and minor acts of violence that she'd put up with for far too long, always half-expecting that he'd go over the edge and turn the violence towards her instead of inanimate objects, sick at the thought of it starting all over again.

Knowing none of that, Beckett had no reason not to feel cheerful as he walked down to Intensive Care, believing Azar was still on the mend and expecting his own good news to bring smiles and handshakes, thinking how he'd be able to keep a friendly eye on the boy when he got back on duty again.

When he pushed open the heavy rubber-rimmed doors he knew before he reached the nurses' station that something was wrong, the sense of it hung in the air like the sound of a silence much more palpable than the bleep and whoosh of machinery. Then he saw the blank monitor screen and joy left him in a rush. The staff-nurse came, rustling lightly, took him into the minuscule office and sat him down, sent the ward-maid to make tea, and said, yes, Azar was dead, had died two hours ago from a secondary brain haemorrhage they hadn't been able to stop. And all that would come into Beckett's mind was the fact that it had changed the case from GBH to murder.

RICHARDSON HAD checked up on Barrett, and hadn't liked the blunt response delivered by his snout. 'You must be joking! Too bloody prissy to fiddle a bus fare that one. If he's been up there holding out his hand, it's a come-on. Forget it.' Richardson didn't like being laughed at, listened to the flat, broad voice and thought that if things really went sour there'd be at least one person left hanging out to dry. Then he found out about Newton's visit to Morrissey from the same source, and by ten that morning he'd transferred the rest of his liquid assets to the kind of overseas account that carried a number, not a name. Three hours later he was on his way to Basle.

In Bradford, Vic Duttin was packing up too. Richardson always looked after his friends, and when he'd called and said briefly: 'Take a holiday, Vic,' Duttin had known better than to dawdle. He packed his few belongings, disinterred his money from under the floorboards, and headed south and fast down the motorway. Leaving Bradford behind didn't bother him, one place was much like another, and he didn't call any of them home, couldn't even think what it would be like to have one. In Nottingham he sold the car for less than it was worth and got a train to Derby, where he picked up a second-hand Escort for cash, doubling back and taking it easy, heading north.

THE FRAUD SQUAD went in heavy-handed, with enough borrowed manpower to let it be known they were serious. Richardson's management team were thrown into a panic that got much worse before it became obvious the man himself couldn't be reached. But when a second group of Fraud officers went into the Town Hall, staff there were more blasé, provoked into nothing more than a collective shrug.

Lowry, and the planning department, Newton had kept for himself, bouncing a little as he handed over the warrant, watching po-faced as it was read.

First the chief planning officer tried bluster, standing on his high horse, naming names in high places, threatening to ring the Chief Constable and bring wrath down on Newton's head, and when that had no effect protested there was nothing in his department that could possibly be linked to a fraud inquiry, feeling beads of dampness grow on his forehead as he said it.

Newton had heard it all before, thought he could probably write a book about it if he had the time, seeing in the man's eyes that the smooth facade hid nothing more formidable than a paper tiger.

Recognition brought a kind of disappointment, the inspector liked to get a wily opponent who'd wriggle and twist and refuse to take the hook.

Watching the speedy way his men worked—leafing through correspondence, selecting files, piling them into cardboard boxes, carrying everything downstairs and coming back for more—and while it all went on around him, standing with Lowry and watching him sweat, trying to guess how long it would take the man to offer somebody else's hide in exchange for his own, and deciding not long at all by the look of him.

Try giving it a bit of a nudge, then, couldn't hurt things any. Saying conversationally: 'That briefcase that went missing—you know the one I mean, the one Chief Inspector Morrissey's been looking for, talked to you about it already, hasn't he? Right?'

'I know nothing about the damn briefcase, for God's sake. Nothing at all. How many times am I supposed to say it?'

'Doesn't matter now, sir. It's turned up.'

'Turned up where?'

'Turned up yesterday. Thought you'd be interested.'

'Where?'

'Where,' said on a down note. 'Expected you'd be more interested in what was in it than where it was. Or was that something you knew about already, knowing everything that goes on in your own department like you do.'

'I don't.' A quick denial, then a backtrack. 'I mean, I don't ask what anybody carries around with them. Could be anything. Ham sandwiches, for all I know.'

'Rubble, sir. Bricks and concrete.'

'I don't understand ... Where was it found?'

'In the canal, sir. Weighting down a dead woman.'

Lowry looked ill. 'Oh, my God, I don't believe it ... Simms?'

'Dead before she was, sir.'

'Then who ... ?' Looking round agitatedly. 'Is that why all this ... ?' Waving a hand.

'No, sir. This is part of an investigation into public fraud and the corruption of Council officials. It's to do with illicit land deals and favouritism of tenders for clearance and building. Sound familiar, does it?' Pushing his face towards Lowry's, chin thrust out. 'And it's to do with a plot of land up near the motorway.' Taking a chance there, but seeing Lowry flinch, pushing harder. 'What we're looking at is prison sentences, not a slap on the wrist. Very long prison sentences, when you count how many people seem to have ended up dead. And all because somebody got greedy. Not nice that, sir, is it?'

'I'm not involved. There's nothing to say I'm involved. Nothing, nothing at all. I mean, all right, I might have turned a blind eye to things, occasionally, but that's all, a case of not over-riding somebody else's recommendations. You can understand that happening, can't you? Yes, of course you can. I can't *afford* to ... to ... Oh, my God!' Fumbling back round the desk and dropping into his chair, voice so low Newton had to strain to hear. 'I don't know who had the briefcase, and I don't know who the woman was.'

'We've served Richardson with a search-and-seize warrant too.'

Lowry's ashen face turned up. 'Richardson.'

'And then there's Thewlis.' Changing it now, feeling lucky. 'Of course if you helped us unravel it all, it'd look better for you when it all comes out.'

'It was an investment,' Lowry said dully. 'A way to make enough to retire on. I'd no idea what . . . what . . .'

'Lengths other people would go to, to get what they wanted,' Newton said helpfully. 'More a victim then?' Suggesting sympathy. 'Anybody else in the deal, was there?'

'Gerald Mason.'

Newton rocked back. Throw a stone in a muddy pool and mud splashed out in unexpected directions. Seeing then, it wasn't going to be just a local scandal, picturing the tabloids turning it into a circus. Blinking at Lowry. 'Anybody else?'

'One of yours.' A small bark of a laugh. 'Supposed to give us wind of this sort of thing,' waving a hand at the now-empty filing cabinets, seeing his life balanced at the brink of the abyss and trying desperately to pull back. 'What's the best I can expect,' he said, 'for saving you a lot of time?'

'A lot better than you could expect if you don't,' promised Newton drily, and began to read him his rights.

THIRTY-THREE

THEWLIS CHAIRED two morning meetings in foul mood, scratching on and off at his groin, eyes rioting with red veins and a hammer pain behind them.

Trawling through dark streets on his way home the previous night, he'd found the only hookers still out were rough trade, and two had backed off from doing business when they caught his breath and the look in his eyes. The third offered a fast knee trembler for a fiver, jammed up behind the station wall, reeking of stale juices and spent semen, and he wilted before he'd near started. When he got back to his unwelcoming house he'd fallen asleep in his chair, the bottle of whisky in his hand spilling over the carpet.

Just before six he woke with fetid mouth and a sour smell in his nostrils, stiff-necked and sore, progress upstairs hampered by pins and needles, painful in his feet. The first shock of cold water on his skin before he turned up the shower's thermostat, brought him shuddering back to his senses. Remembered humiliation generated fresh anger; the prostitute and Monica merged into one image that stayed with him all morning, dulling concentration. Twice he had to be reminded what the committee was debating, flushing irately, arguing contrary to the majority from pure bloody-mindedness, his brain pulsating pain from a hangover.

He wound up the second meeting leaving two items still not discussed, overriding objections, stamping from the chamber without civility, brushing aside two members with a headshake and another with a dismissive hand. Let the buggers wait on his good time, and that wouldn't be yet a

bit. Rode downstairs in a jolting lift and cursed its mechanism, crossed over the road to sit in The Chancellor's with
a pint of bitter and a beef and pickle sandwich, still
scratching intermittently, unaware as yet that last night's
brief encounter had left him host to crabs. He downed his
food quickly and missed the one o'clock news bulletin by
five minutes, driving out of the Town Hall car-park seconds before Newton's squad went in.

He was sitting in his car, parked a short way down the
same back street he'd parked on the night before, when his
wife and daughter came home from their shopping trip. The
sight of them talking animatedly was like an act of provo-
cation, and set him fumbling with the door catch. Then he
set caution over rashness and took his hand away. Impru-
dent in broad daylight, too many bloody people. Wait a bit,
bide his time, get her on her own. Only a matter of patience
now. Thinking on ways to isolate her. Reaching to turn on
the radio, but only half listening until the words 'woman'
and 'canal' on the mid-afternoon news jolted him into paying attention, sweating and swearing, knowing the minute
he heard the police description that Lilian was still fouling
things up for him.

THIRTY-FOUR

BARRETT WAS BACK in his office a bit after two, by which time he'd run Barney to earth and paid two quid to a wheeling-dealing ten-year-old for the privilege of borrowing a book full of registration numbers. An accountant in the making, young Kev, everything dated, make and colour, observation point, bit of gossip thrown in. Rust-bucket. Knackered. The word *wicked*, underlined against a Porsche. Expensive tastes, too.

'No go at Richardson's; he's buggered off,' Barrett announcing his failure cheerfully, before Morrissey's face showed it to be the wrong approach. Adding, 'I might have got a good lead on who hired Guffey, though,' as a kind of ballast before rehashing his abortive confrontation.

'Coincidence, then, you reckon?'

'Sorry, sir?'

'Newton. Coming here and Richardson doing a runner. Coincidence?'

'We don't have anything to say there's a link, do we, sir? Going on what his secretary said, these sudden trips off aren't that unusual for him. I mean, if I'm right, what you seem to be suggesting is he got wind Fraud were nosing round, and, well, he could only have got that from somebody here, couldn't he? Not likely that, is it, sir?'

'You tell me, Neil.' Thinking about Claire, and remembering he'd done nothing yet about finding out who'd been in the precinct. Trusting Smythe to go and do that without putting hackles up.

Barrett asked, 'What's all that about then, anything I should know?'

'If there's anything in it,' said the chief inspector, 'you'll likely be first.'

HILDA GARFITT was busy baking, the kitchen radio tuned to the local station, her husband watching television in the other room and keeping out of her way. Always safest when Hilda was busy, and especially when she was in a bit of mood, which she had been on and off since last evening's visit to the police station. He'd warned her before she dragged him out of the warm house that they'd take no notice of her, and they hadn't. Different, they'd said, if it had been a young person under sixteen, or even an old person, but a healthy neighbour didn't warrant a full-scale search or even a missing poster. Not yet, she didn't. Pretty young lass that policewoman, better than they had been in his young days, right hard-faced battle-axes then. Come back again in a week if Lil hadn't got in touch, she'd said. Seemed sensible enough advice to him. Not to Hilda, though—she hadn't been fit to talk to since. Hadn't even finished her fish and chips last night, he'd had to finish 'em for her. Not like Hilda that, not when they'd come from Stanton's. Dozing off, coming up on his feet with a start when he heard her yelling in the kitchen, dizzy for a minute because he'd got up too fast. Burnt herself, that's what it must be, always telling her to be careful, moving as fast as he could to get to her, angry when he found her standing at the table, her hands covered in flour, yelling at him to shut up and listen to what was on the radio.

Couldn't she just have come and told him, quiet-like, without making all that bother? But he shut up anyway, being peaceable, and caught the end of it.

'Can I just repeat that description again,' came the tof-fee-warm voice. 'Five feet five inches tall, medium build, reddish-brown hair, aged somewhere around thirty-five. If you do know anyone answering that description and missing from home, please get in touch with Malminster police. They'll be waiting for your call. I'll read out the number again at the end of the news bulletin.'

'It's Lilian,' Hilda cried wretchedly, flour from her hands spreading over the floor as she waved them around. 'Somebody up and killed her.' Her eyes overflowed at the enormity of it and dripped in the cherry pie.

'There, there,' said Tom, who didn't believe her but didn't like saying so. 'No need to take on like that, is there?' putting his arms round her and patting her back. He did the same thing every time she got upset, always had. Sometimes it irritated Hilda, sometimes it didn't, getting patted like he was winding a baby. Flour came off her hands onto his maroon pullover, the one with cables she'd knitted for his birthday. Her tears dried up and she pushed him away, flouring his front as well as his back.

'It is her,' she said. 'Doesn't matter if you don't think it; I'm still going to ring up and say so.'

'They won't believe you,' he said despondently, repeating what he'd said the day before, and wasting his breath. Hilda never did take any notice.

ON THE OTHER SIDE of Malminster, Monica Thewlis heard the woman's description too, thought at once of the woman reaching up to draw the curtains in the house on Woodbine Terrace, and the look that had been on Jack's face as he'd stood behind her, dropping a stitch in the lacy white matinee coat, and having to put the knitting down because her hands were shaking. Getting up and looking through the window, wondering again if he were out there, watching for her. If it *were* Lilian Carver—no, of course it wasn't—but if it were, should she...it wasn't right to be lying there with no name, poor woman, whoever she was. She didn't have to give her name, or Jack's. Just ring up and say who she thought it might be. Angeline came in with her coat on while Monica was still thinking, gave her a quick hug. 'Sure you'll be all right, Mum? It's nothing but a last proddle at the doctor's. I can give it a miss.'

'No you shan't give it a miss. Go on, get off. I'll be fine.'

'When Gordon comes,' said Angeline, and stood with her mother, watching traffic go by.

From inside the parked car Thewlis watched Gordon come hurrying round the corner and into the house. Two minutes later Angeline got into the black Citroen, starting up and driving away with a little puff of smoke from the exhaust. Fool, Gordon, letting her drive a car like that. Leaning forward a bit, thinking he saw a shape behind the net curtains, trying to make out if it was Monica. A youth walked round from the yard with a short length of pipe, gesticulating with his hands when Gordon came and shook his head over it. For a minute the lad stood on the doorstep alone. Thewlis dipped his hand to scratch. Damn the bloody sodding itch. 'Ye-es!' Saying the word out loud, triumphant as he climbed out of the car, his son-in-law and the lad going off a trot, leaving Monica alone.

Using Access to gain access, that amused him too, feeling the latch give way. Monica sat quietly knitting and his fury exploded. Fuck her! Placid as a bloody cow in pasture. Roaring at her, cursing, his fists up.

Monica dropped the knitting but didn't scream. No point with the house empty. One minute a frightened jelly the way she always was when Jack got violent, then a funny little shift in her head, like a switch clicking, and she wasn't Monica anymore, she was outside—floaty—watching her-

self shake. Silly fat woman! Stand up to him, done it once
do it again, no knife this time but a poker there. Reach for
it. Stop looking at him and look at the poker. *There!* Cold
and heavy. Who was she? Joan of Arc? No, no! Look what
happened to her! Don't look at his eyes. Think, find another heroine. Why weren't there any? Because men wrote
history—that's why. Angeline had told her that. Didn't
matter. Gordon was nice. Some men weren't wicked. Holding the poker out, brandishing it like a sword. Her father
had been a good man. Good roots, bad roots. Jack's were
evil! I knew you'd come, Jack, but I'm not going with you.
Such a stupid-looking woman with her brass hair. Too fat!
'I know about Lilian, Jack. I know all about her.' The
wrong thing to say. Hit him, hit him! Striking out at the mad
bull rush that sent her staggering, the poker crashing to the
hearth. Were his eyes really red or was it imagination, seeing it all from a distance, calmly peaceful. Never mind her
this time, such a broken face. Splat, splat, spurting crim-
son, a rose for a nose.

Why had he stopped?

Gordon? Gordon?

Beginning to fade, ever so slowly, back inside herself,
feeling pain of such intensity she had to cry out, making
only a faint bubble of sound.

THIRTY-FIVE

SIT THERE twiddling thumbs, thought Morrissey, and nothing happened, but let one thing come, and all else followed on its heels. Wars and rumours of wars were as nothing compared to a paper avalanche of Faxed forensic reports. They began to pile up on his desk, intimidating in their complexity, barely glanced at when news of Hilda Garfitt's telephone call sent him hurrying down to the makeshift incident room. Hilda's complaint had been brief but tetchy, and Morrissey's response mirrored it.

'Yesterday!' he barked. 'Came in yesterday, to this police station, reported her neighbour missing and nobody thought to pass it on? Why the hell wasn't I told? Who in Hades saw her?'

'Er...' Swiftly exchanged glances. 'Seems worse than it was, sir, er...in retrospect, like, well, I mean, er...well, the WPC did, um, follow laid-down procedure, sir.'

'Which WPC?'

'Rosie, sir. WPC Quinn, that is.'

'She on duty?'

'Yes, sir.'

'In the building?'

'Yes, sir.'

'In my office, then. Now.'

Going back upstairs himself at a gallop. Peering into the room across from his own and finding it empty. Where the hell was Smythe? Remembering then that he'd sent him on an errand. Finding Barrett busy on the telephone, he made signs for him to cut it short.

Searching his memory for Woodbine Terrace and checking his briefcase at the same time, a kind of expectation rising up in him, the sensation nudging at his mind familiar
and welcome.

Rosie Quinn's knock was firm, not timorous, but she
came in to face him like a crushed butterfly, eyes downcast
under long lashes. Too pretty by half for a policewoman.
Hearing Katie somewhere in his head calling him a sexist pig
for thinking it.

The chief inspector put on his stern face. 'The missing
person's report you dealt with, last night, can I take it it's on
file?'

'Yes, sir. I'm sorry it didn't come through to you, but the
other description hadn't been circulated, that isn't any excuse, but...'

'Quite right about that; it isn't any excuse. And you didn't
read the dead woman's description and think to connect
both incidents today either, didn't think to put two and two
together and make four.'

'No, sir.'

'Why's that, then?'

'I haven't seen the circular yet, sir. I've been in juvenile
court.' A barest hint of mistreatment in the way she said
that. Morrissey registered it.

'And came back when?'

'About fifteen minutes ago, sir. The sergeant sent me to
have a cup of tea. I'd have read it after that, sir.'

'Hmmph.' Letting the intended reprimand ride and saying less sternly, 'Seen anything of DC Smythe since you got
back?'

'I think I saw him going into Public Relations, sir.'

'Fetch him out for me then, and tell him he's wanted in
here.' Adding: 'That's it then; off you go,' when she hesi-
tated.

Barrett's eyebrows were up.

'You needn't look like that,' Morrissey said. 'She's not a kitten. Not having heard a description's no excuse at all when she knew we'd got an unidentified dead woman. Should have been sharp enough to think twice. She's been let off lightly.'

Barrett chose neither to agree, nor disagree. No sense admitting he thought the chief inspector had gone soft. 'So what's up then,' he said. 'Have we got a lead?'

'We've a missing woman who's the right age, and near enough fits the description, and it'd be handy to have you along when I see the neighbour—if you can spare the time.' Seeing Barrett's suspicious look and adding, 'Nothing pressing with Guffey, is there; nothing that's likely to send you rushing off?'

'Not for a bit, not 'til DVLR get back on names and addresses.' Smiling a bit, thinking that when they did and with a bit of luck, he'd know who'd set Guffey up. 'Are we, er, getting off straight away then or waiting for Smythe?'

'Waiting,' said Morrissey, gathering up loose papers. Barrett picked one out and put it on top of the pile.

'I was having a squint through while you were busy. Looks like the widow was right about Simms. He'd been got at. Digitalis. Foxglove extract that, isn't it? I tend to get mixed up between that and nightshade.'

'Nightshade gives belladonna, not digitalis,' said Morrissey, picturing foxglove in his mind. Fairy bells. Still some in his garden, innocently growing down at the bottom by the wall, the purple unmistakeable. Rare for them to be still in bloom in September, rarer still in October; but this year's hot summer had kept them going right up to last week when the weather changed.

There'd been a bright purple splash behind Claire's home, too.

'Going to tell her then? Mrs Simms.'

'When the time's right,' said the chief inspector, wondering when that would be. Then Barrett's telephone rang and Morrissey left him alone with it. When he came back from talking to Osgodby the detective sergeant was sitting silently, the telephone in front of him, his hands resting on it, head bowed. Barrett had believed things were going well, winding up nicely, and hadn't given much thought to Azar once he knew the boy was on the mend, and off the respirator. Now the telephone call had come from the hospital, hours later than it should have done, wrapped up in apologies for an administrative cock-up.

'Something happened, Neil?' Barrett seemed to shake himself like a tired dog, pushing up from the desk, playing with the points of his waistcoat, fingering his moustache, sure signs that something had sapped the detective sergeant's confidence. He didn't expect the state to last for long; Barrett had a habit of bouncing back fast. But while they lasted, Barrett's anxiety states could be a trial. 'Get it off your chest, Neil,' he commanded, 'whatever it is.'

'Azar died, a couple of hours ago,' said Barrett. 'Secondary brain haemorrhage. Seems funny to think we'd nothing to do two weeks back, and now we've got three murders and a parcel of public fraud to go at. There's no justice in it, is there, sir?' Pulling down savagely again on the grey wool-worsted, not wanting to have to face the Khalids, but knowing as investigative officer he would have to do that, and dreading it already.

GORDON HADN'T expected to find Thewlis in his living room, or to be met by the straight-arm-fend-off that sent him teetering and let his father-in-law get past him. Not for long though—getting his balance back and turning to the door. Then he heard the quiet gurgle of Monica's scream, and gave up on ideas of pursuit when he saw what Thewlis had done. All he could think of then was that he had to get her into an ambulance before Angie came home and saw her. Telephoning first, before he went to Monica, frightened out of his wits when he did. Saying whatever came into his head, babbling almost.

'Oh Christ, I'll kill him for this. I will, I swear I will.' Taking her hand, rubbing it, patting it. 'You'll be all right, mam, ambulance'll be here in a bit. You'll be all right, love. Promise you will. D'you hear me? I promise. You know me, Gordon, don't break promises. You know that.' His hands shaking because she hadn't moved since he went to her. 'He'll never do it again, love, never. I'll put the bugger away for so long he'll be carried out in a box. Just hang on, mam. Just hang on. Won't be long. Think about Angie, Angie and the baby.' Rubbing her hand again, squeezing it in his own. Where the hell was the sodding ambulance? Only half a bloody mile. What took so long? Hearing the siren, louder and louder until the sound filled the room, and being unable to move, frozen on his knees afraid to let go of her hand.

HILDA'S KITCHEN was full of the smell of baking; tangy yeast from bread and the rich syrup of fruit pies mingled with the spicier scent of cinnamon scones and seed cake. Barrett's food-sensitive nose was twitching even before he went inside and got the full blast of it.

'Seed cake,' he said, still sniffing. 'My gran used to make that, regular.'

'I'll make a pot of tea then, to go with it,' said Hilda.

'They'll not have time,' said Tom.

''Course they will. I've told 'em nothing yet!' Turning up the gas under the kettle.

Morrissey said, 'No. Very kind of you, but no,' with a firmness that normally got results. 'Like your husband says, we haven't time. What I do want from you is for you to tell me about this neighbour of yours.'

'You can try a bit of seed cake then while I'm doing it. Tom, get the tea made while I cut this cake up. Come on, then. It's not me what's wasting time now, is it.' Looking at Morrissey. 'I want a cup of tea before I go in next door.'

Thunder rolled around the kitchen and stayed her hand in its cutting. 'Mrs Garfitt!' the chief inspector roared. 'First I want to hear about your neighbour, second I'll want the key to her house. Is that understood?'

Her husband turned off the cold water tap and set the kettle down. 'I told you,' he said. 'I told you they wouldn't have time.'

'Their loss,' said Hilda stoically, setting aside the cake knife. 'Her name was Lilian, Lilian Carver, and she was a nice woman, lovely and cheerful, wouldn't have hurt a fly.' Pushing past him to the back door and shrugging into a short jacket. 'Come on, then, if you're in that much of a hurry,' she said, opening the door. 'But it's no use thinking I'm letting you in there on your own, because I'm not. Lilian wouldn't have liked me to do that at all.'

THIRTY-SIX

LILIAN HAD never gone for style, and her house was a hotch-potch of things bought because she liked them, and never mind if they fitted in or not. Colours clashed with cheerful abandon. A Royal Doulton milkmaid stood next to a bottle of coloured sands from the Isle of Wight. Plaster ducks flew across the wall to get a closer look at Leda and the Swan hanging over the fireplace.

'Lil thought life was a bit of a laugh,' Hilda said, itching to take a duster to the shelf. 'Used to say, ''Might as well get what you can out of it 'cos it'll only kick you in the face.'' Not that I agreed with her. I mean, I've always found if you live respectable you get by. Expect you've found that as well. Wouldn't do though, not for Lil, wanted to get a little place at the seaside, she said, spend her old age watching kids on the sands. I said to her, I said, Lil, you should get married and have some of your own, but she wouldn't, said it wasn't fair having kids without them getting any say in it.' Her eyes defied him. '*I* liked her,' she said, 'and I'm not having anything bad said about her.'

'Why would anyone do that?' asked Morrissey mildly as Barrett went upstairs. Hilda's eyes followed the detective sergeant. She didn't know what sort of things Lilian had got up to, but she hoped there wasn't anything to make her look bad. Wondering if she ought to have made the bed up so it looked respectable. 'Can't think why she stripped it,' she muttered under her breath, not knowing Morrissey's sharp ears.

'Stripped what?'

'Nothing,' said Hilda.

'We need help, not hindrance.'

'I'm not hindering,' said Hilda. 'You've asked me nothing yet.'

'Yes, I have.'

'She hadn't left sheets on the bed, that's all. I was just thinking I should have done it before your lot came so it looked respectable.'

'I'm glad you didn't,' said Morrissey, having viewed the brass plate with a jaundiced eye. 'Kitchen through there, is it?'

'Surgery,' said Hilda. 'Wasn't just a kitchen.' Bustling round in front of him.

'Don't open the door,' Morrissey snapped.

Hilda's hand drew back. 'Don't see why not. I was in there yesterday, tidying round.'

God give him strength! Going in ahead of her and blinking at the pristine whiteness that met him, noting the wall hung with certificates and aged herbal, a shelf of empty size-graded medicine bottles, and another filled with made-up potions neatly labelled. Lilian Carver really had been a herbalist. Feeling slightly ashamed.

'Did wonders for my arthritis,' said Hilda sadly. 'Don't know what I'll do now. Have to go into Leeds somewhere, I shouldn't wonder. Can't think who'd have wanted to do that to Lil. Must have been right off his head, whoever it was.' Adding with a faint glimmer of hope: ''Course, I could be wrong couldn't I? It might not be Lilian at all.'

'What about photographs?'

'I've got her and me at Scarborough that Tom took on a day-trip. You can have that.'

'If you can find it, it'd be a help.'

'Now?'

'Sooner the better.'

Watching her brisk exit with profound relief but knowing she'd be back. Comparing in his mind the randomness of Lilian Carver's living room with the neat orderliness that surrounded him now, the chief inspector marvelled that both belonged to the same woman. Hearing Barrett and Smythe moving overhead, he wondered what the upstairs rooms were like, impatient to find something that would tie the woman who had lived in this house to the woman in the canal, because without establishing a link he couldn't bring in the forensic team. He riffled through the herbal's pages, read the labels on the potion bottles, and found most were simples. Peppermint for dyspepsia, aniseed for coughs, elderflower for influenza, and horsetail for cystitis. A few hundred years ago, she'd have been burned at the stake for gathering such herbs and curing the sick. Thinking about that as he eased open the cupboard under the shelves and found Lilian's dispensing register, meticulously kept in rounded, childishly careful handwriting, flicking back through the last few pages and seeing Thewlis's name come leaping out at him.

Foxglove and thorn-apple. Running his finger across the page to the column headed *Symptoms,* and reading: 'To put down troublesome dog.' Checking the date and finding Lilian had made it up two days before Simms died. Was that how Thewlis had seen the planning officer—as a troublesome dog? Getting a clear plastic bag from his briefcase and sealing the register inside, labelling it and taking it out to his car, able now he'd found his link to call out the forensic team, watching Hilda and her husband come out of their own house and walk back to Lilian's as he called in, catching up with them at the door and seeing things begin to fall quietly into place.

Hilda said, 'This is that photograph.' And as soon as he saw the red-brown hair, Morrissey knew it was the same hair he'd seen in the post-mortem room.

'Thank you,' he said. 'I won't lose it, but I'll have to keep it for a bit.'

'Doesn't matter if you do,' said Tom. 'I can get another off the negative.'

'It's her, isn't it?' said Hilda. 'I could tell when you looked at it. Lord in Heaven, what a terrible way to go.'

'Did she have many men friends?' asked the chief inspector. 'Was it something she talked about?'

'She was a good-looking woman, of course she had men friends. Wouldn't be normal if she didn't, would it?'

'More than one then. Did they come to see her here, or did she meet them somewhere else?'

'Came here mostly: Homebody in some ways, I suppose. 'Course they weren't all men friends, some of them only came for therapy. Like it says on her brass plate.'

'What kind of therapy?'

'Ooh, I don't know; some of it was herbal.' Knowing very well what Lilian did but refusing to be disloyal. 'Couldn't be one of them anyway, could it? I mean it'll turn out to be a stranger, pulling her into a car or something like that. That sort of thing's always getting in the papers now. Don't know what's got into men; never acted like that when I was young. I could go anywhere then, safe as houses. Didn't even need to lock doors.'

'Why don't you go and put the kettle on, love,' said Tom. 'Chief Inspector won't say no to that cup of tea now. Go on now, off you go, I'll come and give a hand in a minute.' Hilda didn't argue. Morrissey watched her walk away with disbelief. Tom said, 'Happen if we go inside she'll not get as upset, seeing us. If that's all right with you, of course.' Going in through the door anyway without waiting for Morrissey to say if it was or it wasn't. 'She was a prostitute, you see. Hilda knows that and it upsets her, thinking it might get out. Very discreet, though, was Lil. Half a dozen regulars and never any trouble.'

'What about names?'

'I never asked. Lil was a grand lass, Chief Inspector. Hilda wouldn't have taken to her if she wasn't. I saw 'em come, and I saw 'em go, and we never had no trouble. Far as I remember Mary Magdalene was in't same line of work, and I'm not in't business of casting stones. I don't mean I'm not willing to cooperate, like. Come up with a name and I'll tell you yes or no, but I'm not doing it t'other way round.' Peering past Morrissey. 'Hilda's back' The chief inspector turned his head. Hilda stopped a couple of feet away and looked at him.

Morrissey went back outside and softened his face.

'Something to tell me, Mrs Garfitt?'

She turned her back on the open door, folding her arms across her chest, hands gripping her shoulders. Morrissey took two strides and came level with her. She squinted up at him. 'Can't do Lilian any harm now, can it, gossip, if it could, I'd not be talking to you.'

'I know that,' said the chief inspector.

'And if I don't tell, I'll not get to sleep easy.'

'Cleft stick,' agreed Morrissey.

'She'd got this client that'd been coming about two months and it'd been a mistake, Lil said, taking him on. Scared the day-lights out of her, she said. So, I said, tell him to go somewhere else for what he wants. Daft not to. My Tom'll sort him out, I said, if he gives any trouble like. Anyway he come round about eight, Monday night, and he left a bit after ten, and I don't know who he was 'cos I never saw his face.'

'And Lilian was all right when he left?'

'Must have been.... "Bye, Lil love," he shouts. "Thanks for everything." And he drives off. So he's the only one I know might have had a grudge.'

'It's helpful to know,' Morrissey said. 'Thanks.'

'Was it quick?' Hilda asked. 'What he did to her—was it quick?'

'Yes,' Morrissey lied. 'It was quick.'

'I'll go get that tea made then,' she said, and shouted 'I thought you were coming to help!' at her husband.

'Two minutes,' Tom said. 'I'll catch up.' Looking at Morrissey when the chief inspector came back to him. 'Tell you about the awkward customer, did she then?' he said. 'Thought she would, given time.'

'Lilian was all right when he left. That's what your wife tells me.'

'Only because she heard him shout goodnight, not because she saw Lil. Anyway, Hilda was asleep when he come back.'

Morrissey's ears pricked. 'When?' he said sharply.

'Near two when he left; don't know when he came. I've got this thing what I call prospects trouble, know what I mean? Gets me up to pee, every flaming night. Anyway, when I comes back I hear this car door bang, so I look out the front window and his car's moving away.'

'You didn't see Lilian?'

'No.'

'And you don't know who the man was?'

'I never said that. Hilda didn't know him, but I bloody did, grew up in' same village, bastard he was, and fathered by another. Only good thing his pa ever did was die, and he took too bloody long doing it an' all. It were Jack Thewlis's car and I'll stand up in court and say it, if you like. I've seen him here before.'

Thewlis again!

'Thanks,' said Morrissey. 'I think I might have a little talk with him.'

'Well, don't go before you've drunk Hilda's tea,' said Tom, 'or I'll never hear t'end of it. I'd better give her a hand.' Looking with curiosity at the white police van that pulled up as he went in his own gate, counting heads as they came out if it, and wondering if Hilda had got that many mugs.

THIRTY-SEVEN

THEWLIS KNEW he'd gone too far; was shaking so much when he got back in his car that he couldn't drive it. Bitch! Bitches! All of 'em, bloody bitches, dragging him down. A heavy hand, like his father, only way to handle women; else they got too clever. A good hiding had never done him any harm. *Brass buckle for thee, lad. Tha wait 'til I coom home t'neet.* Women's faces everywhere he turned his head, in the car with him. *Slags.* Get away, Mother; it weren't me in your belly when you wed him—it were Arthur. Lilian's empty eyes. Whore! Batting at empty air, sweat running from his armpits and trickling round his belly. God! he needed a bloody drink: drink'd clear 'em out of his head. Had he killed her? Would have if bloody Gordon hadn't come. Saved his bacon there. Monica'd never give evidence, not in court. Never had. Always blamed herself, silly cow. Hearing a siren wail, and gripping the seat to ease his shakes; turning the key but unable to keep his jumping foot still enough to use the clutch pedal. Sweating even more as the wail grew louder, until he saw the white of an ambulance and knew it wasn't the police. Silly, bloody fool, Gordon. Drop of brandy and a sticking plaster, that's all she'd needed, not a bloody ambulance. Man had a right to keep his wife in line. Strong as a bloody cart-horse, Monica. Been thumped before and got over it fast enough.

Memory coming back, rushing into his head like a tide. He hadn't just thumped her though, had he. He'd done a sight more than that. Her fault, though. All of it, her fault. Throwing it out like that about Lilian—her fault. What were they bloody doing in there? Should have been out now. Then seeing them come, not seeing Monica though, just a mound of red blanket before the doors slammed and the wailing siren started up again. The shaking quieted. Not dead. Wouldn't waste a siren on a dead woman. Waiting a few minutes more until his mind had control again before he drove home.

In the ambulance with Monica, Gordon's mind ran like a mouse on a wheel. He kept thinking it might have been Angie who'd found her mother, picturing the state she'd have been in if she had. What would have happened to the baby? He'd heard about women losing babies when they'd had a shock. He couldn't keep it from her, though. She'd want to be with her mother. He listened to the faint hiss of oxygen feeding through the plastic mask. She hadn't moved since he'd found her. Didn't look like his mother-in-law—her face was grotesque. His throat ached, his eyes burned, his head throbbed with the anguish of it all.

Always slow to anger, the rage he felt was something new, all he wanted was to find Thewlis and pound him to a pulp. Glad Angie had been spared all this, clinging on to the hard and slippery seat as they swayed round a fast corner and turned into the hospital, remembering only when Monica was rushed through Casualty surrounded by doctors and nurses that when Angie got home she'd find blood pooled on the rug and splashed across the hearth. Hearing himself cry out at the thought of her being there alone, frightened by the sight and smell of it.

BARRETT WAS DRIVING with the kind of circumspection he always practised when chauffeuring Morrissey's car. No fancy braking to cut a dash at corners—he saved that for his own Escort. Turning off the main road and seeing just one other car in front, closing the gap a little before it turned left into Rook's Lane.

'I think that's him, sir, Thewlis.'

'Let's not risk spooking him, then. Hang back a bit and let's get him home and out of his car.'

'Yes, sir.' Easing off the accelerator.

From the back seat Smythe started up: 'Sir, this exhibition van...'

'Later!'

'But, sir...'

'It'll keep, Smythe. Let's get this done first.'

'Think we've got him, then, sir?' asked Barrett.

'Oh, yes,' said Morrissey. 'I think we've got him, wriggle or not,' jolting back in his seat as they rounded a bend and braked hard.

'Bloody tractors!' Barrett tried to see round it and failed; flashed his lights at the driver.

'Not much use doing that,' the chief inspector said mildly, 'not when he's got nowhere to go except a ditch.'

Ahead of them and out of sight, Thewlis garaged his car, the three-parts empty Glenfyddich on the shelf next to the anti-freeze drawing him like a magnet. He drank as if it were ale, not whisky, a long draught that brought some of his belligerence back, squatting on his heels with it in the greying light, not surprised when he heard car wheels scattering gravel at the bottom of the drive. Bloody fool Gordon wouldn't have kept his mouth shut; drinking again while he waited for whatever pink-faced bobby they'd sent to come and find him, watching the wind blow shreds of burnt paper from under the incinerator. When there were no footsteps he vaguely wondered why it was taking so long, unaware yet that it was Morrissey who had come for him, or that news of Monica had only just been relayed to the chief inspector.

Morrissey sat sphinx-like controlling his anger, with Smythe impatient on the back seat and Barrett staring silently through the windscreen. The detective sergeant was exercising discretion where once he would have sallied in without caution; easier for him to guess, now, how Morrissey felt. Didn't he feel the same about Azar?

When the chief inspector got out of the car the wind whipped his trouser bottoms and flapped his jacket, pushing against the open door and almost taking it out of his hand. Against the lowering cloud base a bird—rook?— struggled to make the safety of a tall poplar. The angle of its wings against the wind and its movement across the sky gave it the appearance of a hasty sideways scuttling. It veered and dropped and almost missed the tree as another gust blew it off course. The wind's direction was changing again, coming northerly now. Mike's first game as captain was on Saturday; looking up at the sky and hoping for his son's sake the weather would get better and not worse.

'Come on then,' he said gruffly. 'Let's get it over with,' and moved off towards the flapping side door of the garage.

Thewlis looked at him, but made no effort to get up on his feet. 'Huh. Sent you for bloody errand boy, have they? Well, ask what you like, but you'll get no answers. What happens between a man and his wife is private business.'

Morrissey said evenly, 'I'm arresting you on suspicion of involvement in the murder of Richard Simms, and the death of Lilian Carver. You are not obliged to say anything unless you wish to do so, but what you say may be put into writing and given in evidence.'

'You're bloody mad!' said Thewlis. 'Witch-hunting. You'll not keep me locked up, I've got friends—hear that— *VIPs* a bloody sight further up than you three monkeys. Sod off and think about it.' Taking another swallow and grimacing when the liquid hit his throat.

Barrett took the bottle from his hand.

'Give it back!' Thewlis grabbed and near overbalanced, found himself heaved upright by Barrett on one side and Smythe on the other.

'Shove him in the car,' said the chief inspector contemptuously.

Half-way back into Malminster, Thewlis complained about a painful throat. A bit further along he doubled over and clutched his stomach. Smythe pulled him back against the seat and saw the sweat. 'Looks poorly,' he said.

Morrissey half-turned and wondered if it was just drink that had done it. Thewlis rubbed at his chest. 'I need a bloody doctor.'

Barrett glanced in his rear-view mirror. 'Coronary?' he muttered. Thewlis doubled over and vomited on Smythe's expensive shoes.

'Better go via Casualty,' said Morrissey unwillingly. 'Let's not give him a chance to cry mistreatment.'

'Don't think that's much on his mind right now,' said Barrett as the noises increased.

Gordon was still sitting on an orange plastic chair waiting for news, relieved that Angie hadn't got home before a patrol car got there, and so hadn't seen the carnage in their neat front room. Would *never* see it. The pretty young WPC who'd come into Casualty with Angie had taken a look round the walking wounded and convinced her it would be better for the baby's sake to wait in the visitors' canteen. 'Much nicer,' she said with a brilliant smile for Gordon. 'Quieter and no smells. And when your mother's well enough to have a talk, I'm sure your husband will come straight down and find us.'

'Soon as the doctor gives the word,' he said, stretching his stiff lips into what he hoped Angie saw as a smile.

'Tell me again she's all right,' said Angeline.

'She's all right,' Gordon lied. 'Go on now. Go have a cup of tea.'

Now, seeing Thewlis come in on rubber legs between the two policemen, he was glad Angie wasn't there to witness it. Rage that had simmered suddenly boiled over. Bastard! He flung himself at his father-in-law, fists indiscriminate in where the blows landed, sinking one heavily into the quivering paunch before Morrissey's great hands hauled him off. Seeing Thewlis's vomit arc across the floor. 'I'll kill him,' he told Morrissey. 'Just give me five minutes and I'll kill the bloody bastard.'

The chief inspector, holding him easily, watched Thewlis's face turn blue and wondered if he might not have done that already.

THIRTY-EIGHT

'NOTHING'S EVER easy, is it?' said Barrett with a certain amount of bitterness. 'Makes you think there's malicious intent in the way things continually screw up. Everything coming together, Thewlis bang to rights, and what's he do? Swallows paraquat and ends up in a hospital bed.' Parking Morrissey's car in its regular spot. 'Shall you charge him with assault?'

'Thewlis?'

'The son-in-law.'

'No reliable witnesses, have we?' said the chief inspector gruffly. 'Let's see how it goes.' Getting out of the car with the chill-fingered wind whipping up his hair.

'Snow next, I shouldn't wonder,' said Barrett, still gloomy as they went inside.

'Organise a relief for Smythe, will you,' said Morrissey. 'I want him back here. There's ends to tie up.' One foot on the stairs when the desk sergeant stopped him going any further.

'Sir! Glad I caught you. Inspector Newton said to tell you he'd be in the canteen.'

Where else? thought Morrissey, as he changed direction. And he wouldn't be eating rabbit food either.

Newton wasn't. He'd been filling the inner man on fry-up—was still at it when the chief inspector joined him. 'Have a chip,' said Newton, cheerfully nudging the plate. 'Go on. You're nowt but a shadow. Richardson got wind. Knew that, did you? Thought you would.' Satisfied when Morrissey nodded. 'He's got a little friend in a blue uniform. Somebody's been playing bad apple. He'll have to get slapped down.'

'He'll have to get booted out and charged,' said Morrissey, 'and I want us to get that clear now. There's going to be no rehabilitation and forgiveness on offer.'

'Sounds personal. Done something I don't know about yet, has he?'

'I'll tell you that when Smythe gets back. It's guesswork until then.' Watching Newton placidly stuffing his face. 'Who turned him in?'

The fork to mouth movement stopped. 'I've got your perspiring friend Lowry in custody,' he said. 'Bending over backwards to co-operate, he'd wear his Y-fronts on his head if I asked him to.' Starting the rhythmic transference of food again. 'I heard about Thewlis. Think I'll get to question him? Lethal stuff, paraquat.'

'He'll survive,' said Morrissey darkly.

'Devil looking after his own again then. Took it deliberate, did he?' Seeing Barrett at the counter and putting his hand up.

Morrissey said, 'He's facing double-murder charges, but I don't think it'd give him a rush of conscience.'

'Don't like him much, do you? Lowry's signed a statement. Greedy little turd. Seemed to think I'd go easy on him if he was a good boy.' Breaking off when Barrett sat down. 'What you got there then—tea, coffee or can't tell?' Barrett tried it and grimaced. 'Here, take a chip, take taste off.' Barrett picked one, well salted, and went back to the counter. Newton watched with dolorous eyes.

'Say anything about Simms?'

'Oh, he'd a lot to say about him. Didn't know poor bugger'd been put down and he's scared shitless. Says Simms had conscience trouble, all right, when it was just bending rules, but started making noises when he found out about the Asian business. Pretty much the way you'd worked it out for yourself, isn't it? Clever beggar.' Sighing, 'Ah well,' and patting his stomach. 'Can't manage anymore if I'm going to be any good t'wife tonight.' Winking lewdly as he got up, dropping a heavy hand on Barrett's shoulder as the detective came back with a better-tasting brew, and telling him, 'You want to be careful who you hang around with, you know. Dirt's transferable.' Shifting his attention back to Morrissey before Barrett could get a word in and waving a hand at the ceiling. 'Want me to give sir this latest bit of bad news? Seems to be in my territory more than yours.'

'Feel free,' said the chief inspector wholeheartedly. 'I've off-loaded my share already.'

'What bad news?' quivered Barrett suspiciously.

Newton tapped his nose. 'Ranks above inspector,' he said, and left it for Morrissey to explain.

'What's he on about?' Barrett said.

Morrissey sidestepped. 'Found a relief for Smythe?'

'Woods came in, so I sent him. He hadn't got anything out of his trawl. About Inspector Newton . . . ?'

'I'll shout you to a chip butty and a pot of tea,' said Morrissey, 'if you bring 'em upstairs.'

'Done,' said Barrett, who never quibbled if it meant depriving his stomach. Time enough when Morrissey was mellow and fed to bring up Newton again.

GERALD MASON was pouring himself a whisky in his Pimlico flat, freshly showered and expensively suited for his dinner date, unsurprised when the doorbell trilled its double tone, expecting it would be Annabel come early. Lovely, willowy blond Annabel, who looked better on his arm than a dumpy Yorkshire wife, and was a damn sight more entertaining in bed. Opening the door with a smile that lost some of its pleasure when he found two detectives and a special branch officer on his doorstep instead. Not worried at seeing them there; there were always security alarms of one kind and another causing brouhahas. Throwing open the door and waving them inside.

'What's it this time, lads? Bomb? Personal threat?' Lifting his drink in invitation. 'Fancy a whisky?'

'No, sir.' Going straight on. 'Gerald Mason, I have a warrant for your arrest on charges of public fraud and conspiracy to corrupt.' Reading him his rights while the special branch man watched stolidly, having heard it all before, and not doubting for a minute that he'd hear it all again.

Mason moved backwards. 'Ridiculous! Never heard anything as daft. What's it about, then? Practical joke? I'm not laughing if it is.'

'It isn't any joke, sir.'

'Stuff and nonsense,' said Mason dismissively. 'I've been in Parliament twenty-five years; I'm not a penny ante crook to try scare tactics on. Here'—tearing the warrant across—'bloody silly nonsense.'

'I'm afraid I'll still have to ask you to come with us, sir.'

'Well I'll not! Damned if I will, it's a cock-up, a mistake. Who's laid charges and on what misinformation? Some anonymous crank telephone call, I suppose. No. Go back and get your facts straight. I've got a dinner engagement'

'Certain other arrests have already been made inside your Malminster constituency, sir. If you wouldn't mind now, getting your coat...'

'Of course I'd damn well mind!'

'It's fairly chilly out, sir.' Waiting impassively.

Appealing to the special branch man. 'Can't you persuade them it's a mistake? Come on, they're barking up the wrong tree, man, you know me well enough.'

'I'm sorry, sir. Officially you've already been placed under arrest. My advice is to co-operate fully. I should get your coat if I were you, sir.' Meeting Mason's eyes without sympathy. Bad enough for politicians to be liars without being bent as well. Waiting imperviously for Mason to realise there were no options.

'I want my solicitor,' the MP said stiffly.

'Expected you would, sir.'

Giving in and having to walk out onto the street in procession with them. The humiliation of being bundled into a police car as Annabel climbed out of a taxi, her eyes round blue question marks. Sick in the pit of his stomach as the car sped past familiar buildings. Part of his mind thinking there'd have to be a bye-election, while the rest of it beat frantically to find some small loophole through which he might escape.

'THAT LIST FROM DVLR's on your desk,' said Morrissey, thereby letting himself off the hook for questions as Newton slid from Barrett's mind.

Quietly satisfied when the tactic worked, the chief inspector gave his mind over to white bread and hot, greasy chips and tried not to feel guilty. One butty wouldn't make any difference to his health; it wasn't as if he ate them every meal. Trying to think how to excuse an excuse.

At his own desk Barrett ate one-handedly, his mind on other things. Kevin's book had turned up three goods vehicles he hadn't known about before, and a name and address for the owner of a G-registration Montego.

The detective sergeant's spirits began to revive. It had been worth paying out two quid after all, thinking to himself that this name was the one he'd been waiting for; the end of the trail. Vic Duttin, Manningham Lane, Bradford. Getting the name checked through the police computer and coming up blank on previous convictions. Surprised at that, feeling the first niggle and suppressing it fast. Contacting

Bradford CID and asking for Duttin to be picked up by them. Grinning into his now near-cold coffee in the certain knowledge that by this time tomorrow he'd have all the answers.

LOOKING AT HER father, Angeline found it hard to feel compassion. She had been told he might die, that the poison could have reached his liver and kidneys, that his lungs might already be damaged, that although his treatment had been prompt it still might not be enough, and she had listened to the doctor without feeling anything except that it was no more than her father deserved. He looked ill; he looked *awful*, pallid and clammy, and she said no, no she wouldn't go in to see him. Enough that she had looked through the window in the door. If he died she'd dance on his grave. Seeing herself, arms outflung, slowly rotating, pounding the earth down on him with her feet, cursing him with her woman's magic never to be born again. Believing for a few breaths of fantasy that she held the power to do that, the smile transforming her plain face.

Morrissey had talked to her. She'd wondered why the height and breadth of him didn't intimidate her, and then, watching the movement of his face as he spoke, guessed that he was deliberately softening himself so as not to frighten her. Angeline had been grateful, but she could no more tell him how paraquat had got into her father's whisky than she could tell him how the devil had got into his head. Agreeing that it could have been poured from one bottle to the other by a third party, but denying her mother might have been the one to do it. Then remembering with a kind of apprehending horror how she herself had changed things. Her mother hadn't walked out of her home because of a final act of violence, but because she, Angeline, had told her what Jack Thewlis had done to his daughter—and made his daughter do to him—needing even then to talk of 'his daughter,' instead of crying out, 'He did it to me, Mummy, he did it to me!' *So much guilt on her shoulders.* Crossing her hands over her belly, keeping her baby safe, she cried out: 'I hate him! Oh, God, I *hate* him!'

There'd been compassionate knowledge on Morrissey's face.

She turned her back on the viewing window. Dialysis might clean her father's blood, but what about his hands and the filth in his soul.

'If he dies,' she said dispassionately, 'I'll bury him. Except for that I don't want to know.'

OSGODBY WAS IN a peeve, and Barrett thought he might join him. Where had all the supposed co-operation gone? First Smythe had come back looking surprised that Morrissey wanted to hear about the exhibition van, having made three abortive attempts to pass on his knowledge already. Barrett hadn't been paying much attention until Lister's name came up, then his ears had pricked automatically like one dog scenting another.

'Sure he's the only one after two-thirty?' asked the chief inspector.

'Yes, sir. Sir, about Inspector Lister, is there...?' Cut off short when Osgodby came, blowing as hard as the wind outside.

'Both knew about it, did you? Didn't think fit to tell me, though? Had to find out from Inspector Newton, not even in my Division either, is he. How do you think that makes me look? Chief Superintendent, Head of Division, and I'm last to know we've got a bloody rotten apple! Well? Get on with it then. Explain!'

'I'm sorry, sir,' said Barrett, up on his feet and standing stiffly. 'But I don't know what it is I'm supposed to know.'

'You, Chief Inspector, you knew about Lister?' Giving his full scowl to Morrissey, now standing but relaxed.

'Newton told me five minutes before he told you.'

'Ahh.' Subsiding a little. 'Didn't know before that?'

'No. I'd a suspicion but no name. Yesterday I got a physical description.' *Was* it yesterday? 'DC Smythe has just confirmed it has to be Lister's.'

'Right.' Cooling down rapidly, rocking on his heels a little, locking his fingers and producing explosive cracks. 'Briefing me now, then?'

'Five minutes?'

'Right.' Faint embarrassment showing, closing the door behind him less forcefully than he'd opened it.

'Pissed up the wrong tree,' said Smythe.

Barrett said, 'Dirt rubs off?' Prickly.

'Both from Bradford, that's all Newton meant. He didn't know Lister had had his hand out in Bradford too. But you did, didn't you? You should have shopped him before, stopped him in his tracks before we got lumbered,' Morrissey said severely.

'Oh, yes?' the detective sergeant came back, trenchant for once. 'Young PC Plod, barking at a senior officer who'd got it all sussed? Better to shut up and get transferred out.'

'Do that now, would you?'

'No, I wouldn't. Now I'd have his collar, I didn't know how to, then.'

Smythe listening to them with growing discomfort, knowing he'd made much the same mistake. Squaring up to put it right.

'Sir, I'd started to tell you before the Chief Super came in. about the briefcase.'

Morrissey's neck stiffening visibly. 'Go on.' Tone silky quiet. Barrett, familiar with that, feeling suddenly sorry for

Smythe, and the detective constable picking up on it, confidence evaporating.

'It didn't seem worth mentioning, sir, at the time. When I went round to ask if any of our lot had seen it—the briefcase—in Simms' car, Barclay thought he had. Or at least, he thought he'd seen somebody put *a* briefcase in a police car's boot.' Seeing Nemesis waiting in the chief inspector's face, and saying quickly, 'He was right round the other side, sir, Barclay, with the SOCOs. I thought he'd made a mistake, but I'm not sure now, sir.'

'It was Inspector Lister he saw?'

'Yes, sir.' Waiting for the sky to fall.

'Get yourself home and out of my sight,' Morrissey thundered, thinking of the time that had been wasted. 'I'll deal with you tomorrow morning. In my office, first thing. Go on, then, off with you!' Watching the quick flurry of two-tone shoes, catching an odd little snort from Barrett, and knowing the sergeant was pleased to see Smythe on the receiving end instead of himself. Peering through the wood and seeing only trees—Lister, Thewlis, and Lilian Carver linked together by Simms' briefcase. Frustratedly breaking up the picture he'd built in his head and rearranging the pieces again. Swearing mightily as he went upstairs.

THE SOCO team combing Thewlis's home found Monica's shredded clothes, and chased fragments of burnt paper still blowing out from under the incinerator. When they lifted off the zinc top with its little round chimney, there were shreds of pink poly-cotton fused to scraps of dark wool-worsted. It was emptied with care, its contents bagged. Flames seemed to have burned fiercely round the sides leaving a cone in the centre unconsumed. Pieces of roughly torn paper had survived only lightly charred, some close-typed, some hand-written, some officially headed.

The whisky and the paraquat had been taken for analysis before they got there, but there were other finds for SOCOs in Thewlis's garage—Lilian's neatly labelled bottle, a quarter full, stood next to a pewter hip-flask smelling of whisky. Both had been locked from sight in a metal wall-cupboard that took less than a minute to coax open.

There was much whistling and no long faces.

THIRTY-NINE

BARRETT'S CHEERFULNESS lasted until he found out Duttin's flat was empty as a sucked egg. all he could hope for now was that Duttin had left some good fingerprints, because it was certain sure he wouldn't have left a forwarding address with his neighbours.

Richardson gone, Duttin gone; telling himself the linkage offered some kind of evidence that the property dealer's money had paid for Guffey's death.

Fly away Peter, fly away Paul, and when one came back, so did the other. Would it work for him? Thinking they hadn't done much yet to find Richardson. What was the chief playing at? Why worry about little fish when a shark was getting away?

Looking at his watch. Eight o'clock. Nothing much more he could do tonight except circulate descriptions, nipping down to communications to do that and finding WPC Janet Yarby there busy with the big mainframe.

When she smiled, he automatically looked round to see who'd come in behind him, uneasy when he saw there was no one there. Two years of lusting mightily had taught Barrett that Janet Yarby never smiled at him unless it was a set-up. Tonight it seemed she did.

'We've had a result on this one already,' she said when he got to Richardson, watching the monitor screen fill up with lines of information. 'Yep, Interpol picked him up. He's being shipped back tomorrow. How's the new flat?'

'Who put out the alert?'

More tapping of keys. 'Inspector Newton did, this morning.'

'Wily beggar!' said Barrett under his breath, moving away from her, not remembering she'd asked about his flat until he was at the door and then turning belatedly: 'Come and see the flat for yourself,' he suggested, getting ready to slam the door if she laughed—as he knew she would.

'All right,' agreed his previously unreachable object of desire. 'Next time we're both off together,' she replied and smiled at him again.

There had to be a catch in it, somebody putting her up to smiling sweetly, Smythe, or Woodsy, or some other joker. Then again, on the other hand... letting an impossible scenario develop as he went back upstairs to the office.

Morrissey had just come off the telephone. He said, 'Internal Affairs are coming in first thing tomorrow; Lister's been suspended.'

'Nice to be told about it,' said Barrett, 'since nobody seems to be communicating with anybody else, and I've just heard Interpol have Richardson. Newton put a call out this morning. I think he might have briefed us, especially when he got a result.'

'Ah.'

'You mean he did?'

'I got it from Osgodby. Sorry, Neil. You weren't left out deliberately. It came through for Newton when he was up in Sir's office.'

'No great harm done either way, is there?' said Barrett. 'I suppose what counts is we've got him. Thought I might get on home unless there's something you want me to do first.'

'No,' said Morrissey, shoving up with his big hands. 'I'll come down with you. Lister'll keep until morning.' Walking out of the building companionably and getting into their separate cars, Barrett telling himself how Morrissey was

mellowing, and the chief inspector congratulating himself
that Barrett might just turn into a fair enough detective after all.

MARGARET'S TALK with her son hadn't gone exactly as she'd
planned. For one thing, Mike didn't want to be told he was
misjudging his father. Maybe it was the other way around
and his father was misjudging him; disappointed that his
mother didn't seem to have thought of that. Struggling with
a lot of things, half understanding some, not understanding others at all. Full of burgeoning hormones one minute
and spoiling for an argument, wanting to move backwards
into the safety of childhood the next. He didn't even begin
to know how to handle it all. All right for Katie. Girls didn't
have father problems.

Wishing he didn't either.

Exploding at his mother in anger and frustration. 'Tell me
what you want me to do? Polish his shoes, clean his car, act
like he's the great magician when he's pick, pick, pick, all
the bloody time. Don't tell me about how we're a family,
Mum. Tell him, he's the one who's forgotten. I'm going to
Pete's.' Leaving his favourite pudding on the table and
banging out of the house.

Margaret's stomach did a slow flip-flop.

When Morrissey got home she was curled in the big chair
reading a book, Elgar's *Variations* playing in the background. She looked glad to see him and stayed in the kitchen
with a cup of coffee while he ate, a habit that had always
been hers until these last fraught months when she'd stayed
distantly away. But it wasn't quite the same Margaret, because she wasn't telling him all the bits of gossip that she'd
picked up during the day, soothing him with her voice. Instead her hands were wrapped tightly around her mug and
her vision was fixed silently on some inner point of space.

He said, 'Katie out with Hicks again?'

'When are you going to start calling him Ian?'

'Not yet a while. Where's Mike?'

'At Pete's.' Hesitating. If peacemaking hadn't worked with her son, it probably wouldn't work with his father. Plunging in anyway. 'John, we have to talk about Mike. Things aren't getting any easier between the both of you. Maybe if you didn't jump on him so much...'

Guilt reared up and buried good intentions. Mike! Mother's boy! What about *him?* Slamming down knife and fork. 'Don't tell me how to act with Mike. I'll not have insolence out of him, not in my own home!'

'John, he isn't insolent!'

Seeing shock on Margaret's face, and boxing himself into a corner again. 'Yes, well, Mike never is in the wrong, is he? Not with you.' Watching Margaret get up quietly and go back to the sitting room. Shovelling food so he could go up to the quiet of his study. Sitting at the makeshift desk and feeling anger ebb into a kind of despair. Going back downstairs to say sorry, recognising something had to be done before the whole thing fell to pieces.

The oldest family member should be the most grown-up; gruff and spiky in apology because he knew he wasn't.

THEWLIS LAY propped up on pillows and plagued by torments. Bad enough that emetics and purgatives had left him nauseated and weak, without the shakes of alcohol withdrawal making his wretchedness worse. Hooked up to machines, sweating and trembling, craving for whisky, wanting to sleep and afraid to close his eyes, Hell snapped at his heels. His monkey brain broke loose from reason, throwing up images as solid as reality. The miner's cage dropping through darkness firm under his feet, wind whistling past his ears and his father waiting, burning in flames at the shaft

bottom, belt in hand and buckle white with heat, reaching
out to greet him, swinging the leather, buckle and strap bit-
ing into flesh, while Thewlis scorched and writhed in the
pain of it.

Opening his eyes drenched with sweat, pressing the bell
button, stringing words in an endless obscenity and falling
back into nightmare again. Lilian pirouetted, naked, sightless, laid down in a coffin and took on his face, drifting
through the dark when Monica came, bloody and weeping,
opening her mouth like a great red cave, moving toward it
excited and tumescent and seeing his father there bucking in
the flames.

Waking cold and shivering, convulsing on the bed.

MORRISSEY WAS already awake and listening to Margaret's
quiet breathing when the telephone chirruped. He had it at
the first note but Margaret still shifted and murmured in the
morning darkness. Sighing, the chief inspector spoke his
name, just the one word, 'Morrissey.' Said nothing else until the unemotional voice of the hospital registrar had finished, and then only, 'I'll come now; it'll be twenty minutes.'
Easing out of bed gently in case she'd fallen asleep again,
hearing her pad down the stairs as he shaved. Not unrepair-
able damage that he'd done last night then, not the final
straw, his load lightening just a little with that.

The aroma of percolating coffee reached upstairs and
speeded his movements; impossible not to make an attempt
at eating. Bolting a piece of toast, scalding his mouth,
picking up the soup flask and kissing her with awkward
tenderness, half of him wanting to be gone, the other half
wanting to linger, but the policeman winning as always.

All the hospital lights were on, the car-park near empty,
the big clock over the main entrance had its hands on seven.

Morrissey checked his watch and found it was five minutes ahead.

Thewlis had been moved into a side-room in sight of the nurses' station, he looked like the grey shell of himself, limp and bare chested, electrodes trailing over the bed. Ellis put out a long arm and backed Morrissey out into the corridor again, shutting the door behind them.

'I don't know the ins and outs of what he's done,' the registrar said, rubbing at his eyes, 'but his daughter's on the hospital premises and it'd be a help if she saw him.'

'Told her that, have you.'

'Yes. Told me the sooner he's dead the better all round and refused to come.'

'Is he going to die?'

'We all are.' Raising a hand. 'Sorry, it's been a long night following a long day, and another long day to come. I'm short on sleep. It was a big coronary.'

'Linked to the paraquat?'

'Nobody can be sure, but I'd say no, not directly. Early vomiting got shot of most of the stuff, and he's been washed out both ends and put on dialysis since then. The blood picture was good. If it hadn't been for this, I'd have bet on him being lucky.'

'And his chances now?'

'We're trying.'

'Not fifty-fifty then?' A shake of the head in reply. 'Can I talk to him?'

'I'd rather you talked to his daughter.'

'I need to talk to him,' said Morrissey.

'Five minutes, no more.' Opening the door and going back inside.

'Alone if possible.' Watching the nurses file out.

Ellis stayed, settling himself on a stool in one corner, and closing his eyes.

'Thewlis.' No movement. 'Thewlis!'

His eyes opened. 'Don't want me to die, do you, Morrissey. Spoil your fun.'

'Your wife isn't dead, I thought you should know that, take a bit off your conscience.'

A faint grimace that could have meant anything.

'Lilian Carver. Want to tell me about her?'

'A good fuck.' Sighing.

'But you killed her, and dumped her body? Why?'

'Accident that's all, accident. Didn't think she'd be found. Came to fetch me last night, brought a coffin. I'll not die, though. I dursn't, not with him waiting for me.'

'Who? Simms?'

'Father, father an' his strap.'

Ellis shifted in the corner and looked at his watch.

Morrissey said, 'Clear your conscience then, tell me what you've done. Lilian made digitalis up for you, she wrote it in her book. Is that how you killed Simms?'

A spark of anger came. 'Clever sodding bastard!'

Ellis said, 'That's enough for now.'

'One question,' said Morrissey. 'I'll not leave without it. How'd you give it to him?'

'Spirit of friendship,' said Thewlis and closed his eyes.

'Out,' said Ellis. 'That's it.'

FORTY

IT WAS LIKE a committee meeting, thought Morrissey, himself and Newton, Barrett and Osgodby, sitting at one end of the conference room table, facing Superintendent Lyle and Inspector Jackson from Internal Affairs, picking over Lister's bones before they buried him. Newton said his piece bland and unperturbed. The police were like everybody else, some honest, some not, and he had no iffy conscience about weeding out tares.

For Barrett it was a little different, working under Lister had been an experience he preferred to forget, and he wouldn't have been there at all without some arm-twisting from Morrissey. He looked what he was, nervous; back to a tugging of waistcoat and smoothing of moustache. The chief inspector noted the regression and had a prick of conscience; perhaps he shouldn't have made him speak up after all.

Still thinking about that when it came to his turn, having to marshall his thoughts, turn them back to the beginning of it all, setting out the background to Simms' near-perfect murder, marvelling that without Claire's refusal to accept what she was told none of it would have come out, Lowry would have found another dupe to take Simms' place, and Lilian Carver would still be swaying gently at the bottom of the canal.

'Lister must have been told specifically what to look for,' he said, 'probably by Thewlis, and when Simms' car was lifted from the water, he was seen to remove the dead man's briefcase and put it in his own vehicle. The witness was a police officer. The briefcase then passed into Thewlis's possession, and not long after that it was filled with rubble and used to weigh down the body of a woman named Lilian Carver in the Aire and Calder canal. I haven't yet established if Lister knew about Simms' murder, but I do have evidence that a telephoned threat to harm the widow's young daughter was made by him. I also believe information supplied by him, to a third party, led to the murder of a suspect sought by CID in connection with an attack on an Asian youth.'

'It could well be we'll want to take a look at the whole Division,' said Lyle. 'See who else had his hand out.'

'No one has,' snapped Osgodby. 'Not in my Division. Lister's been sniffed out by us. You'd be better occupied poking round where he came from.'

Lyle looked at Morrissey. 'Thank you, Chief Inspector, I don't think either you or Sergeant Barrett will be needed again.' Flapping a hand to tell Newton to sit down when the big man started to move.

'Now what?' said Barrett as they went downstairs. 'Do they bring Lister in or what?'

'Can't do any other, can they?' Morrissey replied. 'Not somebody to have running round loose.' Feeling frustrated again because all he could do now was wait.

If Thewlis died he'd have nothing to take to court; the files on both Simms and Lilian Carver would be closed. He told himself that even if that happened justice of a kind would have been done, but he knew that without an arrest and the slow due process of law which followed on, he would feel cheated.

And then there was the paraquat.

It couldn't have gotten into the whisky by accident.

Back to whether Thewlis survived his coronary. If he didn't he'd have died from an act of God, not from herbicide poisoning. But suppose it had been the other way round, and the paraquat had been lethal. Different kettle of fish then, and if the finger had pointed at Thewlis's wife, beaten half to death, used as a punch-bag for years—how would he feel then about the due process of law?

Gratified when a flock of Fax sheets landed on his desk, loaded with information he'd been waiting for. Reading the SOCO report first and understanding what Thewlis had meant by 'spirit of friendship'. A mark of the man's egotism to leave Lilian Carver's brew next to a hip flask of whisky he'd laced with it, even if they were locked in a cupboard. Imagining the scene in Simms' office, Thewlis pouring a death drink without turning a hair. Sighing with irritation; the one time he had all the evidence he needed he might never get to use it.

Usually, when a case was ending, winding up, he felt a kind of elation, but this time all he had was vague anger that he'd never really got to grips with it at all. Half resentful that Newton, with two big names in the bag, was already half-way to County court on groundwork done by Morrissey.

Barrett's telephone rang. The chief inspector remembered there was still a reprimand to be delivered to Smythe, and went off to find a quiet place to do it in.

MONICA SEEMED to have been drifting around in some strange and peaceful place. Twice she'd been wrenched away from it unwillingly to find herself in bed. The first episode had been brief, a faint realisation of crisp white sheets before she floated away again; the second time she'd been aware that Angeline was holding her hand. Trying to smile and move her lips had brought a pain so excruciating that she'd spun away from it like a Catherine wheel. Now she felt herself pulled again from the quiet limbo-land.

The first thing she was fully conscious of was a lower level of pain, the second that moving made it much worse.

Opening her eyes. Dark hair, white cap, blue dress. Cool, efficient hands lifting her. 'Not to worry, soon feel better. Did that hurt? No? Oh that's good.' Panic when her jaw wouldn't open. 'Can't talk yet, Mrs Thewlis, you're all wired up.' Cool clean water rising through a straw. A moment's bliss, closing her eyes, then memory flooding back and she wished with all her heart and mind that Jack was dead.

THERE WAS NOTHING quite so catching as despondency, thought Barrett, picking up on Morrissey's mood and falling into it without much of a struggle. All right for the chief inspector to grizzle. At least he'd got results and handed Newton a public fraud scandal to boot. There'd be a nice big favour Morrissey could call in from that sometime. But he, Barrett, had come away with almost nothing. He'd got Badger, but Badger was a tiddler; a nasty vicious tiddler but nothing like the piranha that had swum away. Win some, lose some—that was the philosophical way to view things. Every investigation didn't come to a neat ending, some stayed open for years; a pile of the sodding things, stacked in records, fished out and re-read when things were quiet. Now there'd be another one: Gerald Lee Harpin, known as Guffey. Nobody would point the finger, or say Barrett was to blame, not the way they would if he'd fallen down on the job and made mistakes. But it was his first single-handed case, damn it, and he'd needed it to come out right.

Testing the water.

'Don't think I'll get much further with this Guffey job, not yet a bit. No way to get a lead on the truckie unless we get a whisper. Might take months for that.'

'It'd be the same whoever had handled it, Neil.'

'Not much consolation though, is it? I mean there's Richardson, but I can't see I'll get much out of him.'

'Bugger all, I should think,' said Morrissey, in the same boat himself.

Feeling briefly cheerful when he thought that Claire could now come home; something pleasant to be done then, telling her that. Dropping back into gloom again when the telephone rang and he heard that Thewlis was dead; railing inwardly that he couldn't take vengeance for Simms and Lilian Carver.

'Better in one way,' said Barrett, 'better for his wife and daughter. Them having to have heard all that come out in court... hurt them a lot more than it would him.'

'Let us do evil that good may come,' said Morrissey softly, quoting from Romans 111.

IT WAS Saturday, the day he was going home.

That was the first thought in Beckett's mind when he woke. A new man; that's what Jean would find in him, a new man. He'd told her so again last night; told it to her over and over, enough times now for her to know it by heart. At nine he was pacing, packed and ready to go. 'You've been jilted,' said Jacko, tubed up in the corner. 'She's gone off with a toy-boy. You'll have to catch a bus.' Laughing as he said it.

Beckett grinned sourly and felt annoyed.

He'd asked her to come early, and when she arrived the new man in him was struggling a bit because the old one was disgruntled, but the feeling soon dissipated as he walked off the ward. He put his arm out and hugged her towards him, pulling them both off balance as they went along the corridor. 'You'll not know me,' he said, meaning it profoundly. 'Just wait a bit, and see.' Sitting in the passenger seat driving home, thinking how the house would look dusted and clean, flowers on the sideboard. Couldn't expect a man to think about things like that, not when he was on his own. Apologising gruffly for the mess he'd left it in.

'No point worrying now, is there?' Jean told him quietly. 'You weren't well. You'll just have to make sure you don't get in the same fix again.'

How could he, when she was home to stay.

The first thing he saw was the vase of flowers. 'That's nice, Jean,' he said, 'makes it look just like home.'

Standing in the kitchen, grudging the hours spent in cleaning it, she started making coffee and tried for the millionth time to think how to tell him she didn't mean to stay. If he got into a temper, raged and banged his fists around, that would make it easy, praying he'd do that so she could shed her sense of guilt. She couldn't take responsibility for another adult, no one could, the only life she wanted control over was her own. Setting a tray and adding plain biscuits, carrying it into the sitting room, biding her time because for once the power was hers.

MORRISSEY CHEERED mightily. Standing at the edge of the pitch in the wind, the ground at his feet was soft and sinking, Margaret had rubber boots on and so had Katie, both giggling with virtue as his brogues sank in the mud. The pitch itself was filthy brown, with everybody sliding, more like mud wrestling than a hard-fought game. Hard to tell who was who with the stripes all coloured clay. Trying to keep his eyes on Mike and memorise each tackle, itching to get in there and pound off down the field. Waving his arms and cheering harder still.

Worth upsetting Osgodby to mend things with Mike.

Slipping and sliding, looking where his side were, Mike saw things differently. He'd promised to make a special effort, no flip answers and no twisting tails. Told his mother:

'Dad won't be there anyway, he never keeps promises. I'll give him ten minutes before he's called away.' Taking a pass from Murray and running for the line, hearing Morrissey's bellow as he handed off a half-back, grinning as he slid the ball and got his second try.

Just like a battle truce, fighting suspended for peace talks. But a truce wouldn't last forever such things never did, one side or the other always started up the war again.

PATSY DICKS—'And I don't want any cracks from you about it either,' when the desk sergeant wrote her name down—had been picked up on a police trawl of Manningham Lane. Hipping round the charge-room looking at the notices she saw Vic Duttin's name. *Wanted for questioning by Malminster Police in connection with serious crimes.* Reading his description and thinking it was crap.

She grabbed a passing uniform. 'Him,' she said, 'I know him, right bloody bastard owes me ten quid,' thinking they'd pay her that, and maybe even more. 'He don't look like that, though,' jabbing the description, 'nuthin' like.' Cocking her head like a promiscuous pigeon, painted and perfumed and going for the corn. 'Got a photo you can have if you ask me nicely, him an' me on Blackpool Pier. Right good likeness. Have it if you want it. Only thing is it'll cost you twenty quid.'

Preening and pluming, the centre of attention, she'd made herself a profit and recovered her pride.

DATE WITH A PLUMMETING PUBLISHER
Toni Brill

A Midge Cohen Mystery

First Time in Paperback

FROM RUSSIA WITH LOVE

Normally when Midge Cohen's mother calls from her dental receptionist job with the latest gingivitis-cursed dream date, Midge runs for cover. But Simon Waterhouse, the premiere publisher of Russian literature? Now, *that's a* date.

Sadly, the man is a pompous cheapskate, but Midge gets to meet former Russian hooker and literary sensation Polina Volkova, whose juicy Kremlin tell-all is a book to kill for. And die for, apparently, when Waterhouse plunges from a high rise.

"A warm, observant, breezy talent."
—*Kirkus Reviews*

Available in February at your favorite retail stores.

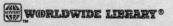 **WORLDWIDE LIBRARY**®

DATE

INTRIGUE®

Tired of predictability?

Then dive between the covers of a Harlequin Intrigue.
Heart-stopping, suspenseful adventures that combine
the best of contemporary romance and mystery.

Always full of drama and suspense, where danger is
spiced with romance. For an absolutely riveting read,
pick up an Intrigue today.

Available wherever Harlequin books are sold.

Harlequin—Not the same old story.

THE PRINCE OF DARKNESS

P. C. Doherty

First Time in Paperback

A Medieval Mystery featuring Hugh Corbett

HOLY TERRORS

The beautiful Lady Eleanor, mistress of the feckless
Prince of Wales, is banished to Godstow Priory by
King Edward, eager to be rid of an embarrassment
while negotiating his son's betrothal.

Whispers of murder echo through the hallowed halls
when Eleanor dies mysteriously. Hugh Corbett, Edward's
chief clerk and master spy, is dispatched to solve the
riddle. Suspicion falls upon the malicious and cunning
new royal favorite, Piers Gaveston. But others also
wanted Lady Eleanor dead.

"…this novel is well-plotted." —*Mystery News*

Available in March at your favorite retail stores.

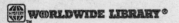
PRINCE

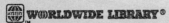

THE LAZARUS TREE
Robert Richardson
A Gus Maltravers Mystery

First Time In Paperback

A PRETTY PLACE FOR MURDER

In the picture-postcard English village of Medmelton, the air remains thick with enchantment of centuries past. Here, women have strange eyes—one brown, one green—and superstition and magic still rule.

When a famous London poet is murdered beneath the legendary Lazarus Tree, Medmelton is forced into the spotlight. Eventually the curiosity seekers drift away, but the mystery still lingers. And Gus Maltravers, at the request of a friend alarmed by the strange behavior of his stepdaughter, agrees to investigate.

"Richardson returns in top form…"
—*Kirkus Reviews*

Available in April at your favorite retail stores.

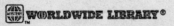 **WORLDWIDE LIBRARY®**